TWELVE DEAD PRINCESSES

a novel

Eleanor M. Rasor

The Telling Room
Portland, ME

TWELVE DEAD PRINCESSES

Twelve Dead Princesses
by Eleanor M. Rasor

THE TELLING ROOM
225 Commercial St., Suite 201
Portland, ME 04101
www.tellingroom.org

ISBN 978-1-7332633-1-3

Book design and cover design by Amy Raina: www.amyraina.com

Author photo by Molly Haley: www.mollyhaley.com
Cover and interior photo under the Creative Commons Zero license (CC0)

Printed in USA by Walch Printing: www.walchprinting.com

To my sister, Lulu,
who pestered/persuaded me
into finishing this book.
I never would have done this without you.
Thank you for believing in my writing
even when I didn't.

"Once there was a king who had twelve beautiful daughters. They slept all in one room and when they went to bed, the doors were shut and locked up. However, every morning their shoes were found to be quite worn through as if they had been danced in all night. Nobody could find out how it happened, or where the princesses had been."

—*The Twelve Dancing Princesses*,
the Brothers Grimm, published 1812

Prologue

Once upon a time, in a tall, gray castle built on the bones of a dead god, twelve princesses lay dying. Fever twisted through their veins until they felt as if they were burning and freezing at the same time. The eldest princess cried out that she saw her dead ancestors standing over her and beckoning her to join them. The second eldest saw her deceased mother whispering things in a language the princess had once known but now forgotten. The third eldest wept and said that she dreamed of her father, drowned at sea in a late spring storm four years before, standing over her with a crown of seaweed and barnacles and calling her his clever girl.

All of them dreamed and saw things that were not there, and all the while their fevers climbed and climbed until they were burning to the touch. Doctor after doctor visited and left shaking his head in despair. The castle around them was hushed and dark, a tomb for those not yet dead, and the young regent barred the doors to his chambers so that he might grieve his nieces in private.

Once the courtiers had gathered in the castle to celebrate the coming-of-age of Larka, the eldest princess; now it seemed they would be there for twelve funerals instead. Some courtiers plotted what power they might seize after their future queen was gone, while others grieved at the untimely deaths creeping closer. They paced the halls of the castle and whispered the names of the princesses as if they were prayers to the gods who were no longer alive to hear them: *Larka Rhiannon Gwynna Auriana Katharine Kristina Karolina Yara Talia Melina Alannah Etain.* They said their names over and over again, as if it might keep death from the girls' doorstep.

It did not work. The princesses grew weaker, until on the seventh evening of their illness, everyone knew they would not live to see dawn.

It was on that day, the seventh and last day, on the evening of the summer solstice, when the sun hung low and blood-red in the sky, that a stranger came to the gates of the palace.

Later, many people, from kitchen maids to merchants to courtiers, would claim to be the first to see him. They would say he came to the castle by many ways, from the north or the south, across the bridge to the island city or stepping foot off one of the boats coming from the eastern islands. They would all say they had been the first to see him approaching the gate. None of them told the truth; the stranger came not by land or by sea, not by foot or by carriage, but by shadow.

It was late evening when he came, the air so still and humid that no one dared to venture outside. And, because of that, there was no one to see the man who walked out of the long shadows of the castle wall that stretched across the city.

He did it with little fanfare, as easily as if he were coming out of some unseen door and not hard, unforgiving rock. The darkness clung to him for a moment; he turned and brushed at it with one hand, irritated, as if it were some overly fond pet that refused to leave him alone. The shadows wavered for a moment, grasping at him with little, black tendrils, and faded back into their normal shape.

The man himself looked a little as if he were made of shadows: He was swathed in a long, black robe that hid almost every detail about him except for his considerable height and a flash of blonde hair poking out of his hood.

If someone had seen him, the viewer would have felt a chill go across them as if standing in a sudden winter breeze. But no one had seen him, even though they claimed to. The stranger walked past the stoically grieving guards at the gate, past the despairing servants hurrying in the halls, past the anguished courtiers clustered in corners waiting to hear the fateful, final news, and none of them saw him. They shivered when he brushed past, but the shadows cradled the stranger close and kept him invisible.

The first person to see him was the young regent. He paced before the locked doors of his nieces' bedroom and listened to the clock ticking away the minutes his family had left to live. For four years, he had kept his country afloat with careful, steady hands and a clear head, but now he was helpless to save his nieces.

Some people say that the stranger cast a spell on the regent, others that he bribed him, and yet others that he threatened the regent with a vision of his own death if he did not unbar the doors.

While those are answers that certainly make the story more dramatic, they are not the truth. The truth is this: The regent was young, not even thirty, and already he had lost his parents and his elder brother, the former king. The last family he had alive lay dying behind that door—the girls whom he had raised as his own since the day the king's ship went down in a summer storm and his body washed ashore twined with seaweed. The girls were slipping away from the regent, inch by inch, and there was nothing he could do to stop it.

So, although spells and bribery and threats make for a wonderful story, the truth is that the stranger only had to say four words for the door to be unbarred for him.

I can save them.

Hope, once ignited, is not easily extinguished. So, despite his fears, the regent allowed the stranger to see the princesses. The door was unlocked, the servants tending the girls rushed outside, and the regent banished somewhere else to pace and wait and hope that he had made the right decision. And the stranger was left alone with twelve dying girls and the promise that he could do the impossible.

Chapter One

Wake up.

Larka awoke convinced she was drowning. Her lungs seized for a second that seemed to last forever, refusing to inhale. She choked on empty air, wheezed, and breath finally rushed into her.

The command was still ringing in her ears as if it had seized onto her soul and pulled. She could no more deny the order to wake up than deny the sun setting. She was bolt upright before she'd even really registered that she was awake.

Larka's forehead collided with something hard. Pain sparked down her skull, and she reeled away, clutching at her head.

"Well, that hurt," said an unfamiliar male voice in a wry tone.

Larka's bed dipped as some heavy weight shifted away from her. She blinked, found her vision oddly blurry, and rubbed her eyes hard. When she blinked again, she found she could see normally.

She was still in the bedchamber that she shared with her eleven other sisters, a long, high-ceilinged rectangle with six narrow, worn beds on each side. The room was dark and humid, the drapes pulled across the windows. It stank of illness: fever sweat and herbs and stale air, and Larka almost choked again. Round, fist-sized orbs of cold, white-blue light were stuck into the wall. They were arcanist lights—fire captured by magic and left to burn forever, bought by one of Larka's ancestors back when the kingdom of Belmarros could afford such things. Still, without the windows, the light was feeble and dim.

Larka saw now that there was a cloaked man sitting on her bed—leaning over her, in fact. That must have been what, or whom, she had collided with, for he had a hand raised to his forehead as well. He wore a black robe, incongruous with the hot Belmarros summer, its heavy folds pulled down low so she couldn't see his face.

The stranger rubbed his forehead again and dropped his hand. "Well, I suppose you are awake." There was a humorous note in his voice.

"Yes," Larka said cautiously. Her voice sounded hoarse. Not surprising—she had thought she would never wake from her fever dreams again, let alone hold a conversation with someone. Doctors had been drifting in and out of the chambers she shared with her sisters for the past week. What little she had been able to understand from under the haze of her illness had included ominous words like "severely weakened," "delirious," and "likely fatal."

"I was afraid you might not wake, for a moment. The rest of your sisters are already up."

Larka's heart seized at the mention of her sisters—were they really alright? Instinctively, her eyes swept across the two rows of beds to check each one as she had done a thousand times before.

The beds were arranged by age, with the second-eldest closest to Larka. That was Rhiannon, who was seventeen. She was still lying in bed; the only things visible of her were one brown arm and a tumble of messy curls, but Larka saw her chest rise and fall.

One bed down from that was Gwynna, who was a year younger than Rhiannon and already sitting up, combing her fingers through her curly hair in a vain attempt to fix it. The fourteen-year-old triplets, Katharine and Karolina and Kristina, were huddled together on Kath's bed, whispering. They were so close together, dark hair and brown limbs tangled, that it was hard to tell where one sister ended and another began. All five of these sisters shared the same mother, the noblewoman Lady Asha, from the tropical archipelago of Astraia, and there wasn't a trace of their golden-haired, pale-skinned father to be found in them.

Larka kept looking. Across from her was Auriana, who shared Larka's blonde hair, blue eyes, and round face—they could have been twins if Auri hadn't been three years younger. Then there was Yara, who was twelve; Talia, who was ten; and Melina, who was eight. They were children of Iris, their father's third and long-suffering wife, and had inherited her stick-straight brown hair and sharp nose. Melina was patting her hands through her bedsheets, presumably looking for the spectacles that gave her an owlish look, while Yara and Talia simply sat on their beds, their weary eyes missing their normal gleam of mischief.

Finally, Larka turned her attention to where the very youngest of her sisters had been sleeping: children of Eithne, the youngest and final wife of King Eldric of Belmarros. Alannah was five and Etain three, not even born when their father was drowned at sea while on his way to the kingdom of Dalbrast, across the sea, to negotiate trade relations. Larka's heart stuttered in her chest when she saw no red curls or freckled skin in these two beds, and then she realized that Alannah and Etain were sitting on the carpet near the triplets.

That was all of them: her sisters, alive and breathing and healthy as she had never expected to see them again. The stranger had not lied. For a moment, Larka's gratitude at seeing them all alive was so great she could only clutch at her bedsheets and breathe.

Her sisters accounted for, Larka turned back to the stranger. She found him still perched on the edge of her bed, watching her. His hood had fallen back, and she had to smother a gasp at what was revealed.

The stranger was a young man, far younger than any of the doctors who had visited in the past few days, and the palest person she had ever seen. His skin was the color of winter snow and his eyes a shade of gray that was almost white. A long, bone-colored braid was thrown over one shoulder. The harsh black of his robe only made him appear even paler.

The reason Larka stared, though, wasn't his coloring or clothing. It was his tattoos. They were deep, stark black, and covered every inch of skin that she could see. Jagged lines like lightning bolts on his cheeks and chin. Unfamiliar, spiky runes overlapping on his brow, disappearing into his hairline, curling over the shell of an ear. He shifted his hand and she saw that the tattoos were on his hands as well. Runes wound around his wrists to mingle with ones on the back of his hand, and twined in ropes down his fingers to join with more on his palms.

His fingers… were there six of them on each hand? Larka blinked again in hopes of clearing her vision, but the sleeves of the stranger's robes now concealed his hands well enough that she couldn't be entirely sure. Perhaps it was just a remnant of a fever dream that had snuck its way into the waking world? She shook the thought away.

When the young man blinked calmly at her, clearly used to being stared at, she saw that the tattoos were even, impossibly, on his eyelids.

There was only one thing tattoos like that could mean: The stranger was an arcanist, one of the elusive magic-users who tattooed their spells onto their very skin so they would stay with them forever. Arcanists were miracle-workers, scholars of magic, an ancient order that had endured for more than two thousand years and only sold its power to the very highest bidders.

Larka had heard many stories of arcanists and the secretive magic they practiced—that they could look into your memories, that they could transform lead into gold with a snap of their fingers, that they remembered secrets from before the War of the Gods—but she had never met one in person before. Never even thought she would. They rarely ventured away from Drekkaria, their island citadel in the middle of the ocean, where they rejected any rule but their own. The last time an arcanist had come to Belmarros had been in the time of Larka's great-great-grandmother.

Now there was an arcanist beside Larka, sitting on her bed with her as if he was just an ordinary person.

"Who *are* you?" Larka asked. She winced at how weak and pitiful her voice sounded after days of barely speaking.

"Oh, how rude of me," said the stranger politely, as if they were exchanging pleasantries at court and not in the middle of her bedchamber where she was supposed to be dying of fever. "You may call me Sol. And you are Larka, the eldest princess who shall be queen soon? I saved your life. Well, your life and the lives of your sisters."

Her mind grasped to understand his words, but their meaning slipped away. He spoke too quickly, too loudly, jumping from one topic to another. Her mind was slow as molasses and she couldn't *understand.*

Nothing felt quite real. The edges of Larka's vision were hazy, as if she was still in the grips of some terrible fever dream. What had happened? One minute she had been burning with a fever, lips cracked with dryness and wracked with shivering despite her temperature. Then… she thought back, trying to remember. What had happened then? Just blackness, at least until she heard the words "wake up" and unconsciously responded to them.

"What happened?" Larka eventually managed.

The pale man—Sol, he had said his name was—didn't get a chance to reply.

"Who in the name of Ysobel the Founder are *you*?" This from her sister Gwynna. The third eldest princess was clad only in her nightgown, brown hair messy and a pillow crease on her cheek, but her expression was fierce and her chin held high. She had climbed out of her bed and was standing next to Larka's. Larka felt a rush of relief at seeing her, far more awake and alive than she herself currently felt. "Do you know who we are?" Gwynna demanded. "What are you doing here?"

"As I said, I just saved the lives of you and your sisters," Sol said mildly, seemingly unfazed by being interrogated by a half-naked princess. "You were dying of a fever, and I saved you."

Larka felt ridiculously vulnerable in her own flimsy nightgown. She edged away from Sol and pulled up the covers of her bed, not caring that they were soaked with sweat. He seemed to notice her discomfort; he got up off the bed and turned to look at Gwynna instead. Larka couldn't help but be a little relieved when the stranger's gaze was no longer directed at her. He appeared about two years older than Larka, no more than twenty or so, yet his eyes looked as if they had seen multiple empires rise and grasp for power only to crumble into blood and dust. She shivered under the intensity of his look. Did all arcanists have eyes like this?

"Does our uncle know that you're here?" Gwynna demanded.

"Indeed, he does. I offered my services to him, and

he accepted. It is thanks to me that you are not being prepared for your funerals now." Larka felt a wave of sickness pass through her at the thought of how close she had been to dying. At how close her sisters had been to dying.

"I—" started Gwynna, but Larka interrupted her.

"How is that possible?" she asked. "The court was preparing for our *funerals*, and now you say you've saved us? How? The doctors said there was nothing they could do."

"Well, I am not a doctor," said Sol simply. Larka found herself able to hold his gaze now that she was more used to his startling appearance. "I have power that even the best doctors in the world cannot dream of. You were steps away from death; I reached out, dragged you back, and burned the fever out of you."

"Are you an arcanist?" Rhiannon said. The second-eldest princess, who had followed Gwynna to gather around Larka's bed.

Sol smiled. "What do you think?"

"I think that all the stories I've heard about arcanists say they won't lift a finger to help a drowning man unless they receive payment for it," Gwynna pointed out, her tone worryingly hostile. The last thing Larka wanted to do was offend the man who'd just saved their lives, especially if he practiced powerful magic.

"Gwynna, be quiet," Larka ordered. She suspected that her authority as the eldest sister and future queen was rather undermined by the fact that her blonde hair was a mess and she still had no idea what was going on. "Don't insult the man who just cured you."

"Yes, you are being rather rude," said Sol, crossing his arms over his chest. "I am feeling rather unappreciated right now; I *did* just save your life."

Gwynna looked as if she was going to say something else, except three-year-old Etain tugged on the hem of her nightgown. Their youngest sister had apparently made her away across the length of the room over the course of the conversation without anyone noticing. The little princess tugged again at Gwynna's nightgown, and Gwynna picked her up. Whatever words Gwynna had been about to say were tossed aside in favor of kissing the top of Etain's head and holding her tightly.

"My sister is right, though," Larka said carefully. "I really do have to ask: What payment do you require? The treasury of Belmarros isn't what it once was, but we might be able to give you a few gold bars, maybe some jewelry."

To her utmost surprise, Sol tossed back his head and laughed, long and hard. Larka saw nothing amusing about the question and could do nothing but watch him, perplexed, until he had finished.

"I have all the gold and gems I could ever need," he said, a secretive half-smile crossing his lips. "I need no more. No, I would rather have a different kind of payment from you."

A chill crawled down Larka's spine at his words. She supposed it was too much to ask that he had saved her and her sisters out of the goodness of his heart. "What *kind* of payment?"

"It would be unfair of me to ask for it now, when you have only just recovered. Greedy, really."

"But—" began Rhiannon. A worried crease appeared between her brows.

Sol turned to her, and she shrank back a little. "What, are you so eager to pay your debt when you have hardly been healed for a minute?"

"But what kind of payment do you want from us?" Rhiannon finished. "What could you possibly want besides our money? I know a life debt means you can ask for whatever you want, but we have nothing else to give you."

Sol raised a colorless eyebrow, the tattoos on his

forehead wrinkling. "Is that truly what you believe? I will come to collect my debt soon, and then you will know what I want. But do not worry; it is nothing very terrible. I just do not think it fair to burden you before you have recovered." He turned on his heel to go.

Larka glared at his back. Gwynna, who'd always been fascinated by stories of magic, had told her many about arcanists, but they had never been so infuriatingly *vague*.

Sol paused. "I nearly forgot. I need you to promise that you not speak of this to anyone, not even your uncle."

"Why?" Gwynna challenged. "We trust Stefan. There's no need to keep secrets from him."

"This is a matter that stays between us. Your Stefan was not one of the people I saved. He does not owe me anything, and I do not want him to. Now *promise*."

Gwynna must have been startled by the intensity of his words because she did as bidden: "I promise I won't tell anyone about the debt between us."

"All of you." Sol cast a look around at the other sisters, who were still sitting on their beds, and pitched his voice louder. "Say it. Say, 'I vow on the name of Truth, Lady of Promises, that I will not speak of this debt or its collection to anyone outside of this room.'" With the oddly formal way that he spoke, the vow almost sounded normal coming from his lips.

Larka hesitated to repeat his words.

"Go on," said Sol. A trace of irritation crept into his voice. "Swear it."

Larka parroted the words along with her sisters, even as her stomach clenched in uneasy knots. From the troubled looks she saw around her, she wasn't the only one who had misgivings about swearing this vow. But what choice did they have? They owed Sol a debt so large Larka could scarcely comprehend it.

"Again," commanded Sol. They spoke the words

three times before he was satisfied, and as she spoke the last word, Larka had the uncanny feeling that a net had just drawn tight around her chest. She even looked down and poked herself with a finger to see if there was really something there. The only thing she saw was the thin fabric of her nightgown. The feeling persisted for a moment, the net drawing tighter—she could feel every knot and twist of it around herself yet could see nothing—and then it was gone as quickly as it had appeared.

"What was that?" blurted Rhiannon. Clearly Larka had not been the only one to feel the impact of the promise.

"Promises made under the name of Lady Truth are binding, even if the goddess herself is long dead," said Sol. "Though they may have warred and died two thousand years ago, the old gods still have sway in this world. I would have assumed you all knew that."

No, we didn't, Larka thought. It had been generations upon generations since the War of the Gods. The only source of magic in the world now was the arcanists, and they were a candle compared to the sun that the gods had been. Humanity had been without its creators long enough that it was beginning to forget its own history, and Larka had the uncomfortable feeling that, by swearing the vow, she and her sisters had just done something—*agreed* to something—that they didn't understand in the slightest.

Sol flipped up the hood of his robe so his face was covered in shadow except for his eyes. In the darkness, they had a faint glow to them that reminded Larka of the arcanist globes.

"I expect I will be seeing you again before long," he said and strode toward the doors of the bedchamber. The double doors swung open at his approach, and he disappeared into the twilight hallway beyond them, swallowed up by the shadows as if he had never been there at all.

The door clicked shut. Sol's absence left a stunned quiet in its wake.

Larka rubbed her arms, feeling chilled even in the stuffy air of the bedroom. The heat of her fever had left her so abruptly that her body still hadn't adjusted, and neither had her mind. She had trouble believing that, simply by laying his hands on her, the stranger had been able to draw the illness from her as easily as pulling a loose thread from a dress.

Larka looked around at her equally puzzled sisters. "Does *anyone*," she said at last, "have *any* idea what just happened?"

Only silence greeted her at first.

"No," said Gwynna finally. She was still glaring at the door that Sol had walked out of.

Auri asked, "Do you really think our uncle let that man in here? Sol, he said he was called?"

Gwynna shrugged and shifted Etain sleepily in her arms. "Probably. You remember how… how desperate Stefan has been. I think he would have done anything if it meant we would live."

They all fell silent, remembering.

Larka had been the first to fall sick. At first she had thought it was just a passing illness, but it had quickly revealed itself to be one of the wicked summer fevers that periodically burned through Belmarros like a wildfire, leaving just as much devastation in its wake. Her sisters had quickly become victims of it as well, and all her memories after that were a haze of nightmares and despair.

Two or three days ago had been the first time Larka had heard a doctor whisper the word "dying." It was during one of her few lucid moments. She was fairly certain Stefan had thrown the man out of the castle, but the word had stayed with her, and then it had been clear that the doctor was right.

Larka had been dying—they all had been dying—and she had been surprised to learn it. It had seemed impossible that she and her sisters could be healthy one week and the next one slipping ever closer to death no matter how hard they fought to hold on. But even as she had tried to deny it, a deep, gut-clenching dread deep inside of her had forced her to confront the truth. So, she had lain there, lurching in and out of fever dreams, and had known that she was going to die, and her sisters along with her.

Auri cleared her throat, jerking Larka out of her memories. "Do you believe him?" Auri asked nervously. "About how we shouldn't tell Uncle?"

Kristina, who was fourteen and skeptical of everything, snorted. "No. I doubt he wanted to do anything except frighten us. Doesn't everyone say that arcanists are too arrogant and melodramatic for their own good?"

"I'm pretty sure people only say that when the arcanists can't hear them, and for good reason," pointed out Katharine. "They are powerful, Krista. And unpredictable."

“Be quiet, Kath,” said Kristina, but there was no bite behind it. The triplets quarreled all the time but never really meant it, and besides, it was hard to be angry when they all had nearly died less than an hour before.

“Besides,” butted in twelve-year-old Yara, “what could he possibly want from us? Didn’t he say he didn’t want money?”

Larka stopped trying to finger-comb her hair into something that made her look less as if she’d been dragged through several hedges; it was probably beyond saving without a hot bath and a brush. “Yes, but there are plenty of other things he could want from us besides money. A favor to call in, a title, an acknowledgement of gratitude…” She trailed off as a thought occurred to her. “A marriage, maybe.” As soon as she’d said the words, she regretted them. Kristina stiffened, indignant at the mere idea of someone forcing her into a marriage, and Rhiannon paled.

Gwynna frowned. “I thought arcanists only married other arcanists. They have some weird ideas about not diluting powers and bloodlines.”

“There’s a first time for everything,” Krista said darkly, twisting a black curl around one finger.

“And if he *does* want to marry one of us, it’s not like we could stop him,” said Katharine. “Arcanists have enough power to do what they want.” She drew her brows together with worry.

Rhiannon rolled her eyes. “Well, he’s not marrying me, for one. I’ll only marry a woman.”

“If he married Larka, he’d be king-consort,” pointed out Kath.

Larka’s stomach lurched unpleasantly at her sister’s words. Not just at the idea of marrying an arcanist—Kath had reminded her that most of the country was expecting the eldest princess to pick a consort soon, as it was tradition that any ruler not already married by the time he or she ascended the throne would marry as soon as possible. Even if she didn't marry an arcanist, Larka would be expected to pick someone who would create an advantageous alliance for Belmarros. They certainly needed allies: Belmarros was an old, strong country, but her late father's lavish spending and boredom with the day-to-day reality of ruling had left the treasury empty and the Royal Council frustrated. Her Uncle Stefan's four prudent years as regent hadn't been enough to restore Belmarros to normal, and even in a time of peace, a weakened Belmarros wasn't good.

"No one is marrying anyone," said Larka as firmly as she could. "Never mind all of that. I shouldn't have mentioned it. It was just a theory, and anyway, Stefan and I wouldn't let any of you marry a strange arcanist if you didn't want to. Speaking of Stefan, we should probably let him know we're alright." She slid off the bed and winced at the sight of herself in one of the mirrors. Well, at least she was alive. She ached at the idea that Stefan—loyal, careful, comforting Stefan—had nearly been left alone.

"Oh, dead gods," said Auri in horror. "Stefan's probably worried out of his mind about us." She stood up, too, and Larka was reminded yet again that her little sister had somehow ended up almost as tall as she was.

Larka gathered the rest of her sisters around her and walked out of their bedroom for the first time in a week. She half-expected to find Sol lurking in a dark corner in order to eavesdrop on their reactions to his appearance. The hall was empty, though—eerily empty, in fact, with no one in sight. The tapestries had been taken down from the walls and replaced with the blood-red drapes that symbolized a household in mourning.

"A bit premature, don't you think?" Larka heard Gwynna murmur under her breath, and she couldn't help but agree. It was as if they were walking in some parallel universe where an arcanist hadn't conveniently appeared with magic at his fingertips and the fever had sucked the life out of them with nothing to remain.

Larka resisted the urge to tear down the hangings

and continued across the cold stone floor.

They found Stefan in the room right down the hall from their bedroom. It was normally a brightly lit place used for their tutoring sessions. That evening, however, the curtains were drawn, and the mess of books and papers strewn across the long table and drifting onto the carpet had been cleaned away. It was as if no one had expected the girls ever to come back and prop their feet on the table while complaining about how their tutors had assigned a ten-page essay on how the alliance between Belmarros and Astraia had begun or about how difficult it was to memorize intricate court politics, full of dozens of families and nobles who still harbored anger toward their family after King Eldric's disastrous reign.

Larka's Uncle Stefan sat at the table with his husband, Dario. Stefan was twenty-eight, only ten years older than her, but four years of being the regent responsible for getting the kingdom back on its feet after his brother's mismanagement had taken a toll. There were already lines around his blue eyes, and a few strands of gray were mixed in with the blonde-brown hair only a few shades darker than Larka's.

Dario had his head bent close to Stefan's. Larka had rarely seen him so unkempt; his green tunic was rumpled, and the many small braids his dark hair had been arranged into were unraveling at the end. Dario was the eldest son of an Astraian merchant who'd settled in Belmarros, and Larka had barely ever seen him look other than perfectly groomed.

Dario was whispering something in Stefan's ear and rubbing his shoulder in a comforting way. Four years ago, Larka had been glad that Stefan had someone as solid and filled with common sense as Dario to support him as regent. Back then, she had never dreamed that Dario might have to comfort Stefan through losing his remaining family.

It took Stefan a moment to look up and see who stood in the doorway, but when he did, he cried out in astonished joy and leaped up from his chair to try and embrace all of his nieces at once. Larka hugged him back, as hard as she could, and laughed when the rest of her sisters flung themselves at him. Dario joined in, and soon all fourteen of them were enveloped in a hug so tight and large that it threatened to knock them all over. Larka and Stefan were nearly lost in the crush.

Larka let herself stand there for a moment and simply be surrounded by everything that she loved. When the princess had first fallen ill, she had wished with all her heart that her sisters not follow suit. If the gods had still lived, she would have lain before them and begged that she would be the only one to die. As it was, when the fever swept across all of them, her one comfort in those endless days full of sweat-soaked nightmares was that at least her uncle would be spared.

At last, Stefan squeezed her one last time and stepped back. Years had dropped off his face in mere minutes. He looked young again, not a haggard old man faced with losing almost everything he loved.

"You're alive," he said, a note of amazement in his voice. "I—I told that arcanist man, Sol, to do whatever he could, but I didn't really *think*..." The hand he reached up to brush away his tears was shaking.

"We're alright," said Larka. "But—" She bit her lip. How could she phrase this?

Stefan looked at her with worry sharpening in his eyes. "But what?"

"Did that arcanist... did he ask you for any kind of payment?"

The worry fell from Stefan's face. "Don't worry about that. He said he didn't want anything from me; I suppose he was the rare arcanist who cares more about doing the right thing than getting paid for it."

"It was damned strange," added Dario, coming up behind Stefan and leaning against his husband. Their hands twined together in an easy, natural gesture of affection. "He just walked up to Stefan and said he could save you girls.

Didn't even tell us who he was or how he'd gotten here so quickly from Drekkaria. We would have agreed no matter what he wanted, but I'm not complaining that he said there would be no debt between us."

"That's—" *That's not what he told us*, was what Larka wanted to say. She could picture the words, picture telling her uncle that Sol had demanded some unknown payment from them, but they caught in her throat as a sensation like an invisible string drew tight around her until she could barely breathe.

Larka suddenly bent double, hands on her knees, coughing and gasping for breath. The string drew tighter and tighter. She fought against it for a moment longer and then gave up trying to talk when black spots began to dance before her eyes. The moment she ceased trying to speak, the invisible string relaxed and she could breathe again.

She straightened to find Stefan and her sisters regarding her with alarm.

"Larka!" Stefan said. "Are you alright? Are you ill again? Do you need a doctor?"

"No, no, I'm fine. I just… I just need some water; I think my throat is dry." She waved him away with the lie spilling from her lips with surprising ease.

"Of course!" said Stefan in relief. "I'll go find some. Wait just a minute."

Dario untangled himself from his husband. "And I should probably go tell the court that you're all going to be fine. The last I saw, half of them were on the verge of a breakdown, and the other half were plotting with Lord Braddock about who was going to be ruler after you."

Larka winced. "Please don't remind me of Aengus Braddock right now." Braddock was the leader of a small but vocal group of courtiers who'd spend the last four years subtly, or so they thought, trying to come up with some reason that Larka was unfit to be queen. Half the time she thought they were probably right; the other half of the time she was furious that they would try to judge her by the reign of her father, which had been marked by scandal and spending and ended with a dead king who didn't have to deal with his empty treasury. He'd barely even remembered he had daughters most of the time, let alone passed on his hedonistic ways to them.

She was not her father. She would not *be* her father. She'd spent years telling herself that, and years resisting the urge to yell it at the court.

Dario patted her on the shoulder apologetically. "Sorry, I shouldn't have brought that up." He and Stefan slid past the cluster of her sisters and into the hallway.

Larka immediately went and sat down on one of the chairs and pinched the bridge of her nose in an attempt to ward off a headache that was already forming. Not even an hour cured, and already her problems were building up again.

The rest of her sisters followed and sat down on the floor, with the triplets leaning against her legs. Rhiannon and Gwynna sat on chairs next to her.

"So, what *was* that?" asked Gwynna. "You sounded like you were being strangled."

Larka touched her chest, lightly, where she had felt—where they had all apparently felt—the binding of the promise. "It was the promise, I think. I was going to tell Stefan and Dario about Sol. And I just… I couldn't say the words. It was like something was stopping them from coming out."

Rhiannon's eyes widened in understanding, Gwynna's in indignation. Auri looked physically ill.

Melina squinted behind her spectacles and asked, "But we can still talk about it to each other, right?"

"I don't know," said Larka. "Let's try. I just met an arcanist named Sol who might have had six fingers on each hand and said he wanted to collect a debt from us….. No, thank the gods, I can still say it."

"I'm sorry, what?" Rhiannon sounded as if she herself was being strangled for a moment. "He had how many fingers?"

Larka raised her hands. "I'm not sure! I just thought, when I first woke, that he had six fingers on each hand. I didn't get a good look, though, and I might have been seeing things. None of you noticed?"

"He was sitting on your bed, not mine," pointed out Kath drily. "I don't think I ever saw him as close as you did."

Larka frowned. "That's true. I… I suppose I could have just been seeing things. My vision was a bit blurry when I first woke up."

"No human has twelve fingers," agreed Auri. Larka made a noise of agreement, but privately, she was conflicted. It hadn't *seemed* as if she was imagining his strange hands. Then again, despite their powers, arcanists were people, nothing more. They just happened to be people born with a spark of magic inside them that they spent their whole lives cultivating.

"Whether or not Sol has the correct number of fingers isn't the important thing," said Gwynna. "The important thing is that it wasn't just some ritual promise he had us swear. It actually *works*."

They were silent, considering the predicament.

Promises made under the name of Lady Truth are binding.

Larka thought Sol was exaggerating or joking. Clearly he hadn't been, not if the consequence of her vow was the inability to speak the words he had forbidden. The things that endured beyond the gods were strange—invisibility cloaks woven out of their hair, songs in the language they had spoken, and, apparently, unbreakable vows.

Finally, Gwynna said, "I'll do more research. The library is so large, there *has* to be a book about undoing god magic. Maybe we can get to the bottom of this and find out if there's a way to break the promise we made."

"Good idea," said Larka, relieved that someone else was coming up with a solution. Every time she had to—whether it was the Council asking her about trade tariffs or a maid just wanting to know what color her new dress should be—Larka feared she was doing something wrong.

Kristina said plaintively, “Does this mean we’re going to have to lie to Stefan and Dario about what’s happening?”

“I suppose so,” said Larka, heavy-hearted. Stefan was more like an older brother than an uncle to her; the idea of keeping something from him made her stomach feel sour.

“It might not be for long,” suggested Yara. “Maybe Sol will just go back to Drekkaria and forget all about us. And then it won’t matter that we promised not to talk about him.”

“Perhaps,” Larka said, more to humor her younger sister than anything else. Yara was twelve and not quite old enough to understand that in the world of royal politics no one did anything without a purpose. If Sol had a debt he wanted to collect from them, then collect it he would, somehow.

And much as she disliked to admit it even to herself, she was curious about Sol. She wanted to know why he had chosen them out of all the people in the world to save, and how he had come to Belmarros. She wanted to know about the tattoos that had traced their way across his skin and the sadness she had glimpsed in his eyes.

Before anyone else could speak, Stefan returned holding a pitcher of water and some cups. He didn’t seem to notice the gloomy atmosphere in the room and simply poured Larka a cup of water.

Larka drank it in two large gulps; she hadn’t realized until the moment the cool water touched her lips how thirsty she was. Stefan refilled the cup for her two more times, and she drank more slowly, thinking.

So, Sol had forbidden her and her sisters to speak of the debt he wanted to collect from them. They would simply have to wait and see what he wanted.

And hope that it was, as he promised, nothing too terrible.

Chapter Three

Larka's eighteenth birthday was a week later. A week that she should have been dead for, a week when Sol did not appear and they still could not speak of him, and a week during the entirety of which she could not stop dreading what was to come. When she was younger, birthdays had been occasions to savor. She would get presents and smiles and even a rare visit from her father, King Eldric. On her fourteenth birthday, the last one they had celebrated together, Eldric had thrown her another one of his lavish parties. And for one evening at least, she had been the center of his attention.

But this one? This one she couldn't help fearing, silently, hopelessly, a tight knot of anxiety deep inside her chest.

This year she would be eighteen, the age of womanhood and inheritance and marriage. The age where she would finally be declared Queen of Belmarros and crowned at the end of the year. In between her coming-of-age and her coronation, she would be Little Queen, a time meant to let the new ruler become more accustomed to her new duties and titles without having to deal with preparations for her coronation.

Larka appreciated the sentiment, but she didn't think ten years would be enough to prepare her to be queen, let alone a few months. She was fairly certain the court knew this, too, and that was why they had agreed to let her have the period of being Little Queen instead of jumping straight from four years without a proper ruler into finally having a new queen. Well, that and the hope that she would spend those months entertaining suitors so she could pick a consort to rule beside her.

Larka couldn't help but think that it was unfair that she had to deal with all the expected problems of being queen and the constant tension of not knowing what kind of price Sol wanted from her and her sisters. Not even queen yet and already she had more secrets and responsibilities than she knew what to do with.

Rhiannon did up the last button on Larka's heavy silver dress and moved around to stand next to her sister. "Everything alright?" she asked quietly, slipping an arm around Larka's shoulders. "You look worried."

Larka, gazing at her reflection in the mirror, forced a smile. Heirs couldn't just declare that they didn't want to be queen. It wasn't done. She was the eldest legitimate child of the late King Eldric of Belmarros. This duty was in her blood, for better or worse, whether she wanted it or not. Even if she abdicated, the crown would only pass to one of her sisters, and she couldn't bear to be that selfish.

"I'm fine," Larka said softly. "Just a little nervous about the ceremony, I suppose." That was probably the biggest understatement she'd said in her whole life. Some people said they had butterflies in their stomachs; at the moment, Larka felt as if there were half a dozen snakes twisting inside her. "What if I mess up or forget the words or trip over my dress?" *What if the thought of being queen makes me want to throw up or cry or run until I reach a place where no one has ever heard of Belmarros?*

Rhiannon squeezed her shoulder reassuringly. She was almost a year younger than Larka but somehow always ended up being the one giving comfort to her older sister rather than the other way around. "You'll do fine," Rhiannon said reassuringly. "Here, let me do your hair."

On a normal day, the dressing of the heir was something done by two or three maids, but on the day of his or her coming-of-age, it was traditional for the heir to be dressed by relatives. Larka appreciated this tradition as she appreciated few Belmarros traditions; it was comforting to have someone who really knew her present for the preparations, as opposed to the unfamiliar hands of servants. Unskilled though she may have been, the feeling of Rhiannon's fingers weaving Larka's hair into a long braid was oddly comforting. A reminder that Larka was real, not a ghost. A reminder that she was not dead, and neither were her sisters.

Rhiannon had just finished tying the end of Larka's braid with a white ribbon when their sister Yara bounded in. To her, Larka's coming-of-age was an adventure and a chance to flirt with court boys, not a solemn, dreaded time. Larka had put Yara's hair in a tight crown braid that morning, but it had been for nothing; already most of her brown hair had fallen loose across Yara's pointy, freckled face.

"I got the herbs from the priests," Yara said breathlessly. Her brown eyes gleamed with excitement as she dumped a double handful of slightly wrinkled sacred herbs onto the dresser. Larka had memorized their names and purposes and what they represented months ago for the ceremony. Her mind drew a complete blank now. She felt as if she'd forgotten everything she'd learned in preparation for this day.

"Can I weave them in? Please?" Yara gave the same wide-eyed, hopeful look that she had once used on a court boy to get him to climb into the king's orchards and steal a basket of fresh peaches. The boy had been caught, but Yara had gotten her peaches. Yara always got her way.

"Alright," Larka relented.

Yara beamed and picked up the herbs. Her hands were nowhere near as gentle as Rhiannon's, pulling strands of hair this way and that in an attempt to get it exactly the way she wanted. Still, the end result didn't look like someone had stuffed random handfuls of herbs in her hair and Larka considered that a success.

"Where is everyone else?" Larka asked as she turned her head from side to side to judge how well Yara had done.

"Waiting for you in the hall," Yara said. "They have been for ages. You're going to be late if you don't leave soon."

"I know," Larka snapped. "I've only been preparing for this day for, oh, my entire life. Don't tell me things that I already know." She instantly felt bad about the words when she saw Yara's face drop, the smile gone and instead replaced with hurt. "Sorry," she said, smoothing her hands through her hair and feeling the herbs catch against her palms. "I guess I'm still nervous about… everything that happened when we were ill, and if I'll perform the ceremony well. But that's not a good excuse. I'm sorry."

"It's alright," Yara said. "Really, it is." She took one of Larka's hands and Rhiannon the other.

Rhiannon squeezed Larka's fingers. "Come see what you look like before we leave for the ceremony."

Obediently, Larka allowed her sisters to pull her away from her dresser mirror to the full length one in the corner of the room. The girl in the mirror wore a wide-skirted dress of silver and white silk; with her pale hair, she looked like a creature of moonlight. There were pearls around her neck and silver in her ears, and her hair was caught up in a single long braid. Maybe someone else would have seen a princess and worthy heir to the throne of Belmarros, but all Larka could see was a frightened girl playing dress-up and being thrust into so many responsibilities at once that even thinking about them made her feel as if she were drowning.

Why was it that she could play the role of queen so

easily in the scripts that she read? She had learned so many roles in court productions, before she got too old for it to be proper for the future queen to play at being an actress. Kyra and Adelina and Corinne and Danaya and even Ysobel the Founder all came to her without the slightest effort. She would speak their words and memorize their lives and learn their parts, and it was so easy. Yet she couldn't seem to be her own ruler. Princess Larka of Belmarros, heir of a whole country, was not a role that she knew. This one part, the one she actually was, or at least was expected to be, was a stranger to her.

All she knew how to be was Princess Larka, daughter of Eldric, the worst king Belmarros had seen in generations, and Marion, the lower-class actress. All she knew how to be was the daughter of two people who had left her behind to struggle into her birthright on her own. She didn't know how to be Queen Larka, someone who felt that she belonged on the throne.

Larka took one last look at the girl in the mirror before her and turned away. She felt sick. "Lovely," she said abruptly. "We'd better go now."

The walk to the temple seemed to take only seconds though it was on the other side of the palace. One moment Larka was stepping out of her rooms with a sister holding each of her hands, and the next Rhiannon and Yara had split off to enter from the side and Larka was walking up to the high walls of gray stone and through the open doors of the temple.

Larka was greeted with silence. It was tradition in Belmarros that a ceremony could only be celebrated after it was done, and not the slightest bit before. She still couldn't help feeling that everyone in the temple was watching and judging her unworthy with their silence. And there were many eyes to judge: those of the priests, the council, her sisters, and what seemed like every courtier and merchant in the city, all dressed in their most expensive silks and brightest jewels. There were easily five or six hundred people crowded into the temple to watch her come of age.

Larka squared her shoulders and tried to look like a princess and not a lost little girl as she walked through the doorway. The Temple of the Fallen Gods had always reminded her uncomfortably of the maw of some massive beast. It was decorated almost entirely in a bloody shade of mourning red, and the ceiling, arched high above like the roof of a mouth, was dotted with tiny arcanist globes. A long, red tongue of a carpet led her down the center of the temple and through the middle of the rows of seats. The altar was waiting for her at the end of that walk: a massive slab of perfectly flat, perfectly smooth, perfectly white marble like a giant tooth.

The only thing that didn't remind her of a mouth were the tall windows lining the hall. Larka focused on those, taking in the view of the city on one side and the endless expanse of summer sea on the other. It was better than concentrating on all the curious eyes watching her—or the task that awaited her at the altar.

So, the windows it was. It was only from the temple, the highest point of the city, that it was possible to see that the city was built on an island shaped like a massive figure sprawled in the ocean. This was Vaelkarra, Belmarros's capital city, built upon the bones of a fallen god: the palace and temple on his head, the sprawling markets and townhouses on his chest. One arm stretched out to make a causeway to the mainland, and another curved to create a crescent harbor against the dead god's side. Larka could just barely see the tips of sails bobbing in the port and the sturdy wall built atop the arm.

On clear days, it was possible to look all the way down the body of the fallen god to the poorer neighborhoods that were built on the narrow lengths of land that had once been legs. These had landed sprawled in such a way that people said the god was dancing, and so that area had been nicknamed the Gallow's Dance. Her mother had been from this neighborhood before she caught the eye of a king.

Larka made herself keep walking past the windows. She went past the rows of shaven-headed priests in red robes and lavishly dressed nobles craning their necks to look at her, past her sisters and Dario, past the visiting ambassadors, until she had climbed up the shallow steps to the altar where her uncle was waiting.

Stefan smiled at her reassuringly, the laughter lines around his blue eyes crinkling. He wore blue and green, as all the rulers of Belmarros had down through the ages. Just thinking about what kind of ruler she would make someday, the inevitable comparisons between her ancestors and her, made Larka almost want to turn and flee.

Stefan moved to stand next to her, and Larka's gaze fell on the knife between them. She swallowed hard and tried not to think of what would come soon. Not yet but soon.

Stefan held out his hands to her. Larka took them. His palms were rough with calluses from years of sparring with Dario and the royal guard.

"My queen-to-be," Stefan said, "are you ready?"

No. Not now. Not in a thousand years. "Yes. I am ready to come of age. I am ready to pay the price and take the duties of Belmarros from the ones who carried it before me." The traditional words were so heavy she could barely force them off her tongue.

"Then let us begin. Tell me, my queen-to-be, of how Belmarros came to exist. Show me that you know the history of our people and the long years that lie upon us."

Larka licked her lips. How did the beginning of this story go? What line began the words that countless kings and queens had recited? This was only the first part of the ceremony; she could not afford to forget something now. She had spent such a long time practicing this that she could have said the words in her sleep. And now? Now, her mind was utterly, horribly blank. She couldn't remember a single word. Wherever they had been was just mindless fear.

Some of her panic must have shown on her face, be

cause her uncle said, "Larka. Courage. You can do this." He said it quietly, so that none of their watchers could hear him, but even those scant words of comfort were enough.

There it was, suddenly—the first word of the story came to her and then the one after that and the one after that, as if recalling the one line had summoned the rest. She knew what she had to say. Larka gave a great gasp of relief as the words came rushing back. Stefan stepped away so she had the altar steps all to herself, and she began.

"In the beginning, there was only divinity," Larka said. She heard her words echo off the stone walls of the temple. The upturned faces of the audience before her were rapturous. "There were only the gods above us, King Earth and Queen Sky and Lady War and Lord Love and all the rest of the pantheon that created the world." Those weren't the real names of the gods, of course; they were only Belmarrian translations of their names from the Divine Tongue. The language of the gods was only scattered fragments these days, rarely spoken.

Larka paused for breath—all the eyes in the temple focused on her were a weight crushing her chest—and continued. "In time, the gods grew bored of living in an empty world and created humans in their image. The humans built cities and palaces and temples. We worshipped our creators, and the gods were pleased. But we also stole, lied, killed, and committed such terrible deeds that some gods believed that, although we were made in their image, we were made imperfectly." Privately, Larka disagreed with this idea; after all, what happened next proved that gods were just as capable of atrocities as their creations, perhaps even more so.

"The gods met in council and debated if the world should be rid of humans and wiped clean for a fresh start. They argued long and fiercely over it, the worst argument the world had ever known, although the world would see worse to come. Perhaps they would have argued even longer if Lady Sun had not sent tendrils of fire down to the earth to burn away those she considered impure."

There were paintings of Lady Sun in the palace, based off stories people had passed down for centuries. They showed a woman made of light, skin blazing like coals and her three eyes the blue of the hottest part of the flame. It was said that to even be in her presence was to burn away to nothing before you realized what was happening. Stories like these almost made Larka glad the gods were dead.

Larka went on. "It is said that the two sisters who lived in the moon, called Full Moon and Dark of the Moon, did not want to see the world burn. They had seen the worst of humankind, the things we did in the shadows when we believed no one else could see us—murders and robberies and unspeakable crimes—but the goddesses had also seen mothers tell their children bedtime stories and lovers meet by moonlight. They knew that the world was composed of both good and evil, and one did not cancel out the other.

"So, when Lady Sun sent her fire down to the earth, the two sisters of the moon stopped her. They cried silver tears of moonlight to extinguish the fire that would have devoured the world and left it a charred wasteland. They cried so long and hard that they wept away their very essence, shriveling up until there was nothing left of them. The fires were put out, but the moon was empty and Full Moon and Dark of the Moon were gone.

"The sisters in the moon were the first deaths of the war, but they would not be the last. For it was only then, with fire and rain falling from the sky, that the war truly began. It split the gods apart, for more than ever, half wished humanity dead and the other half wished them to live. The gods raged against each other and ruined the world in the process. They tore up continents and drowned each other in the oceans. The land ran gold with ichor, the blood of the gods.

"In the end, the gods who wished humanity to live fought so long and so hard that they killed those who wished to see us dead. They won the war at the cost of their own lives, however, and when humanity emerged from the hidden cracks of the world to which we had run during the fighting, we found an unrecognizable world empty of our creators. We were left alone."

The rows of priests along the walls inclined their heads in respect, acknowledging the sacrifice the gods had made, and the rest of the crowd did the same. Larka herself had done it so many times before that it had become a habit.

"In the land that we now call Belmarros, there emerged many warring tribes who fought for what resources remained after the war and continued to fight for almost a thousand years afterward. A woman was born into one of these tribes: Ysobel was her name, although she was not yet called Queen." Larka saw an excited ripple pass through the crowd at the name of the first ruler of Belmarros.

"As Ysobel grew, she was touched by death. By the time she was twenty, she had lost much of her family, including her husband, to wars and raids." This was perhaps the only thing that Larka felt she really had in common with Ysobel, her ancestor, her role model for the perfect queen: that they both knew what it was like to lose their families.

"Ysobel was angry that humanity had survived the gods' war only to become the selfish beasts our creators feared we would be. She wanted only peace between people, to prove that we could be more than the gods thought we would be. She rode out in storms, in winter, in bitter wars, and slowly she drew together the tribes that lived across the land into one people. She married again and built a great city where there had once been only bones and the memory of death. She created the traditions that we follow to this very day. So it was that Queen Ysobel the First created order out of chaos and named it Belmarros, after the word for "whole" in the tongue of our creators. And so, we of her blood have kept it, for these thousand years, and may we continue to keep it for a thousand more."

Larka fell silent. She felt drained and oddly out of breath, as if she had been swimming a long way through dark waters and had only just reached the shore. The faces of the nobility before her were unreadable except for the encouraging looks her sisters were giving her; still, she knew she had told the story right. She had spent a long time memorizing it, reciting the words back to her tutors and writing them down over and over again. Even her near-death hadn't been enough to make her completely forget.

When Larka turned to Stefan, though, the glow of her satisfaction fell away. He was smiling at her, but his eyes were solemn, and that was enough to remind her that this wasn't over yet. The hardest part was still to come.

Larka took a few steps back to stand against the altar and turned to face her uncle. "Very good," Stefan whispered to her. She gave him a tired smile back and wished that the ceremony was over. Sometimes she thought the worst part of her coming-of-age was that she'd had so very long to dread the inevitable.

Stefan picked up the knife that lay before them on the altar. Larka's heart beat against her ribs like a trapped bird in a cage at the sight of the weapon. It was no ordinary blade but one even older than Ysobel herself, pure white despite the years. Legend had it that the knife was carved from the thigh bone of Lady War. Every ruler of Belmarros carried it at his or her side throughout their reign. She remembered seeing it in the hands of her own father; he had treated it as a toy, wagering it when he gambled and using it in games of knife-throwing. How her ancestors must have been horrified by him.

"Larka of Belmarros," Stefan said, his words ringing clear through the temple. "My niece. Heir to our land. Daughter of Eldric and Marion. Do you accept this sacrifice that will bind you to our land and people?"

"I do," she said. Her voice came out hoarse, and she wished she had something to drink.

"Very well. We shall commence the binding." Stefan gestured to the altar.

Larka obediently laid her hands on the altar palm-up. Her slender fingers looked so fragile against the chunk of marble, and the altar was so unexpectedly cold, that she couldn't help twitching a little.

"Hold still," Stefan ordered her. Larka sucked in her breath and did her best not to move as he held the knife above her left hand and judged it with a careful eye.

Then, before she really had time to prepare for it, he slit her palm open.

Larka bit the inside of her cheek as hard as she dared to stop herself from crying out in pain. She'd spent a long time fearing this part of the ceremony. It wasn't a terribly deep cut, but it hurt even more than she'd dreamed it would, a searing, white-hot line across her palm. Pain was so much worse when you were expecting it.

It wasn't over yet. Even as bright red blood began to well from the long cut, Stefan raised the knife again and drew another cut down the center of her right palm. Larka resisted the urge to cry out as her whole world narrowed down to nothing more than two lines of pain and a bloody knife.

Stefan set the knife aside and the copper bowl beside Larka as she braced herself for what she had to do next. Before she had time to think about how much more this was going to hurt, she lifted one hand and held it over the bowl. With the other hand, she squeezed the edges of the cut so that blood would drip faster into the shallow bowl. Both hands throbbed. She gritted her teeth and got on with it. She could not afford for anyone to see her as weak. Not now, not ever.

Pain made her clumsy enough that a few drops of blood spattered onto the white marble instead of into the bowl. She moved her hand so it was over the bowl and tried again, and then she began to sing.

Chants in the Divine Tongue sounded less like individual words than a steady rush of sound, dipping down and up, some parts long and others short but all still one single piece that flowed together like a river to the ocean.

Though the words were in another language, everyone present knew what they meant. The chant was a vow, one that could never be broken, of loyalty to Belmarros. A vow which meant that whoever spoke it agreed to become

Little Queen and later ruler of the country. A vow to be, until her dying day, the leader that the country needed and to love Belmarros with all her heart.

It felt as if chains were tightening around Larka, or nails were being hammered into her coffin, with every word she spoke. With these words, she was finally declaring that she was willing to be queen someday. She couldn't avoid it anymore. And once Larka had started, she could only continue. The words flowed out of her without stopping, as if she'd opened a dam that couldn't be closed. Larka thought that even if she had tried to stop, she wouldn't be able to.

There was magic in the old chants. Once she started them, Larka was no longer a girl reciting them but simply a vessel for the words. She had never needed to memorize this song as she had had to memorize the story of Belmarros. Once she sang the first line, the rest of it came spilling out of her like an unwinding ribbon. One couldn't stop in the middle of the song; it wasn't *possible.*

On and on and on until her jaw ached and her tongue was dry. Larka's voice was clear, echoing along the ceiling of the temple as the voices of a thousand years of rulers had before her. And still the words came, and still the blood dripped from her hands into the bowl. The pain was almost forgotten now that she was in the grips of the remnants of god-magic.

Finally, finally, the chant was over. The last note cut off, and her mouth snapped shut, and she was silent. Larka took a minute to lick her dry lips and get used to the feeling of her body being her own again. Even during her practices for the ceremony, she'd never been overtaken by the magic quite so strongly. The pain came back in a burst now that she no longer had the Divine Tongue moving through her as a distraction. Her hands burned as if she had grabbed fire in them and squeezed.

Out of the corner of her eye, Larka saw that the Astraian ambassador was frowning in discomfort. She supposed that to an outsider, even if he was an ally, the customs of Belmarros seemed cruel. Knives and blood and bowls to catch it was an awfully barbaric way to declare an heir, but it was the Belmarrian way. The royal council cared more about tradition than the fact that other countries thought it was distasteful or how much the heirs hated the ceremony.

There was a fair amount of blood at the bottom of the bowl. After only a short pause, Stefan dipped one finger into the blood and set it to Larka's face. He drew one symbol on her chin, another on her brow, and two others on each cheek. When he began to trace runes on her forearms and the backs of her hands, Larka couldn't help thinking of Sol's arcanist tattoo. His runes were spells stored on his skin, and hers a transcription of the vow she had just spoken. She wondered if they had anything in common.

Stefan finished the last line of the rune. They were done. Larka was officially Little Queen. She had declared that she would rule Belmarros someday. She smelled blood and tasted it, too, from where she had bitten her cheek in an attempt not to cry out.

Larka turned away from the altar and the bowl and the bloody knife. She raised her hands and tossed back her hair to show the temple that she was Little Queen now. To show them the blood that she had shed to gain this right.

The roar was deafening. The gathered nobles rose to their feet, shouting and clapping, rejoicing for their new queen. Her sisters clapped hardest of all, and Gwynna stuck her fingers in her mouth to give a piercing wolf whistle.

They were all celebrating, joyous, and Larka wanted nothing more than to run and hide. She looked out at the crowd. *Will you cheer for me when I am queen?* she couldn't help wondering. *Will you cheer for me when it becomes clear that you've chosen the wrong person to rule Belmarros? Will you cheer then?*

Larka made herself smile even through the pain, even though she wanted to cry.

Chapter Four

If it had been any other court dinner, Larka would have already been seated at the head of the table, making small talk with whomever the council had decided was worthy of her attention. Not today. When everyone else was feasting, she was at the infirmary to have the cuts on her hands tended to. The infirmary was a comforting place, quiet and cool even in the hot summer months, smelling sharply but not unpleasantly of herbs from the jars of medicine lining the shelves and clustered in the cupboards. This was where Larka's scraped knees had been bandaged as a child, where she had consoled her younger sisters about their own injuries. When Larka married, this was where she would drink a medicinal tea to keep from becoming pregnant until she wished to have heirs. The infirmary was a familiar place—and certainly more peaceful than the crowd of well-wishers waiting for her outside its doors.

As Albin, the court physician, rubbed salve on her

hands and carefully bandaged them, Larka thought about the ceremony. She had known about the bloodletting part of her coming-of-age—it had been no secret—and she remembered seeing the scars on the palms of her own father. He had rubbed them whenever he was thinking hard about something.

Still, the sheer barbarity of the moment had taken her breath away. The copper tang of blood in her nose and watching it dribble down into the bowl. The regret in Stefan's eyes as he held the knife over her hands.

But it was a tradition, and Belmarros was nothing if not traditional. Barely a word or step of the ceremony had changed since Ysobel had united the warring tribes of their land into one kingdom. Sometimes Larka thought traditions were all that held the country together after the world had been left with a gaping hole where the gods should have been. Belmarrians were steeped in tradition. Oversteeped, even, like a pot of tea left to sit too long. Her father's reign, where he had done what he wished with no concern for what was expected of him, had made Belmarros even more determined to cling to its rituals.

"All done, Your Majesty." Albin tied off the bandage on her left hand and stepped away.

Larka winced at the formal address. "Albin, you don't have to call me by my title." Her sister Rhiannon had apprenticed with Albin for several years, so Larka considered him, if not a friend, at least an acquaintance.

Albin blinked at her, gray eyes wide behind his spectacles. His light brown hair was standing up in spikes, and it made him look younger than his forty years. "Yes, I do," he said, and there was unexpected gentleness in his voice. "You're not a child anymore. You need to get used to the idea that you'll be queen soon, and part of that is realizing that it wouldn't be proper for me to call you by your given name."

"I suppose so," Larka said. She flexed her hands experimentally. They hurt but only a dull throb; the salve Albin had given her had done its work well. She just hoped that she could get through the feasting without dropping her silverware or bleeding again.

She slid off the examination table and left the infirmary with reluctance.

The moment Larka entered the feasting hall, she was hit by a wall of light and noise so intense that she had to blink and adjust. This room had rarely been used since her father's death, and it was like walking into a half-remembered dream, familiar and strange at the same time. She remembered the giltwork shaped like trailing vines across the walls, the tapestries depicting rulers from centuries past, and the heavy gold chandeliers, filled not with candles but with caged arcanist light, hanging from the high ceiling.

She had forgotten the sheer scale of the room, though. The unlit fireplace was big enough to fit two oxen. Then there were the feasting tables, three of them, constructed of wood made heavy and dark by the years and long enough to fit fifty people on each side. Each one was stuffed full with members of the court. The tables stretched into the distance, toward the fourth, shorter table where her family and the high nobility awaited her to fill the empty spot.

Larka had hoped to make an unobtrusive entrance to the feast, but she paused just long enough in the doorway, stunned by the heat and light, that people noticed she stood there. To her embarrassment, someone began to clap, and so she made the whole long journey to her place at the front with her cheeks burning and her ears full of praise she wasn't sure she would ever deserve.

Things got worse when Larka sat down. She'd missed the first course of the dinner, and they were onto the soup now. She picked up the spoon and hissed in pain when it dug into one of the cuts in her palm.

"Having trouble, Your Majesty?" Larka had been so fixated on the problem of her soup that she'd failed to notice who was seated next to her until he spoke in a polite tone that still had a sardonic edge. It was also a very familiar voice.

Larka sighed and put down the spoon, dejected. "Oh, not much, Lord Braddock."

Aengus Braddock had always looked more like a soldier or farmer than a man of politics. He was tall and broad-shouldered, his dark brown hair cropped short and his skin tan from years in the sun. Still, anyone who thought he'd be better suited to hauling bales of hay or drilling with a sword would be sorely mistaken. He might have been square-jawed, and his nose might have had a break in it—from a youthful brawl with Larka's own father, if rumors were true—but there was a gleam of intelligence in his slate-gray eyes that could not be ignored.

"You seem to be having some trouble with your hands," Braddock continued.

"Well, I did just slice them open," Larka said testily. "That would give anyone a bit of a problem, I'd think. And the cook who made this feast didn't seem to consider how difficult eating cold vegetable soup with bandaged hands might be."

"You sound ungrateful," said Braddock, a falsely mild note in his voice. "One might think you don't appreciate the traditions of our ancestors."

Larka bit back something rude and wished that she'd been seated next to anyone else in the entire court. It wasn't exactly a surprise—the Braddocks were rulers of most of the southern vineyards and were an old, powerful family—but she hated having to pretend that he wasn't trying to unseat her.

At last she said, "I'm not complaining. I know what's expected of me as queen." *I just wish I had food I could actually eat without worrying I would spill it on myself.*

"Good. I would hate to think you ignorant of your duties."

That's the whole problem, Larka thought, giving up on the silverware and dunking a slice of bread into the soup instead. *I know what I must do, and I don't think I'm enough of a queen to do it.*

She ate her soup as carefully as she could, attempted to steer Braddock's conversation onto something inane and boring, and tried to think of a way she could escape without making her unhappiness too obvious.

The night after her coming-of-age, Larka claimed a headache, dismissed the maids, and retired early with the rest of her sisters. It wasn't entirely a lie—lately, bright lights had been making her head throb and her eyes water—and anyway, there were more important things to do than deal with Lord Braddock for the second night in a row. The court wouldn't miss her for one night.

Larka kicked off her tight shoes and sat down on her bed with a sigh of relief. "So, what do you have for us?" she asked, turning to Gwynna.

Her sister was already lying on her stomach on her own bed, with her legs kicked in the air and skirts around her knees. A pile of leather-bound books from the palace library sprawled across the sheets, and Gwynna turned the pages of yet another with the frantic energy of someone searching for answers she couldn't find.

"Well?" prompted Larka again.

Gwynna set the book down in front of her and glared at it. This was a bad sign. Gwynna had practically swooned at the idea of looking through dusty old tomes in search of information on arcanists and their magic. Things must have really been going badly, Larka thought.

"Nothing!" Gwynna burst out. "Absolutely nothing that I didn't already know! I've read histories about the order of arcanists, first-hand accounts of their magic, books on the fallen gods, lists of the relics they left behind..."

Larka frowned. "And there was nothing useful?"

Gwynna shook her head. She'd cut off a chunk of her hair the previous spring, complaining of the weight of it and the fact that most court hair styles were made for straight, fine Belmarrian hair and not her thick, curly Astraian hair. Now it barely reached her ears. Larka thought the new look suited her sister; it made Gwynna look like the portraits of Astraia, the fierce queen whom her sister's mother's country was named after.

"I even found records of the graduating classes from the Citadel of Ink, though I have no idea how our ancestors managed to get them. There's no mention of an arcanist named Sol graduating from there, but they're very old records. Still, it's frustrating!" Gwynna stabbed one finger against the cover of her book for emphasis.

"Are you sure you didn't miss anything?" asked Karolina—or Karo, as she preferred to be called—who was dangling upside down on the edge of her bed with her hair spilling onto the floor.

"Positive!" Gwynna raised up her book again. "Look, this one is called *The Secret History of the Arcanists*. You'd think it might have something interesting, right? Want to know what it says?"

"Sure." Karo shrugged, something that Larka thought looked dangerous given the girl's precarious pose.

Gwynna cleared her throat. "Alright, here goes. 'No one knows exactly how old the school of magic which rests upon the craggy island of Drekkaria is. It is an ancient order. All that is known is that it has perched upon this island since before the War of the Gods. Perhaps we may never know; the arcanists keep their secrets firmly to themselves. When the kaiser of Dalbrast sailed across the sea two hundred years ago to conquer Drekkaria with his warships, the arcanists laughed at him. They told him that their island was a holy land, the place where one of the last gods had fallen, and they would not allow it to be controlled by someone who was mortal. Whether this is true remains to be seen—the city of Vaelkarra is one of the few locations in the world known to be the death site of a god—but the point remains. The arcanists of the Citadel of Ink bow to no authority but their own and follow no law except their pursuit of knowledge and power.' It just goes on like that for chapter after chapter of speculation with nothing certain."

"So, I take it you haven't found out anything useful?" This was Rhiannon, sitting cross-legged on her bed while she brushed Melina's hair. Mel was eight and constantly traipsing about in the palace gardens, so brushing her hair usually dislodged a handful of twigs and flowers, at least one dead insect, and on one memorable occasion, a small frog.

Gwynna rubbed a hand across her eyes, looking tired. "Just old history I already knew. There's not much about magic left over from the gods, either. We lost so much knowledge when they died that it's impossible to understand everything."

"I've sworn on Lady Truth before," commented Larka, "but I've never done it three times, and it's never been unbreakable. Did you find out anything about that specifically? Or how to release us from the promise?"

"Yes, is there a book called *How to Free Yourself from Debt to an Arcanist in Ten Easy Steps*?" chimed Auri.

"Nothing that easy. Though according to this book," Gwynna indicated another one, so old the binding was falling off, "there are types of god-magic, such as invisibility cloaks, that can be used by anyone, as well as other types whose true use can only be unlocked by someone with power of their own. So, you probably could have sworn on Lady Truth all you wanted, but without Sol to prompt you, there'd be no real magic in."

"That makes sense," admitted Larka. "Was there anything about how to undo god-magic?"

"Nothing."

Larka fell back against her pillows in annoyance. "Gods forbid a library that large actually have something *useful* in it."

"And you're not even the one who spent all week combing through it." The teasing expression on Gwynna's face fell away. "I did find one odd thing, though. I read that arcanists prefer not to use god-magic, and that they'd rather rely on their own rune tattoos. It made me wonder why Sol had us swear on Lady Truth, if that's god-magic."

Krista, sitting at the dressing table trying on Rhiannon's earrings, snorted. "Because he wanted us to shut up. It's that simple, isn't it? He didn't want us to talk about the debt, and swearing that vow was a way to do it."

Gwynna frowned down at her books. "I don't know. It was very clear that arcanists prefer to use their own power whenever possible. They can control it better. I thought maybe—"

Larka never had a chance to hear what Gwynna thought, because at that moment, the arcanist globes in the chamber dimmed for a second before flaring brighter than the noonday sun. Light blasted across the room, erasing every trace of shadow. It wasn't a flickering orange light like a fire, or the comforting gold of the sun. It was a white light so harsh and clear it didn't seem to belong in this world.

Kath fell off her bed completely, and Larka heard her other sisters cry out in surprise as she herself raised a hand to shield her eyes from the flare. She could hear the arcanist globes making a high-pitched humming noise. She blinked and tried to brush away the tears that were streaming down her face from the harsh brilliance. Each of the lights was a falling star, burning so bright that she couldn't even look at them.

"What's happening?" Larka heard one of her sisters say in confusion. The answer snapped into place in her mind: Sol.

This had to be the doing of Sol. It had to be. There was no other reason perfectly good arcanist globes would suddenly malfunction, all at the same time and all in the same way. The cold fire in them was supposed to burn forever. As a child, Larka had been fascinated enough with the lights to go as far as to pry one out of the wall and try to break it. Nothing she'd used had made a dent, and certainly it hadn't changed the steady light.

Larka started to climb off of her bed—to see if her sisters were alright, to see what was going on with the arcanist globes, to try and do something, at least, because she was the eldest and she was supposed to fix things—but then a hole opened up in the middle of the floor.

There was no rumble of parting rock as the hole opened up, and the earth didn't tremble like the accounts of the earthquakes Larka had read. It was simply that one moment the floor of their bedroom was stone cushioned with numerous rugs, and the next moment a wide black hole gaped in the center.

Trembling, Larka forced herself to climb the rest of the way off her bed and cross the floor to the edge of the pit. She knelt beside it and peered down only when she had her hands firmly planted on the ground. The cuts on her palms throbbed, but she refused to let go. The hole was at least six feet wide, plenty big enough to fall down as she looked into it.

Even with the arcanist globes acting so strangely, she could make out one thing for certain.

It wasn't *just* a hole. Or at least, not completely.

There was a spiral staircase winding along the sides of the pit, down and down and down until she couldn't see the bottom of it. The staircase was no illusion; she reached out to touch the first step and felt the cool black-and-gold metal under her finger. If Larka hadn't known better, hadn't seen it appear right in front of her, it would have looked as if there had always been a staircase going to some kind of basement below their rooms.

"Larka?" asked ten-year-old Talia nervously from where she was standing against the far wall clinging to Yara's hand. "What's going on? What is that?"

"I think it's a doorway," said Larka. "But to where?" She leaned out farther over the pit, curious about it but not curious enough to set foot on the stairs yet. There was a wind blowing up from the hole, cold and moist, smelling of dirt and rock.

"What's it doing here?" whispered Kath. "Do you think Sol did it?"

"Who else could it be?" said Auri, a hint of anger in her voice.

"Who else, indeed," agreed Larka. She was about to climb to her feet—stairs or no, being this close to a very dark, very deep pit was nerve-racking—but a sudden gust of wind blew up from inside the pit.

This wasn't the gentle flow of air that had been coming out before. This was a violently howling gust that tore through the entire room. It pushed Larka hard enough that she fell back, skirts flapping and hair beating against her cheeks. It ruffled the blankets on the beds, took one of Auri's discarded dresses lying on the floor and swirled it in the air, and rippled through the pages of the open books on Gwynna's bedside table. The wind was strong and cold as a winter storm, and they were all helpless to stop it as it whirled through the room.

Then, as abruptly as it had begun, the screaming wind was gone. All together, the arcanist globes flickered and dimmed until they were back to the brightness they had been before.

The sisters were silent for a moment, open-mouthed

and gaping in surprise. Even little Etain and Alannah were quiet, though wide-eyed. Larka finally managed to get to her feet and rearrange her twisted skirts and tangled hair.

She stepped farther away from the edge of the pit, and that was when she saw the paper that had definitely not been there before the wind howled through. It was just a scrap, so small and pale against the white stone floor that she wouldn't have noticed if the toe of her slipper hadn't nudged it.

Larka leaned down and picked it up, handling it gingerly with two fingers as if it might bite her. Had she not known better, she would have thought it was one of the invitations she'd been receiving lately for salons and balls, the paper fine and white, the handwriting elegant and nearly incomprehensible. But she did know better. The swirling black designs around the edges were runes, not random, pretty decorations.

"What does it say?" asked Rhiannon.

Larka steadied her shaking hand, cleared her throat, and started to read.

"Well," said Rhiannon at last. "At least we finally know that he does want to call in his debt."

"Yes," said Larka hollowly, dropping her hands to her side. "But we still don't know what he wants. I suppose we should find out."

To the Princesses of Belmarros,

I have given you a week to recover, and I expect you to begin paying your debt to me tonight. Go down the stairs and you will find yourself on the path to my home. Do not go off the path. Do not take anything you see. Do not try to avoid paying your debt.

Regards,
Sol

Chapter Six

They went. Of course, they went. Sol had told them to come, and none of them wanted to know if there were consequences for refusing to pay their debt besides a guilty conscience and unanswered questions.

So, they climbed down the staircase, the older girls clutching hands and the two littlest girls carried tightly in arms and Larka leading them all into the darkness. They made sure that their bedroom door was locked securely; it would no doubt cause a panic if a servant wandered in and found them missing but a large hole in the middle of the floor.

The metal of the staircase was chilly under Larka's thin slippers, and her thin summer dress of blue cotton was no match for the cold air that had a bite to it. Down they went, one after another, into the near-darkness barely lit by tiny arcanist globes set into the staircase.

The princesses climbed down so many stairs that it felt as if they'd been descending forever. Larka shuddered to think of having to come back up them and kept one hand clutched securely on the railing to keep from falling. She tried to count how many steps there were but lost count and gave up. After that, she just looked down at the darkness below and fearfully wondered how much farther they had to go. When Auri leaned out in the darkness with Kath holding onto her waist, they were unable to find the side. A breeze sometimes ruffled through their hair, and their whispers didn't echo as if they were in a small chamber.

Larka began to think of this not as a tunnel or hole but as a portal. This place did not really exist; it was just a space joining their bedroom to wherever Sol lived.

And still, they went down.

When Larka's foot hit solid ground rather than another metal step of the stairs, she almost didn't believe it. She took another tentative step forward. No, it was definitely soft earth that she was on now, not a staircase.

"I've hit the bottom," she called out to her sisters, and one by one they joined her milling on the ground. All around them was the whispering of wind and the clatter of something stirred by the breeze. Larka's mind shuddered to think of monsters in the dark, lurking just outside the light and poised to devour them. She shook the thought away. Still, the unease remained.

"It's so dark," she heard Yara say fearfully, clearly thinking along the same lines. "Aren't there anymore lights down here? Wherever here is, I mean. Does Sol expect us to wander around until we find him?"

As if on cue, a row of new lights flickered to life before them. Larka squinted, ready for a repeat of the blinding arcanist globes from their bedroom, but these merely fluttered to life and remained a steady white glow slightly brighter than the tiny ones on the stairs.

Now they could see where they had been led.

Two impossible things became clear. The first was that they were in a forest. If they were anywhere, it should have been a cavern underneath the palace, but there was no denying that they were surrounded by dark trees. The second thing was that the leaves and trunks of every single tree around them was made of silver. This was the clattering sound that they had heard before: the leaves brushing against each other in the breeze, making a sound like silverware clinking together. Even the dirt had silver flecks.

There was a cobblestone path before them, lined on both sides with arcanist globes that cast everything in a ghostly light and made the leaves of the trees sparkle. Larka caught her breath in wonder at the strange beauty of it all. She was still afraid of how Sol might want them to fulfill their debt, but that didn't mean she couldn't admire the place they had found themselves in. An underground forest with leaves of silver? It sounded like something not from this world.

That, of course, was the question. Were the sisters in their own world anymore? In their world, staircases did not appear in the middle of bedrooms, and trees did not grow leaves made of metal. Yet, if they weren't in their own world anymore, where were they? And how would they get back home?

Only then did it occur to Larka to look at the staircase. She whirled, her heavy skirts dragging on the ground, and turned back toward the steps. What she saw made her head spin. The staircase looked horribly out of place in the dark forest, going up and up so far that even when she craned her head back she couldn't see the top of it. It just kept going, suspended by nothing at all that she could see, out of the light of the arcanist globes and into the fog. The mere idea that she and her sisters had willingly descended that staircase without knowing how far down it went made her head spin with dizzy fear. If one of them had fallen, it would have been her fault. She was the eldest sister; she had to keep them safe, even in this unfamiliar place.

"Larka." It was Talia, tugging on her arm. Larka realized that she had been staring around for several moments without saying anything. "What do you want us to do?

Where should we go now?”

Larka squared her shoulders just as she had a day earlier in her ceremony. This was entirely different, entirely more unknown and far more frightening, but people were still relying on her. “We go forward,” she said with as much confidence as she could muster. “Where else? It does seem like the lights are trying to lead us in that direction, so let us see what they want us to find.”

Talia’s small hand curled into hers, and Larka held onto it like a lifeline. They went forward down the cobblestone path.

It didn’t take long for the forest to change. Not to normal leaves, no, but to leaves of shining gold. Alannah, ever fascinated by everything shiny—Gwynna always liked to joke that she would be the court treasurer someday—wandered up to one and tried to tug off a leaf. Auriana managed to snag the back of Alannah’s dress before she could so much as touch one. “Lannah, don’t,” she scolded, pulling her back onto the path. “Sol said not to take anything, and we don’t know what could be dangerous here. You too, Mel!”

Mel had also wandered over to one of the trees and was holding a fallen golden branch to her bespectacled eyes. “I’m just looking,” she said, sounding hurt. “Sol said not to take anything, not not to touch anything.” She brandished the twig. “And look, Gwyn! It’s not a statue; it’s growing. I can see new buds on the trees, and this bit here is rusty. I thought gold didn’t rust. Maybe it’s like rot? Or maybe—”

“Maybe you shouldn’t touch it?” suggested Gwynna, gentle yet firm, and Mel dropped the golden branch on the ground with a disappointed look.

The sisters went on. After another minute of walking, the forest abruptly changed again, this time to clear, sparkling diamond. Larka distinctly heard Gwynna mutter, “What next? Rubies? Emeralds?”

Instead, they reached the end of the forest. The trees thinned out, and the path suddenly plunged down to an expanse of still black water. No plants stirred in the shallows or grew along the dark, pebbled shore. It was barren and empty. There was no telling how wide or long the water stretched on for; the feeble light of the arcanist globes did nothing to penetrate the gloomy mist that hovered before them.

"Should we wait here?" Auri asked doubtfully. "Or keep going?"

"There's nowhere *to* go," pointed out Kath. She was right. Although a dock made of silver wood and white stone jutted out over the water, there were no boats tied up there or bumping against the shore. There was no way across.

"We wait here, I suppose," said Larka.

Almost as soon as she finished the words, the mist before them stirred and the prow of a small black rowboat became visible. Then another and another, until a whole row of boats—twelve in all—had emerged, paddled by shadowy figures. Neither Larka nor her sisters could bring themselves to call out across the water and split the silence, and so the scene was silent.

When the figure paddling the first boat reached the meager light of the arcanist globes, Larka had to stifle a gasp. For a split second, she saw runes scrawled across pale skin and thought that it was Sol himself. Then her eyes caught up with her mind, and she realized that it wasn't Sol but rather a completely unfamiliar man. He looked to be about thirty, with cropped brown hair; a narrow, clever sort of face; and a pointed chin. He wore only a plain, dark coat and trousers, nothing like Sol's dramatic black robe. Besides his arcanist tattoos, the most eye-catching thing about him was his scars: silver, crescent-shaped slashes, one on each cheek.

The arcanist tied his boat to the dock with a nimble knot and vaulted up onto dry land. He tilted his head to one side and considered the wall of girls facing him with an appraising expression. Larka appraised him as well. Now that he was closer, she noticed something odd about the arcanist that wasn't just his scars or the runes on his skin. He seemed faded and hollow, as if he didn't exist in the same way that Larka did.

"You're not Sol," said Karo accusingly, which Larka thought was rather obvious.

"No, my name is Galen Dietrich," said the arcanist. "Sol did send me, though. You're the princesses of Belmarros, I assume?"

Larka nodded. "Where is Sol?" she asked. Introducing all of her sisters to Galen could wait until later. Until they'd found out exactly what Sol wanted from them and what this strange place was.

"He sent me to make sure you arrived safely. After you, Your Majesty." Galen gestured to the boat he'd just stepped out of.

"Wait," said Rhiannon before Larka could step into Galen's boat. "What about explanations? Sol said that he'd explain our debt if we came, but he isn't even here."

"And so he will," soothed Galen. "He's waiting for you across the lake. It's not a long journey, really, and then you can hear what he has to say. I swear it upon my name."

"Sol had *better* explain," Larka heard Gwynna mutter under her breath.

"Fine," said Rhiannon. Though she cast Galen a distrustful look, she didn't stop Larka from stepping into Galen's boat, and when another silent, solemn-faced boatman pulled up at the dock, Rhiannon followed suit.

Mel and Talia helped lift Alannah and Etain into their boats so they didn't accidentally tip into the water. Once all twelve sisters had climbed into their crafts, they set off again across the water. Galen rowed, for which Larka was grateful. Her palms were still healing from her coming-of-age, and they ached at even the mere idea of touching an oar. Instead, she kept an eye on the boats around her and made sure none of the younger girls tried to trail their fingers through the water. Larka didn't trust the lake. Who knew what could be hiding inside its depths?

The only sound was the splash of oars in the lake, and even that was muffled by the fog. There were no bird calls or fish leaping through the water, only silence as the mirror-flat lake glided past them. Gaps in the fog revealed a sky as black as a mirror above them. Larka hadn't realized until they had stepped out of the forest that there were no moons or stars in the sky. It was eerie to see that the sky above them was as empty and dark as the lake they rowed across. She thought they hadn't been traveling for very long, but there was no way to judge the progression of time, not without being able to follow the progression of the moons. Time might as well have stopped.

Larka hoped they would return by dawn and that there even was a way to get back to Belmarros from… whatever this place was. Stefan and the court were still on edge after the princesses' illness; if the castle woke to discover they were all missing, it would be utter pandemonium.

"Galen," said Larka, after they had been rowing for what felt like hours but might have been only minutes and she had worked up the courage to talk to him, "what land is this?"

"Sol's home, and mine too," he replied promptly.

"But where are we? There are no stars or moons, and it's much colder than Belmarros here."

Galen let go of the oars for a moment and leaned forward. "Majesty, Sol will explain everything shortly. It's not my place to tell, but I promise that you and your sisters have nothing to fear from this place, or from Sol. Do you believe me?"

There was such earnestness to his words that she couldn't help but say, "Yes."

"Good." Galen took up the oars again and continued to row.

"Do you work for Sol?" asked Larka.

"In a way," said Galen, and she didn't think she was imagining the evasiveness in his voice. "We've known each other for a long time. I'm more of a partner than a servant."

She wanted to ask Galen more questions, press him for answers about what Sol truly wanted from her and her sisters, but she didn't think he would give her a useful answer. Larka settled herself more comfortably on the hard seat of the boat and wrapped her arms around herself in an attempt to stay warm. Even though she could see the other boats cutting through the water behind them, the heavy fog gave the uncomfortable impression of being adrift and completely alone in the world, and she was relieved when they reached another dock only a few minutes later.

Galen tied up at the dock and helped Larka out of the boat, a tricky endeavor with her bandaged hands. It was only when Larka stood on the stony shore that she saw the palace before her: massive, sprawling, and built out of black rock that made it nearly invisible against the night. When she tipped her head back to try and find the top of the high, jutting towers, they blended in so well with the surrounding night that it was impossible to tell where the palace ended and the sky began. Or perhaps the building simply went up forever, just as it extended as far along the edge of the lake as Larka could see.

The only part of the palace not made of black stone were the massive double doors before her. One was of silver wood, the other gold, and both were studded with pieces of diamond leaves. The doors loomed two or three times taller than Larka, as if the whole building had been made for giants instead of men.

"Holy gods," Larka heard Auri whisper behind her, and she couldn't help agreeing with the sentiment.

"It's so big," marveled Yara. The rest of Larka's sisters were also staring up at the castle, equally amazed. Galen seemed unaffected by the sight; then again, he said this land was his home. He was likely used to such awe-inspiring sights.

"Should we knock?" asked Larka when she saw the large, black-and-gold door knocker, shaped like the head of a jackal, that hung from the middle of one of the doors.

Galen shrugged. "Go ahead. He's expecting you."

Before she could lose her nerve, Larka marched up the steps to the door, grasped the knocker, and rapped hard three times. The sound echoed loudly through the still air.

The doors swung open on silent hinges, and light poured through the open doors. Not cold arcanist light but flickering firelight. Larka felt warmer just looking at it. "Come on," she said, trying to sound braver than she felt. "Let's find out what kind of man lives in a palace like this."

One by one, the princesses stepped through the open doors and into the castle. Galen followed behind them, a quiet shadow.

The door swung shut behind them soundlessly, and Larka was too stunned to notice. They were in the entrance hall of the palace. It, too, was colossal; the ceiling was at least forty feet high, and the room was as long as the feasting hall where Larka had eaten after her coming-of-age. Even though it was only an antechamber, it was far more sumptuous than anything in Belmarros. The white tiled floor was clearly made of pure marble, the brackets of the torches polished silver, and pieces of engraved ebony were embedded in the walls.

The light Larka had seen came from a wide fireplace on one wall. The fire was a ghostly imitation of normal flames; it seemed to burn without fuel, but it gave off heat. The younger girls dashed from the doorway to warm themselves by it, and Larka followed them to hold her hands over it. Krista bent down toward the flames, and Kath closed her eyes like a contented cat. For a moment, they all simply savored the warmth. It might have been high summer in Belmarros, but it felt like late autumn or the beginning of winter here—wherever they were. They had forgotten how to be cold.

Galen, though he followed the sisters across the room, didn't seem to care about the fire even though his plain brown clothing looked thin.

Once Larka had warmed herself a little, she stepped back from the fire and asked, "Where's Sol?"

"Right here, as a matter of fact."

None of them had heard the other door at the end of

the room open, yet it had. Sol stood in the doorway. It was simply that one moment he wasn't there, and the next he was.

Larka's heart started to thud as soon as she saw Sol. He looked the same as he had on the day he had saved their lives: a long, snow-colored braid trailing over one shoulder, black tattoos vivid against the white of his skin, gray eyes that seemed immeasurably old despite his youth.

"Hello, princesses," Sol said. "You look well." To Galen, he said, "You are late. I was wondering how much longer it was going to take you to get here. It is terribly lonely without any company, you know."

"It—it took us a long time to walk through the forest," Larka stammered. She cursed the blush that she could feel rising in her cheeks and to the tips of her ears; with her father's coloring, she always turned the color of a tomato. "Our—our apologies." She reddened even more at her continued stammer and the penetrating way that Sol was looking at her. Only their first visit to this land, and already they'd made a mistake.

"Your apology is accepted," said Sol with a wave of his hand. "I understand my home can be overwhelming for first-time visitors."

The questions that had been burning inside Larka burst out of her. "Who are you really? And what is this place? Is this the Citadel of Ink?" She immediately regretted being so hasty; whatever this place was, it clearly wasn't the Citadel. Larka had never been to the headquarters of the arcanists, but Gwynna had read her descriptions. These spoke of a tall, foreboding castle located high on the island of Drekkaria, with gulls circling about and the surf crashing below. Not a place with no stars or moons in the sky and with trees made of precious metals. Certainly not a place that you could arrive at by climbing down a staircase that appeared in the middle of one's bedroom.

Sol crossed the antechamber. Larka's sisters stepped back from him as if they were magnets and Sol another one that repelled them. Not Larka, though. She did not move. If Sol repelled her sisters, then she was drawn to him like metal to a lodestone. She could not seem to move away.

Sol held out his hands to warm them over the fire as the princesses had just done. Larka stared, and not just because the dark tattoos wound even under his fingernails. No, it was because she saw, with a jolt of horrified shock, that he really did have six fingers on each hand, and far too many joints. She had dismissed her memory as unreliable, the imaginings of a fevered mind, but now she saw that she'd been right.

"Who are you?" she asked again. "What kind of arcanist has six-fingered hands and lives in a palace surrounded by metal trees? Why wouldn't you let Galen answer any of my questions?"

"Well," Sol said at last, slowly. He pulled his fingers, long and spindly as a spider's legs, away from the fire. "About that. I thought it best you hear the truth from my lips. This is not the Citadel of Ink, Little Queen, and I'm afraid I lied to you about who I am. You see, I'm not an arcanist at all. I'm a god."

Chapter Seven

For a moment, all Larka could do was gape at him. Then she got her voice back and drew herself up to her full height, although even then she wasn't quite tall enough to look Sol in the eye.

"I don't believe you," she told him and was surprised at how cold her voice sounded. She was tired of whatever game this man was playing, tired of his half-truths and out-right lies. "The gods are dead and gone, and I'm not enough of a fool to believe that even the most powerful arcanist is anywhere close to one. The priests would happily put you on trial for claiming heresy like that."

"It's not heresy. It's the truth," said Sol quietly.

"You can't expect me to believe that's the truth. All the gods are dead," she repeated.

Every child in Belmarros—every child in the world—grew up hearing the stories. The gods had split, the gods had warred, the gods had died. Humanity had been saved at the cost of the lives of its creators. That was what the records stated. And now this… this man… was telling her that what she had known her entire life was not true.

Larka whirled to face Galen, who was lurking near the wall of the room as if he was hoping to be forgotten. "Please tell me he's joking," she said.

"He's not," replied Galen quietly. "I know it seems mad, but it is the truth—"

Larka spat out a furious laugh and spun back to Sol. "Why should I believe you?" she challenged. She could feel the gazes of her clustered sisters behind her and was desperate to do something for them. To release them from the fear that had been weighing them down ever since they had woken in their sickroom. If the only way to do that was to declare this man a fraud and a liar, then so be it. "You have no proof."

Sol met her eyes steadily. He did not have the look of a man who was lying. He did not even look surprised at her words. As if he had been expecting her to say something like this all along. "Yes, I do."

Sol held out his hands to her. "Let me show you."

After a moment's hesitation, Larka took them.

Sol wound his twelve fingers through her ten and held on tightly. His hands were cold—colder than any skin she'd ever touched. Combined with his pale coloring, she could almost think that he was a man carved of ice and snow.

For a moment, Larka and Sol simply stood before the blazing fire, their hands bridging the gaps between their bodies.

Nothing happened.

"Well?" said Larka. "Where's your proof, Master Sol?"

There was a secretive smile on Sol's lips. "Patience, Little Queen. You will see soon."

"I don't—" Larka started, but "see anything" died stillborn on her tongue as she felt a wave of power explode out from Sol. It crackled through her like white-hot light ning, so strong that she half-expected her hair to stand on end.

Larka gasped and took an involuntary step back against the sudden force of the power flowing into her. An odd, blue glow rimmed the edge of her sight, and she blinked, hoping to clear it. When she opened her eyes, she saw…

A man standing in the midst of a heavy northern blizzard. He was unbothered by the cold and howling wind, for he was made of jagged ice and snow. In front of him was a tiny hunting lodge tucked deep in the mountains. Inside, three hunters huddled around the flickering fire, their eyes dull with cold, fingers clumsy and frostbitten. The wind blew a particularly harsh gust, and the pitiful fire blew out, leaving the hunters alone in the dark. The icicle man raised his hand to knock on the door…

Another man, with skin like ebony and eyes like rubies, dressed in an elaborate Astraian robe of many colors. He did not have the same face—yet somehow she knew this was still the same person. He walked under a harsh, blue sky, through a field of battling Astraian warriors who did not see him yet shuddered and fought harder when he passed. Wherever he went, shades rose from the corpses of the dead and followed him…

In the grasslands across the eastern sea from Belmarros, riders with light brown skin and straight, dark hair picketed their horses and set up their tents. They crouched around their campfires, looking fearfully over their shoulders and whispering stories of a man with the head of a vulture and hands of bone who prowled just outside the circle of light, waiting to drag them away…

She saw a hollowed-eyed man with greasy, ink-black hair and gray-white skin. He looked nothing like the previous figures, yet she knew it was still the same man—Sol. He stalked through the streets of a city that had long since burned to ashes and ruin. He wore dull black armor and carried a battle-ax in one hand, a stiletto dagger in the other.

A massive murder of crows followed him, blotting out the sky and turning it dark as night, and she knew they were here for all who had died as this city burned.

She saw this man walk among massacres and shipwrecks and plague, through the halls of infirmaries and across endless battlefields. She saw him standing in the corner of sickrooms, saw him take the hands of fallen warriors and usher the dead away from the sunlight. He was there when children slipped away in their mother's arms, when a tyrant's throat was cut and a kingdom roared its delight. He was everywhere, a shadow wearing a thousand different faces and a thousand titles.

All the while, as those thousand aspects walked the living world, the true one stood in the underworld and ushered in the dead. He guided old men and young children alike, heroes fallen valiantly and gloriously in battle, and those who had been unjustly betrayed with a knife in their back. He cared not how the dead came to be there, only that he must guide them to a place where they might rest forever now that they were not among the living. He was not cruel and vicious, only calm and implacable. He was patient, for he knew that all came to him in the end...

Larka let go of Sol's hands with a gasp, nearly stumbling in her haste to get away from him. Her knees felt weak, and when she blinked, she could still see the images he had shown her on her eyelids, like impressions from staring into the sun.

She looked back up at Sol and had to keep from flinching. When she'd first met Sol, she'd thought that his eyes were ancient for someone not much older than she was. Now she knew that although his face looked young, his eyes were the only thing that showed his true age.

Only that wasn't his only face, not really. Because he wasn't Sol the arcanist. He was Death Himself, He of Many Faces, the One Who Waits for All. He had as many faces as the sky had stars, and she had only seen a fraction of them. The records said that he was dead, cut down by his sister, Lady Sun, with a spear of fire through the chest, and yet here he stood before her.

Larka had doubted him before, doubted his claims that he was no mere arcanist but the last of the surviving gods. She had doubted Galen for believing him. She didn't doubt Sol now. No one except a god could have such power. There had been such force behind the visions she'd seen that she knew they were true. The divine power that had flowed through her was as real as her own flesh and blood.

Had this all been a test of the princesses' loyalty? The illness, the strange bargain, the revelation of who he was only after they had refused to believe his word? The old stories were full of these kinds of anecdotes: the gods, when they were alive, disguising themselves as humans and questioning the faith of their followers. Lady Truth, it was said, would cut out the tongues of humans who called her a liar, and the Lord of Mischief would turn disloyal followers into deer to hunt. It was never a pretty fate.

"Do you believe me now?" Sol—no, Death Himself—asked.

Larka had doubted the claims of a god. She had called him a liar and a fraud. At best, it was blasphemy for which she would be punished. At worst… she didn't want to think about what the worst consequences could be. If she would be punished for her crime, she hoped that she would take the blame and not her puzzled sisters standing clustered behind her.

"Yes," Larka said, trembling even harder at her thoughts. "I believe you, my—" what was the correct way to address a god? "—my lord."

Larka was horrified to realize that she was still standing. Still looking a god straight in the eye, as if the Little Queen of Belmarros was an equal to Death Himself. She bowed her head and knelt before him so quickly she almost fell. One of her knees throbbed painfully from landing on the hard stone, but she did not get up. Instead, she bowed her head even lower and stretched out her arms before her, in the traditional pose of one submitting to a much higher authority.

"Please," she whispered, her head still spinning from the visions she had been shown until she could barely piece together her words. "Please don't hurt my sisters. I'm sorry for doubting you. The fault is all mine. It's my blasphemy; they didn't know. How could we have known? The histories all say you're dead—"

Larka's words stumbled to a halt when Sol—she could not quite get out of the habit of thinking of him as "Sol"—crouched before her. She wasn't brave enough to look up, not until he put one finger under her chin and very gently tilted her face toward his. Even then, she did not quite dare to meet his gaze at first and instead looked at a point somewhere over his left shoulder.

"I am not angry," Death said quietly. Despite herself, Larka's eyes darted toward his face. He did not look angry. Merely a little sad. "Little Queen, I am not angry with you. I do not blame you for not believing me. I know it has been a long time since the gods walked your land, and you had no reason to believe me. *I am not angry.*"

The whole world had narrowed to a sliver, and the only things in that sliver were the cold stone under her knees and Death's finger under her chin.

She swallowed. Hard. "You are not angry, Lord Death?" she repeated. The relief she felt was staggering.

"No." The barest smile was upon his lips, and then it was gone. "Fear not. You won't be punished for not believing my words. A fool queen you would be someday if you did not question claims based on words alone." Sol took his hand away from her face and took both of Larka's hands again. "Come, get up. There's no need to kneel before me. You are my guest."

She did as he said. Once she was on her feet again, he let go of her hands and she stepped back among her sisters. Rhiannon reached over and took her hand in a crushing grip that hurt her palms, yet Larka did not let go.

"You do not need to call me Lord Death," he said,

after a moment. "The only realm I rule is one that you are not yet beholden to—and should not be for many years yet. Call me by the name that I gave you all when we first met. Call me Sol."

"Sol," she said experimentally. She had used the name before—he had, after all, given her and her sisters no other, and they had talked about him frequently after their recovery—but it was different now that she knew who he really was. It shook her to know that the whole time they had been speaking of him as a mysterious arcanist he had really been a god.

"Larka, what did he do to you?" asked Rhiannon, breaking into Larka's thoughts. "I don't know about you, but staring into someone's eyes for a few minutes isn't enough to convince me he's a god."

Sol sounded deeply offended when he said, "I did not do anything to her. I merely opened my mind and showed your sister my memories. I showed her the truth."

Rhiannon snorted. "The truth. More like an arcanist lie. I don't know what you are, but—"

Sol directed the full force of his gaze at Rhiannon. For the merest of seconds, his face flickered into that of a leering skull and then back to the man before them, young and pale-haired and covered in arcanist markings.

"Do you believe me now, clever princess?" he said.

Rhiannon only nodded. Her expression was much more shaken than a mere glance should have made her; Larka wondered if Sol had shown her some of his memories as well. She squeezed Rhiannon's hand as reassurance.

"Don't frighten them," said Galen from where he was still leaning against the wall.

To his credit, Sol looked contrite. "My apologies. I only wanted you to understand who I truly am."

"Well, you can do that without frightening them out of their wits." Galen spoke in an easy, almost familiar way that Larka found a little shocking now that she knew he was addressing a god. She looked at Galen again: dark hair, plain clothing, runes twining across his skin. He didn't look eerie and vaguely inhuman like Sol. Still, she had to ask. "Are you a god as well?"

At that, Galen tipped his head back and laughed, stretching the silver scars on his cheeks. "No, Little Queen. I'm nothing of the sort."

"Then what are you?"

"Oh, nothing very interesting. Just another dead man."

Rhiannon dropped Larka's hand in surprise. "You're dead? But you look so—"

Galen raised an eyebrow. "Normal? I assure you, princess, I'm very much dead. Look closer."

Larka didn't need to. She had noticed how faded Galen looked while they crossed the lake, as if he was lacking something vital that other people had, but she had assumed that it was her imagination. It hadn't been—the thing that he lacked was life.

"Now, the night will not last forever, and there is still much other business to cover," said Sol. "I'm sure you have more questions. Follow me, and I will answer them." Sol didn't wait to see if the girls were going to follow him before ducking down one of the narrow hallways branching from the antechamber. Galen darted after him.

Larka exchanged a suspicious glance with Rhiannon as they followed the god. Despite Sol's claims that they were safe, it was hard to forget that he was still Death Himself. It was not an aspect you took on and off as easily as a coat.

The hall was dimly lit with a scattered handful of arcanist globes placed at intervals, casting the walls in patches of bright light and deep shadow. Larka was grateful for the soft lighting; ever since her illness, her eyes had had trouble adjusting to bright light. She took a moment to wonder if Sol could see in the dark, being a god rather than a mere mortal, and then shoved the thought away. That was the least important thing to consider.

What little light there was revealed that the hallway

was pure white. The tiles, the wall hangings, the statues of strange figures leering from alcoves in the wall, all of them were white. Though the color was less harsh in the pale light of the arcanist globes, it was a little unnerving. Larka heard Kristina behind her whisper that it made her feel as if there was something wrong with her vision, and Larka had to agree. The hallway seemed to stretch on forever, too, adding to the strange feeling.

It was a minute before Larka dared to quicken her step and catch up with Sol. His legs were so much longer than hers that she could barely keep up, but he slowed to match her pace.

"You have questions, I am sure," he said, glancing her way. "Go on. Ask what you wish. I will answer."

"How is it that you lived when the other gods died?" she asked breathlessly. "The records and scriptures that the priests have, they say that the slaughter was complete. That no god survived the war. Why did you live?"

Sol barely spared her a glance, keeping his gaze fixed on some point in the distance.

"Death," Sol replied, "is under my rule, just as War oversaw every battle in the world and Wisdom every citadel of scholars. Other gods ruled the sea or the sun or the stroke of an ax. Death is what I oversee. It is the one thing I can control."

His voice was calm, maybe too calm. Until the words were already out of her mouth, Larka hadn't considered that the deaths of the other gods could be a sore point for Sol, even two thousand years later, but what was done was done. And he had said she could ask whatever questions she wanted.

He glanced over at Larka, and her confusion must have been evident because he elaborated, "It wouldn't be very dignified if Death Himself could die, would it? There are a lot of things I can do, Little Queen, but dying isn't one of them. War never lost a battle in her entire life, until she fought against her own family. Wisdom never heard a riddle he didn't know the answer to, and I cannot die."

"Ever?" asked Larka. She tried and failed to wrap her mind around the idea of never dying, of going on and on and on, even as the world changed around you.

"Ever," Sol agreed, a touch grimly. "Trust me. I should have died in the War of the Gods—certainly others tried hard enough to kill me—yet here I stand."

They walked in silence for a minute more until another question itched at Larka so much that she couldn't help but ask it. "The other gods… what happened to them after they died?" She had wondered this her entire life. The histories only spoke of the gods until they fell in battle, and then they were gone. Now that she had a chance to learn, she had to ask.

Sol's voice was still calm. Nonetheless, Larka could sense a roiling thunderstorm of emotions just below the surface. "I guided them along the path that all dead walk, to the far side of the lake where the afterlife for mortals resides. The other gods journeyed farther past that, to their own afterlife, but I could not follow them for I was not dead. So, they are gone, my brothers and sisters and enemies, and I…" Sol's voice caught, grief leaking into his words. "I remain here forever, guiding souls to the lands beyond my kingdom. I am the last god, and I am alone."

At first, Larka was chilled by his response. He was Death, old as time and more powerful than she could comprehend. He had been there when the sun first rose from the sea. He had lived through the War of the Gods and the centuries after it. By the time Queen Ysobel had set her capital upon ancient bones and carved her throne from the mountains of Belmarros, he had already been unknowably ancient. But when he spoke of what it was like to be alone after all the other gods had died, his sorrow made him seem much more present, more human.

Sol seemed to mistake Larka's silence for fright. "I did not mean to frighten you, Little Queen," he promised.

"You didn't," she said, and it was the truth. Even

if he was Death, it was impossible to fear him when he had grief in his eyes.

He smiled at that a little, just a twitch of his lips. “Of course not. I would expect nothing else from the woman who will be the next queen of Belmarros. And look, we’re here.”

Chapter Eight

Here, Larka realized as she stepped out of the corridor, was a massive room. She winced and raised a hand to shield her watering eyes from an explosion of brilliant light. Squinting, she looked around as the rest of her sisters filed behind her. Like the hallway before it, the great room was decorated in shades of white. The floor and pillars were white marble, the walls covered in swirling designs of silver and gold, the chandeliers high above made of twisted white metal. They were the source of the blinding light, and she quickly had to look away. Next to her, she saw Karo rubbing her eyes and blinking, and Yara throwing back her head to look past the chandeliers to the ceiling. Larka did the same and saw with amazement that the ceiling was made of glass, a sweeping stretch of pure black sky visible far, far above them.

"It's beautiful," said Rhiannon, sounding surprised.

"I know," breathed Karolina. There was wonder in her eyes. "Look at that sky. And the walls—I bet that's real gold and silver!"

"Shhh," said Larka, though she wanted to join in her sisters' admiration. "Rhee, Karo, we're not here to admire the decorations. Come on."

Sol stood out like an inkblot on a blank page as he walked farther into the room and up the shallow steps to a dais. Galen followed him and seated himself on one of the steps as if he had done it a thousand times. Larka looked past the dead man and saw a tall black throne at the top of the dais, seemingly carved out of a single slab of shining stone. Sol sat down on it, arranged the folds of his robe around him, and rested his hands on the great clawed armrests.

Gwynna barely waited for him to settle before she asked, "So this is the underworld? How come we're here if we're not yet dead?"

"The underworld is a world unto itself, princess. It has layers, and the seat of my power is not terribly deep into it. Walk farther, along the paths the dead take, and only then will you go so far that you cannot return."

"How far would we have to go?" asked Gwynna. Her voice was full of distrust that Larka didn't blame her for having.

"Very," promised Sol. "Past the forests you walked through, past this island, to the very far side of the lake. Farther than you or your sisters could ever go by accident. Trust me, you will be able to return to your own lands after this."

"That's good to know," said Gwynna. She crossed her arms and tipped her chin up. Larka recognized that her sister was trying not to show that she was intimidated by Sol. "Now tell us, Lord Death, why are we here and what do you want with us?"

"As I've told you before, you're my guests here." Sol appeared unfazed by the unfriendly way Gwynna regarded him. Of course, as Death, he was probably used to fear and contempt, Larka thought.

Gwynna didn't look impressed. "Yes, but why? I know you want us to pay off the life debt we owe you, but how do you want us to do that? Why does paying off a debt mean that we have to come all the way to the underworld?"

Sol shrugged. "I'm lonely, princess. My brothers and sisters have been dead for so long that I am starting to forget their faces. The only visitors I have received since I led the last of them along the path into the afterlife are other souls going along the same journey. So, I would like some company. Your company, to be specific."

Larka blinked in confusion. "What do you mean, 'company'? And why us?"

"Why, that's how I want you to pay off your debt." Sol tilted his head, his long braid spilling over one shoulder. "Little Queen, I am not the kind of person to demand some outrageous reward for saving your lives. You may think of death as cruel, but I am not. All I want in return is for you and your sisters to be my guests. For at least a few hours a night, I would like to not be alone."

"You don't need us to come to you," Larka pointed out. "You were perfectly capable of leaving the underworld just last week. Why not leave it again and seek out company for yourself that way?"

Sol sighed. "The day I saved you was the summer solstice, the longest day of the year. The world begins to turn back to darkness after that. On certain ritual days—the solstices and All Hallows' Eve—I may leave the underworld. That is why I only came on the very last night of your illness. The rest of the time—" he shrugged, resigned, "I am as much trapped down here as if there were chains around my ankles." He kicked one foot for emphasis. Larka saw that he wore no shoes and that yet more arcanist tattoos curled down his leg and across his pale, slender toes. "A long time ago, I used to be able to leave the underworld to guide the dying, but no longer. I am diminished now that I cannot draw on the power of the other gods to let me walk in the living world."

"Is that why you saved us?" asked Gwynna. "Because you wanted company and we just happened to be dying on the right day?"

"No!" Sol sounded so taken-aback by the idea that Larka had to believe him. "Well, not entirely. I could… I could *feel* you dying, you understand. You have all been touched by so much death in your lives, and in such a short time, that I could feel it when it started to come for you as well."

"Really?" asked Larka. Though she and her sisters had tossed around many theories as to why Sol had saved them, she'd never considered that the endless progression of death in their lives—their father and all five of his wives, one after another—had anything to do with it.

Sol ran one finger down the carved armrest of his throne. "Besides that, the dying of a future king or queen can be felt all across this realm, for the hopes and dreams of their reign die along with them. I felt that dying, and I… I did not want to watch you journey down here, not when you are all so young. I waited for the solstice so that I might walk in the daylight world. And I hoped that you would still be alive by then."

"You can't seriously expect us to believe you saved us only out of the goodness of your heart," said Gwynna flatly. "Good men don't make people swear undying vows not to speak of them."

Sol sat up indignantly. "I did not know you were not aware of the power of Truth's vow! Humanity has fallen lower than I thought if you cannot remember even that much. I only made you swear it so that this agreement between us would remain private. I want nothing more from you than company and entertainment."

"I see," said Larka, cautious and a little baffled. "Company and entertainment. I don't think that's the usual way of paying off a life debt—"

"It is tradition that I may choose the manner in which you pay me, and you Belmarrians are all terribly obsessed with tradition, are you not? No matter how many centuries go by, that, at least, does not seem to change." Sol nonchalantly leaned his chin on a hand.

Larka found herself saying in defense, "It's our way. The foundation that our kingdom was built upon. When Queen Ysobel united—"

"Yes, yes." Sol waved a dismissive hand. "I know all about Ysobel from the stories the dead tell me. Not that her great deeds did her much good in the end. Everyone comes to my realm, no matter how noble they are. Whether peasant or warrior queen, all come to death eventually."

Gwynna shot Larka a glance, rolling her eyes, and Larka could practically hear her sister say, *That's pretty grim, don't you think*? Larka gave her a little shrug in reply. He was the god of death. That was bound to make anyone a little morbid.

"Do you expect us to begin repaying tonight?" Larka asked. Her hands throbbed from the ritual cuts, a lifetime ago in the daylight world. She wished that she could just go home and put some of Albin's numbing salve on the cuts. The idea of entertaining Death while her hands hurt was exhausting.

"No, I don't think so." Sol's gaze went to her hands. He must have been thinking the same thing. "Not when your hands are so injured. I want your company, not your blood. I would not have called you here tonight if I had known you were hurt."

"It's not Larka's fault," Gwynna said, annoyed. "She had her coming-of-age, and the heir has to spill blood to prove his or her loyalty to Belmarros."

"How savage." There was real distaste on Sol's face, and Larka couldn't help but be amused that Death Himself disliked their traditions while the rest of Belmarros insisted on following them. "That is very like humans, I suppose, to cause yourselves pain for no reason. Is it supposed to make you feel noble about yourself because you are willing to suffer for your crown?"

"Yes, that's about it." Larka absentmindedly rubbed a finger over one of the bandages and winced at a burst of pain.

Sol hesitated and then asked, almost timidly, "May I see your hands?"

Larka mounted the dais, past where Galen lounged on the steps, to stand before Sol. She uncurled her hands and showed him the strips of white bandage wrapped around each palm.

There was an unexpected look of kindness on Sol's face. "Fool that I am, I didn't even wonder what those were for when I first saw them. Do they hurt much?"

"Yes, but I only got them a few days ago. The doctors said they will heal soon enough, though they'll scar." It had made her uneasy at first, the idea of having these markings on her body that would so publicly declare, This girl shall be queen someday, but she did not really care anymore. She had spent her entire life being shaped in a thousand different invisible ways to be queen; two visible scars were the smallest of it.

Sol touched the tip of one finger to the bandage, so lightly that it didn't hurt. "I might be able to help with these. I have not fallen so far in my power that I cannot heal a little."

Larka wondered what had happened to his power to leave it so decreased. She was tempted to take up his offer, until she remembered that she would somehow have to explain the miraculous recovery to her doctors. Recovering from a fever was one thing, if there was someone to claim credit; cuts that healed overnight would be a little harder. "No, thank you," she said politely. "I'm not sure how I would explain that."

"If you're sure." There was something like regret in his voice when he continued, "I suppose you should go now."

"How soon should we come back?" This from Kristina, sounding worried.

"Oh..." Sol tilted his head back. "Say, a week. I wouldn't have your sister to entertain me if she still hurts."

"Alright." Rhiannon this time. "Auri, do you mind if you keep carrying Alannah? I think she's fallen asleep."

Larka looked back and saw that, indeed, Alannah was asleep in Auri's arms.

"Until next time, Little Queen," said Sol softly, bringing her attention back to him. "If you go out that door," he jerked his head in the direction of a door opposite the one they had come through, "you should find yourselves on the path to your home."

Larka looked at the doorway, gaping and black as the maw of a monster. "That's not the way that we came in, is it?"

Sol shrugged. "There are many different entrances to your world in my realm, and they are constantly shifting. Death is not supposed to be an easy realm to get to if one is not dead, for we cannot have every mourner come searching for their lost love. That particular passageway was not there an hour ago, and it will not be here in an hour."

Larka blinked. "I've never heard of that before."

"Humans have forgotten a great many things about myself and my realm since the war, not limited to my actual existence."

Sol raised her hands to his lips and kissed her palms delicately. Larka could not suppress a slight shiver, and not just because his lips were colder than a human's. Plenty of courtiers had kissed her hand before, but always the back of it, not the palm. It felt much more intimate. Sol's mouth lingered a little on the second kiss, and then he let go.

"Goodbye, Lord Death," she said, with as much regal dignity as she could muster even though she now felt shaky.

"I thought I said to call me Sol," he said, though there was no reproach in his voice. He sighed. "Goodbye, Little Queen. I will see you again soon."

She started to step from the dais and toward her sisters when Sol said, "One more thing, Little Queen. When you walk back through the forests of silver, gold, and diamond, take a leaf from each one. In a week, when you wish to come here again, merely set them on the floor of your room and think of this place to open the portal."

"No magic I've ever heard of works like that," protested Gwynna from where she stood with the rest of Larka's sisters.

"The trees have the magic of my land in them and can remember their way home, even in another world." Sol sounded serene, as if it was entirely normal to talk about trees as if they could think. Then again, this was the underworld. "You have that same magic in you. Together, it's enough to open the portal."

"None of us have magic," pointed out Larka. "At least, not that we're aware of."

"Oh, it's not your magic. It's mine. There's a trace of death in all of you now."

"What?" Rhiannon cried. Larka turned to see shock written across her sister's face, and her brown skin had an ashy undertone.

Sol tilted his head to one side. "Are you alright, princess?"

"I don't want your death magic," Rhiannon snapped, rubbing a hand across the bare skin of her forearm. "Take it out of me!"

"I can't," said Sol patiently. "And I wouldn't, even if I could. It's a remnant of the power I used to heal you all. I am not the god to whom life comes naturally. In order that you might live, I had to bring you a little closer to death."

Larka's skin prickled unpleasantly at his words, and she looked down at herself, trying to see the power he'd left inside. She'd felt a little different ever since her illness—more drawn to the shadows, eyes stinging at bright light—but she'd never dreamed it was because she carried a touch of death inside herself.

"But what will it do to us?" persisted Rhiannon.

"Nothing," said Sol. "You will, perhaps, be drawn to death and the underworld a little more than you would be without it. That's all. You are still yourself. I promise you."

Rhiannon still looked unsettled, but she sighed and

said, “Good. I just wish you’d told us that earlier.”

“I have told you,” said Sol. Larka wondered if all gods were as puzzling as he was. “Remember, pick the leaves and take them with you. Galen will show you out.”

“Of course,” said Galen. He climbed to his feet and began to walk to the door. Larka noted that his boots made no sound on the marble floor. She and her sisters followed Galen to the door. Just before stepping out of the room, she turned to look back at the throne and saw that Sol was still sitting there, a single dark figure against the vast, white emptiness of the room. God he might be, but he was also so alone that she pitied him.

Chapter Nine

Sure enough, the passageway that Sol had pointed out to them lead straight out to the lake, where Larka and her sisters immediately climbed back into the boats paddled by still, silent men—men who, she now realized, must also be shades like Galen. The princesses stopped only to pick three of the leaves, which Larka put in her pocket. She thought perhaps she would make a necklace out of them; no one would believe they had come from real trees, and turning them into jewelry would be a good way to disguise them.

Tired as they were, the climb up to their bedchamber seemed to take the sisters twice as long as the descent. The moment the last girl climbed off the staircase—Talia, who had been lagging behind and complaining of exhaustion the whole way—the hole in the floor sealed as if it had never been. Their room was exactly as they had left it, Gwynna's books piled haphazardly on her bed and clothing strewn across the floor.

To Larka's relief, the door was still locked. The entire time she'd been in the underworld—she was still having a bit of a hard time wrapping her head around the fact that they had just been in the *underworld*—she had been silently worrying that someone would notice the girls' absence and raise a panic. It seemed that no one had, and the clock said that only a few hours had passed. Underworld or no, it seemed that time still passed the same way.

Larka sat down cross-legged on her bed and began to undo the pins in her hair with clumsy, aching fingers.

Auri covered her mouth with one hand as she yawned. "I don't think I've ever been up this late before."

"Try and get some sleep," Rhiannon said gently. "Everyone should."

Larka thought that Auri was probably going to have to get used to staying up late, if Sol really did want them to entertain him every night. Still, although it was a strange way to call in a life debt, it wasn't the worst she'd heard of. No marriage, no drained treasury.

Larka helped get the younger girls settled in their beds and was about to get to bed herself when Gwynna pounced.

"Not so fast," Gwynna declared, seating herself down on Larka's bed, immovable as rock. "We're not going to sleep until we talk about what just happened."

Larka rolled her eyes. "Really, Gwyn? In case you didn't notice, it's late."

"Rhee, back me up," called Gwynna. "We have to talk."

"I hate to say it, but she's right," said Rhiannon, coming over to sit beside Gwynna. Larka resigned herself to not sleeping any time soon. Still, she didn't really mind it; the three of them had stayed up late talking often enough when they were younger, before Larka was consumed by her role as heir.

Larka and Rhiannon and Gwynna. Before the others were old enough to be part of court, it had been the three of them together. They had the clearest memories of their father, who'd been a figure in the distance for most of his other daughters, and that bound them together in some way none of them could really explain.

They curled up together then as they used to do before King Eldric died, Larka resting against the headboard, Gwynna and Rhiannon leaning against each other and facing her, all their legs tangled together under the blankets.

"So," said Rhiannon once the room was filled with the soft sound of the breath of nine other sleeping girls. "They're not all gone."

She didn't have to say who she meant. All the princesses had been raised on stories of the dead gods. Two thousand years, and the world still echoed from their absence.

Gwynna shook her head. "I just can't believe it. One of the gods still lives. Death Himself, no less. All this time, and we never knew. All this time he walked in the underworld and we grieved the gods, and he *still lived*."

"And we can't speak of it," said Rhiannon glumly. "I suppose he thinks humanity doesn't need to know he's still alive, not if he's so diminished in power and can't even come to our world." She paused thoughtfully. "You know, we must be keeping the greatest secret in the world. If we could speak this truth, it would upend everything."

All three of them were silent. The speeches the priests read on Remembrance Days, the books in the castle library, the children's tales they had once read, the plays and ballads and monologues, the history the entire world believed... it was all wrong. For two thousand years, humanity had thought it was alone, and it was wrong. The revelation that it wasn't, that one god still remained, was so staggeringly enormous that Larka could barely wrap her mind around it.

"I wonder why the records say that Death is dead if he still lives." Gwynna stared into the darkness of their room. "You would think our ancestors would have noticed if the body of one of the gods was missing. The death of a god is usually, well, large and dramatic and hard to miss. I mean, Lady War's body turned into an entire island."

"He told me that the other gods did try to kill him," admitted Larka. "But apparently Death can't die. In the chaos of the War of the Gods, everyone must have just thought he was gone. "

Rhiannon sighed. "And none of the other gods lived to tell the truth."

"I suppose I should have wondered who he really was, having heard all of those stories about arcanists and their love of money, but it didn't occur to me," said Larka.

"Yes, most people's first thought when confronted with a man with mystical healing powers and arcanist tattoos isn't that he must be a forgotten member of a pantheon that was supposed to have been destroyed thousands of years ago." There was a wry note in Gwynna's voice.

"I just thought he was strange," Larka admitted.

Rhiannon pulled the blanket a little higher up to her chin. "And you don't think he's strange now?"

"Of course she doesn't. She thinks he's handsome."

Larka flushed at Gwynna's words. "I do not!" she protested.

"Oh, really?" Gwynna gave her an amused look. "Then tell me, what exactly was going on with you two down there? He didn't care when you challenged his authority. He told you to call him by his name. Then the god of death, an actual god, kissed your palm. And you didn't seem to mind. So, what, exactly, was that?"

"I don't know," Larka muttered. "It's all very sudden."

Hastily, Rhiannon changed the topic, and Larka was grateful to her. "Strange and sudden is right. If three weeks ago you'd told me that one of the gods survived and would save my life, I would have laughed and suggested a visit to a mind doctor."

"What did he do to you, by the way, to convince you?" asked Gwynna. "I do believe now that he's a god, but all he did was grab your hands, stare into space, and suddenly you were convinced he was telling the truth."

Larka blinked, and she could still see images that Sol had shown her behind her eyelids, although they were fading. "He showed me his history. His true essence. All the aspects that he used to be seen as when he walked the world before the war. It was… it was like nothing I'd seen before. He showed me, and I just knew. Even the arcanists don't have power like a god does."

Rhiannon curled her feet under the blanket. "It was a good disguise for him to come in, really. No one dares question arcanists these days. He couldn't have chosen a better cover to get to us if he tried."

"I don't think it's a disguise," said Larka suddenly. She had been thinking of this on the walk back to their bedchamber, puzzling over the conflicting information that refused to fit together. "I mean, he still had the tattoos even when he was in the underworld, and he wasn't pretending then."

"Maybe he does have some connection to the arcanists after all," said Gwynna. Even as tired as her sister was, Larka could tell that a thousand new thoughts about arcanists and gods and everything in between were whirling through Gwynna's head.

Rhiannon nudged her. "Gwyn, I know you're a scholar at heart, but I think research and theories can wait until you've had some actual sleep."

Gwynna sighed. "I know, I know." She and Rhiannon got up and picked their way across the messy floor to sleep.

Larka settled into her own bed, tucking her cut hands on top of the blanket so the bandages didn't snag on the cloth in the night and wake her. She'd thought that she would have a hard time sleeping after the revelations of the evening, after having crossed into the underworld and back again, but instead she was asleep so quickly she didn't even have time to be surprised.

Chapter Ten

The next morning, Larka was dragged out of bed after a few short hours of sleep and marched, at seven o'clock, to the first meeting of the Royal Council since she'd turned eighteen and earned the title of Little Queen by cutting scars down her palms.

Council meetings were held in a narrow, rectangular room of gray stone with a long wooden table running down the center and early morning sunlight falling across the gathered councilors. Though Larka's seat at the front of the room was a chair so gilded and elaborate that sitting in it was normally so uncomfortable as to be a challenge, she was so exhausted and overwhelmed by the previous night that she was having difficulty paying attention to the day's proceedings.

Larka did understand, however, what the general subject on the table was that day, or at least a little. It was about whether or not to continue selling wine from the southern vineyards to the island nation of Veanara. Councilor Eugenio was in favor; Councilor Davin was not. Lord Braddock, who owned many of the relevant vineyards, had been invited to the meeting, but so far, he had been content to sit quietly in the midst of the arguing council while Davin and Eugenio battled out their opinions.

"You misunderstand me," Eugenio was saying. "I'm not arguing that we should favor Veanara over other countries. I'm saying that they have an increasing demand for fine wine, which we are currently able to supply." Eugenio was a tall, middle-aged man with a receding silver hairline and a tendency to stand and gesture wildly while illustrating a point. He was doing so currently, and his neighbors on both sides had to keep ducking out of the way in order not to get a meaty hand to the face.

Councilor Davin was the youngest member of the council, only six years older than Larka, although his wide hazel eyes and brown curls made him look younger. His arms were folded resolutely, one hand fiddling with the gold braiding on his wrist. He looked nervous, but there was a stubborn streak in him that Larka had seen come out to play more than once. "Yes," Davin said, "but I'm not convinced that we need to reinforce our alliance with Veanara quite so much. There are other countries to be thinking of."

Larka stifled a yawn and tried to keep track of the debate. The two councilmen went back and forth several times more, others cutting into the discussion to share their opinions. Eugenio gestured so furiously he almost hit Councilor Mariana in the face, and Councilor Davin began to sweat under the hot lights of the chamber. Stefan, trapped squarely in the middle of the argument, began to have a rather long-suffering expression. Lord Braddock looked bored.

Larka couldn't blame either Stefan or Braddock. From what she knew of court politics, Eugenio tended to favor Veanara since his family was originally from there. Davin, while idealistic, was overly cautious. There were seemingly endless benefits and problems that could come from this one trade issue, and the council seemed determined to go over every single one that morning. It was entirely possible that Larka would be sitting there until evening while they argued.

The two councilmen continued arguing for the next few minutes, so quickly that Larka's sluggish mind could barely follow the points they were making. Eugenio listed every alliance they'd ever had with Veanara for the last two hundred years, and Davin replied with a reprimand about Veanara being known for debauchery and little else.

"Why don't we ask Lord Braddock for his opinion on the vineyards?" suggested Councilor Mariana diplomatically. "While I appreciate your dedication to our agriculture, Davin, your own estates are not as far south as the vineyards are. I would greatly appreciate the opinions of someone with a more personal stake in this."

Davin's mouth snapped shut in the middle of an explanation about the amount of water he believed it took to grow the vineyards.

Lord Braddock leaned back in his chair. Larka saw a flicker of self-satisfaction cross his craggy face now that he was the center of attention, just as he always liked.

"I believe we should continue trade with Veanara," Braddock said easily, shooting Eugenio a conspiratorial look. "My people are dedicated to this kingdom. They're willing to do the work, and the land can support it. Hopefully, this could cover the debts with Veanara that our beloved late king produced."

Larka winced at the barbed tone of his last sentence.

"Very well," said Mariana. "All in favor of continuing to sell to Veanara, please raise your hands."

Braddock, Eugenio, and more than half of the council raised their hands. Davin did not, instead folding his arms and looking as if he was resisting the urge to glower like a child that hadn't gotten his way. Stefan did not vote due to his role on the council being purely ceremonial now that he no longer held the powers of regent. Larka did not raise her hand either, although that was mostly because she was too flustered to decide which way her vote should fall.

Mariana, counting off the votes, paused when she turned to Larka. "Dear girl, don't you wish to have a say in this decision?"

"I'm not sure which way to vote," muttered Larka, trying and failing to shake off the exhaustion that coated her words. "Both sides give good points." Something about Mariana always made the princess feel like she was still the child that played with blocks of colored wood under the council table while her father disregarded advice given by his desperate councilors.

Lord Braddock leaned forward in his seat, burgundy tunic shining against the dark wood of the table. "Well, it's a simple enough decision, isn't it? Do you wish Belmarros to pay off our debt to Veanara through the sale of fine wine, or do you wish to watch that debt to continue to grow with no way to pay it off?" Braddock spoke kindly enough, yet Larka heard a note of the same condescension that was always present when he spoke to her.

Our beloved late king. The words played in her ears again, and Larka remembered every extravagant party her father had ever hosted, every portrait commissioned, every inch of rich imported brocade bought, every day that he had sat before the council and toyed with his jewelry instead of listening.

She refused to be her father. She refused to be the one wearing the crown while Belmarros sank into debt like the ship that had carried her father to his doom.

"I want only the best for Belmarros," said Larka, barely able to squeeze the words out of her throat. "Of course I want to settle our debt with Veanara. I support continuing trade."

"Good, that's settled." Mariana wrote down the final vote in her impeccable handwriting and smiled, a triumphant baring of teeth. "Braddock, thank you for your honest opinion of your lands."

"It was the least I could do," said Lord Braddock. He was smiling, too, the satisfied smile of a cat that's caught a mouse with greater ease than expected. "You will excuse me, if you don't mind. I have other matters to attend to." He rose from his seat and marched out of the Council Room with more confidence than Larka could ever dream of having. She breathed a little easier at his absence and turned back to the council.

Of course, the meeting wasn't over yet. No sooner had the doors shut behind Braddock than Councilor Trajan brought up the next topic on the agenda: whether or not to raise the pay of Belmarros's army. This issue was not so easily settled. Even Mariana and Eugenio, normally allies, were split on it, and the conversation dragged on and on with no end in sight. It wasn't even an interesting debate; the councilors went over the same points more times than Larka could count. Empty treasuries, the possibility of revolt, the necessity of an army even in peacetime—Larka was astonished at how many ways they had to say the same thing. She found herself nearly falling asleep at the table.

Just as Larka was starting to think that she might be forced to get over her paralyzing fear of speaking in the Council Room and tell them to make a decision and move on, one of the council pages arrived. He was a boy of about ten or eleven with curly brown hair and a nervous kind of energy that reminded Larka of a royal kennel puppy, very excited yet not entirely sure what it was doing.

Larka watched the page as he entered the room. She'd never seen a council meeting interrupted before; it had to be something important. Could it have something to do with Sol? Had someone discovered her and her sisters' disappearance last night? Or maybe it had to do with her ceremony?

Her tumbling thoughts were abruptly interrupted when the door slammed shut behind the page. The boom of the closing door was clearly much louder than he had intended it, because the page jumped and then blushed as Eugenio was cut off mid-sentence and the rest of the eyes in the room turned to him.

"Well? What's so important, boy, that you're barging into the middle of the Little Queen's own council?" Eugenio snapped, annoyed at having been interrupted in the middle of a rant about the ridiculous size of army pensions. Larka resisted the urge to snort—at the rate things were going, this was more

Eugenio's council than hers.

The page turned bright red at Eugenio's hostile tone and shrank in on himself.

"Councilor!" Stefan said angrily. "You overstep your boundaries!" He turned to the page and, more gently, said, "What is it?"

"Some guests have arrived, Majesty," the boy blurted. "A nobleman. He says that he's here to see the princess. Um, I mean, the Little Queen." Larka's heart jumped with a combination of apprehension and surprise, and for a split second she thought of Sol, the last person who had unexpectedly turned up demanding to see her. The page continued, "He says that he's come as one of Little Queen Larka's suitors."

Chapter Eleven

The entire council froze at the boy's words in a way that would have been comical if Larka's gut hadn't lurched unpleasantly. Not so soon, she pleaded, though she wasn't sure with whom. Please, not so soon. I've only been eighteen for a few days!

"Are you sure about this?" asked Mariana, making her way around the table to stand before the boy.

The page stuck out his chest indignantly. "Yes, Councilor! I heard him myself, and the steward confirmed it."

"Where is this man from?" asked Davin.

"Dalbrast," said the page. An interested murmur washed through the room like a wave.

"Risky for a Dalbrasti nobleman to come here seeking our Little Queen's hand," whispered Councilor Edana, leaning over Larka to speak to Councilor Corbin.

Larka scrambled to remember what her tutors had

taught her of the country. Dalbrast: a kingdom that lay on the other side of the vast ocean from Belmarros. The islands between the two kingdoms had once been a continent, but ever since the land mass had been destroyed in the God's War, Belmarros and Dalbrast had become the two biggest powers on either side. Dalbrast was a coldly puritanical country obsessed with damnation and virtue, filled with snowy mountains and ruled by a kaiser with a heart of ice and a fist of steel. Larka had spent many days memorizing details of the countless wars and skirmishes between Dalbrast and Belmarros, though the kingdoms' relations had calmed in recent years. Still, that history of animosity lingered. It was hard to forget years of blood spilled across the waters of an ocean.

"This Dalbrasti man, did he come alone?" asked Eugenio urgently. "Did he bring an armed escort?"

The page gulped at Eugenio's intensity. "No, sir. He brought only himself and his sister. He says that he comes in his own name, not his kaiser's. He told the steward he only wants to be allowed to compete for the hand of the queen of Belmarros."

"I see," said Eugenio, though there was a hint of grimness in his voice. "Well, this is certainly a surprise. I think—"

"This isn't a matter for the council, Eugenio," interrupted Stefan from where he sat at the edge of the council table. "Suitors never are, and I don't think this man's country of origin changes that. You're all dismissed. Someone find this man and bring him to the East Sitting Room so that Larka can be introduced." The page left, but no one else moved. "You're all dismissed," repeated Stefan, a hint of annoyance in his voice. "This meeting is over." Finally, the councilors rose with a scrape of seats and the sound of low voices. Even Eugenio didn't protest; he had clearly learned his lesson about undermining the royal family, at least for the moment.

After the councilors left, Larka and Stefan took a shortcut to the East Sitting Room through a door at the back of the chamber. Legend had it that a previous king had the door installed so he could visit his mistress during breaks between meetings. Larka thought it more likely that the king had simply wanted a quick escape from the council.

Compared to the other sitting rooms, the East Sitting Room was small, but it was still larger than Larka's bedchamber. It was crammed with velvet-upholstered chairs, tables full of expensive knickknacks, and shelves of leather-bound volumes that Larka doubted anyone had ever read. The entire room was decorated in shades of forest green and blue, the royal colors of Belmarros, and the wide windows looked out over a garden courtyard that was a flourishing riot of colorful flowers despite the heat.

Larka winced as she looked at the wall hangings: a series of tapestries depicting a deer hunt, ending with the embroidered huntsman parading back to his mountain lodge holding the bloody head of the stag. Her father had favored this room for meeting with ambassadors and nobles newly arrived at court, perhaps as a way to intimidate them. As a child, though, the tapestries had terrified her. The dead eyes of the stag had always seemed to follow her no matter where she'd sat in the room.

Larka sat down on one of the overstuffed chairs with her back to the wall hangings and wished that she could open one of the windows. The air was hot and stuffy, and the scent of dried herbs drifting from the bowl beside made her want to sneeze. Still, she knew it wasn't proper, so she didn't ask. She waited until Stefan had settled down next to her before saying, "Stef, isn't it awfully early for suitors? I mean, I'm only *just* eighteen."

Stefan crossed his ankles and tugged absently on a handful of hair in a way that Larka knew meant he was thinking hard. At last he said, "It is odd, I have to admit. Most would-be suitors have the decency to wait a couple of weeks to make sure it doesn't appear they were waiting to pounce."

Larka shivered despite the hot room. "Ugh, don't say that. It makes me feel like some sheep being stalked by a wolf."

Stefan put a comforting hand on her shoulder. "Don't worry about it too much. There will be a lot of people to choose from, and you won't have to marry until you feel ready. Maybe you'll even come to love your choice. I certainly did with Dario."

"Yes, but you weren't the future ruler of Belmarros when you married Dario. Everyone's going to care a lot more about the person I choose than they did with you. Maybe they'll even—maybe they'll even try to choose for me."

"Larka. Look at me." Stefan used the hand on her shoulder to turn his niece in her seat so that she faced him instead of the doors to the sitting room. When he met her blue eyes with his own, both so similar to Eldric's, he was serious in a way she rarely saw him with her. "I know you're not used to this. I know it hasn't been long since you came of age, and I know that you technically haven't been crowned yet. But you need to remember no one can force you to do anything you don't want to. I'm not saying you should be like my brother and ignore every piece of advice the council begged him to listen to, but you also don't need to answer only to them in matters like this. They're not going to be the ones married to the man picked as royal consort. Understand?"

Larka made herself breathe in and out, as her tutors had taught her to do when she got overwhelmed. "Yes, I understand." She made herself sound calm, though inside she was anything but. In the weeks leading up to her birthday, she'd been worried that she might falter or embarrass herself during the ceremony. Now, with that past, Larka had even more to worry about: that she would hate all her suitors or that she'd accidentally seem to favor ones who weren't respectable enough and start rumors that she was going to be just like her father. Add all her confused thoughts about Sol and the debt she owed him, and it was as if she was carrying a mountain on her shoulders day in and day out. Still, she tried to smile at Stefan and conceal any of her nervousness.

"I understand, Stef. I'm the Little Queen now. I have power, real power, now. I'll try not to forget."

Stefan smiled back at her, and for a second she saw a hint of the younger boy he'd been back before her father died. He'd been regent for over four years now, and it was taking its toll. Sometimes it was hard to remember that he was only ten years older than her. "Good," he said. "Gods know I let myself get bullied by the council enough for both of us when I first became regent."

He had barely finished his sentence when there was a knock on the door. Larka swept her hands nervously down her gown one last time and called, "You may come in." Her stomach felt as if there were a dozen warring snakes in it.

The door swung open again, and the page from the Council Room entered. In his green and blue clothing, he practically melted into the background of the room. He bowed, then said, "His Grace, Duke Miron Brandt of Dalbrast."

Larka's first suitor entered the sitting room. He, too, bowed before Larka and Stefan, then stood waiting before them. Larka used it as an opportunity to study her unexpected guest.

The Duke held himself proudly, almost arrogantly, though he was in the presence of royalty. He was perhaps five or six years older than Larka, certainly not the oldest suitor she could have. He was pale-skinned like most people from Dalbrast, his dark green wool tunic far more suited for the cold mountains of his home than the hot summer of Belmarros. His reddish-brown hair was worn longer than Belmarrian fashion, almost shoulder-length, and his eyes were dark brown and keen. He was handsome, she had to admit, though his eyes were perhaps a little too knowing for her taste.

The Duke's eyes swept up and down her, taking in every detail of her, from the bandages on her palms to her circlet of braids that was beginning to fall apart after hours in the Council Room.

"Your Highness," he said. "It is an honor to meet you." He spoke Belmarrian well, with only a hint of a Dalbrasti accent, which snagged harshly on the ends of his words.

"It is the same for me," Larka murmured politely.

"I only wish that my ship had arrived in time for your ceremony yesterday. Unfortunately, it was caught in a storm and I only arrived today," the Duke continued. "Otherwise, my sister and I would have surely attended."

"I'm sure that would have been lovely," Larka replied, scrambling to find some hidden meaning in his words. "I do hope your journey was not so bad, besides the storm." The Duke waved a careless hand. "For me, no worse than any other trip. My sister, though, became quite ill. She's never done well during sea travel."

"Speaking of your sister," Stefan said, frowning, "why didn't you bring her along to the palace with you so we could be introduced?"

"I did, actually," the Duke admitted. "She is still quite sick, though, and I thought it would be better to have her escorted to one of the healers rather than embarrass herself in front of our hosts by becoming ill. She is often embarrassing herself, my sister," he added scornfully.

Larka arranged her face into a look of serene calm to hide her revulsion. Perhaps it was just the Dalbrasti's way of being obsessed with guest protocol, but she didn't like that this man's first concern was his appearance before them rather than his sister's health. If Stefan felt similarly about the Duke's words, he hid it well.

Larka said, "Your Grace, I must say, I'm surprised to see you here so early. I only turned eighteen recently, and you mentioned that you would have been here earlier had your ship not been delayed. If I am remembering my lessons correctly, the journey from Dalbrast is more than three weeks."

The Duke nodded. "It is indeed. Longer, sometimes."

"Then you must have set out even before my coming-of-age."

"Yes." The Duke was beginning to look puzzled.

"Well, I don't know if it is different in Dalbrast when your monarchs come of age, but here in Belmarros, it is customary to allow the new ruler a few months to get used to her new position before any courting occurs." Larka's father, of course, had married scarcely two months after his coronation, but that had been mostly so his advisers wouldn't have time to force him to marry someone else. Never mind that the king marrying a common actress from the Gallow's Dance had been one of the largest scandals in living memory. "So, you see," continued Larka, "I'm afraid you've arrived rather early. I likely will not be entertaining any official suitors until mid-fall."

The Duke smiled. Larka thought, spitefully, that he looked like a ferret in that moment, with his thin build and narrow face. She immediately regretted the thought; it was very uncharitable, and besides, she hardly knew the man. "Oh, it's no trouble at all," the Duke said, sounding almost pleased at her pronouncement. "That will just give us plenty of time to get to know each other before courting officially starts."

Larka scrambled for something to say in response. She wasn't sure that she wanted to get to know this man at all. "I'm afraid we don't have any guest rooms that a man of your station would require," she blurted. "The castle is quite full with all the guests from my coming-of-age. That's another reason we don't usually have suitors for a couple of months—there's never enough room for them right after the ceremony. I doubt that there will be rooms free for another few weeks."

The Duke was still smiling. "Oh, that won't be a problem. My sister and I are perfectly capable of finding rooms for ourselves in the city. We will be able to visit whenever you wish us to and to take rooms here once the guests are gone."

"Oh," said Larka lamely, all her plans foiled. It seemed that she would be stuck with this man after all. "Well, alright. Give your sister my best wishes for her recovery. It was… it was a pleasure to meet you."

"Likewise," the Duke said. He bowed again.

"As you said, we have plenty of time to get to know each other, and I'd hate to keep you here when you should be settling in."

The Duke's mask of courtly charm slipped for a bare second, and she saw an annoyed muscle work in his jaw. Well, it had been his decision to arrive early, she thought. She could hardly be faulted for trying to get rid of him when he shouldn't even be there, could she?

"Of course," he said. "I suppose I should see if my sister is doing better. My thanks for this audience, Your Majesty." He bowed again, a fluid and beautifully practiced movement, and turned to go.

Larka followed him with her gaze as he walked to the door and left. Her heart was filled with dread, not because of the man himself, however unpleasant he had seemed, but because of what he represented. It was starting. She couldn't deny it any longer. The beginning of her reign was starting, and there was nothing she could do to stop it. Soon, an entire nation would look to her for guidance and wisdom. Soon, she would marry someone who might be no more than a distant, awkward stranger. Soon, the crown of Belmarros would rest on her head, and she did not feel ready to have that burden. Sometimes she felt like she was still the same girl reeling with the news of her father's sudden death, drowning in all her new responsibilities and expectations and all the eyes upon her.

The world was changing around her faster than she could keep up with it.

"Larka, are you alright?" asked Stefan, and she realized that she had been staring into space for several long seconds.

She folded her hands to stop them from trembling.

"Yes," Larka said, her voice sounding distant to her own ears. "Yes, Stefan, I'm fine." As bitter as the lie was on her tongue, there was no way for her to take it back. There were too many people relying on her now.

The rest of the week passed in a blur—attending court, lunches with Stefan and her sisters, council meetings, more court. It seemed to Larka that one moment she was in the sitting room with Stefan and the Duke and the next she was back in her bedchamber with her sisters on the night they were to go back down to the underworld and begin to pay their debt to Sol.

In tense silence, Auri checked that the doors were securely locked as Larka fished the three leaves out of their hiding place behind her wardrobe. The leaves gleamed brightly in her open hand, looking more like fine jewelry than something from another world. Larka placed them on the ground in their room where the portal had opened the first time and sat cross-legged before them. Her sisters did the same with a rustle of skirts, and they all clasped hands, Gwynna holding one of Larka's hands and Kath the other. Kath was trembling, and Larka squeezed her hand in a man ner that she hoped came off as comfort instead of strangulation.

"Alright," said Larka, acutely aware that everyone expected her to be in charge and that she had no real idea what to do. "I suppose we just… close our eyes and think of the underworld? And hope it works as Sol said it should?"

Larka watched her sisters close their eyes before she did the same. Then she thought of the underworld: the long staircase connecting their bedroom to the land of the dead, the strangely beautiful trees, the sound the dark waters made as they broke against the side of their boats. She could see it so strongly that it was as if she was already there, traveling across the strange realm toward the sad-eyed god who awaited her.

Let us in, she thought. *A part of us belongs there, or so you told us. Let us in so that we might pay our debt.*

Light flickered against her closed eyes, starkly white, and a gust of chilly wind washed across her face.

Even knowing the portal was there, Larka flinched in surprise when she opened her eyes to see the hole in the middle of her floor. No matter how many more times this happened, she didn't think she would ever get used to the yawning blackness in the middle of her bedroom. Or the fact that there was something inside her that had summoned it.

The rest of Larka's sisters looked worried as they gathered around the edge of the portal. Larka knew she should feel the same, yet she didn't. What she felt was closer to excitement—or no, not excitement, but the wild feeling that makes someone walk along the edge of a cliff, wind tugging at her hair and the ground far below. A reckless kind of curiosity toward something that might be dangerous.

She shoved the feeling away. It didn't matter if she was curious about the underworld they were about to visit or the god who ruled it. The princesses had agreed to this. They owed Sol a debt. They had promised they would come, and come they must.

So, Larka and her sisters went down into the darkness. At the bottom of the staircase, they found themselves in the forest of silver again. The sound of metal against metal whispered all around them as the trees stirred in a cool breeze.

Their journey was the same as on the first night. First the forest of silver leaves, then the forest of gold, and finally the diamonds that faded away to the still and silent lake. Galen and the other boatmen waited at the water's edge to bear them across, and Larka looked at them with new eyes now that she knew they didn't number among the living. She wondered what tragedies had brought them there.

At the end of the lake loomed Sol's palace, a silhouette blocking the sky above. Reaching the door, Larka hesitated briefly. Then she stepped up as she had before and gave three sharp, solemn raps.

Even though Larka had seen the grandeur of the room beyond just a few nights before, her breath caught in awestruck wonder as the doors swung open. The sheer scale of it, the starkness of the black and white—it was like nothing they had in Belmarros, nothing she'd ever seen before.

This time there was no fire in the hearth and no Sol standing in the doorway to greet them. Larka and her sisters stood in the antechamber awkwardly. "Should we wait for him?" asked Kath, casting a wistful gaze at the now-empty hearth.

Galen shook his head. "No, I'll bring you. I've been here long enough that I know my way around just as well as Sol."

"Good," said Rhiannon shortly. "I don't like this place, and I won't spend a minute longer down here than I have to. I just want to pay our debt, leave, and never see Sol again until he comes for me the day I die." Not even waiting for Galen, she marched through the doorway that Sol had taken them through a few days before. Everyone else hurried after her.

The princesses walked through the halls long enough for Larka to wonder if Galen really knew where they were going, or if she was destined to spend the rest of her life fumbling through corridors in search of the god of death. Thankfully, once they had turned a few more corners, arcanist globes began to glow in the walls, illuminating everything with an eerie white light.

Finally, the girls turned another corner and stepped out of the dim hall and into the blazingly bright throne room. Larka saw Sol immediately, seated on the throne at the other end of the room. Clearly waiting for them.

"Good, you brought them," Sol called across the expanse of the empty room, his voice echoing and bouncing along the high ceiling. The whole long room, from the vast floor to the towering columns lining the walls, was made of blindingly white stone, and he stood out like an inkblot with his dark robe, perched upon a black throne.

"Of course," said Galen. "I could hardly leave them to find the way on their own. They might never leave here alive." Larka wasn't sure if he was joking or not.

Galen led them across the floor to the throne, and Larka shivered as a cold breeze smelling of dust and earth curled across her shoulder. She halted before Sol's throne and curtsied gracefully. That, at least, her tutors had drilled into her; whether for a foreign ambassador or the god of death himself, she could be counted on to curtsy perfectly.

"Lord Death," Larka said. Even her soft voice was amplified by the acoustics of the room. There was a slight tremble to her words that she couldn't stop. Sol had straightened on his throne the moment she spoke and was looking at her intensely. "We know the debt we owe you," she continued. "Of course we came. What do you want from us?"

She had been asking herself the question for the past few days. No matter that he didn't seem wicked or cruel, he was still the god of *death*. What kind of entertainment could he possibly enjoy? Sending plagues to the living world? Disemboweling people? None of the options were good.

Sol leaned forward on his throne, an angular black slab carved from a single piece of shining rock, and beckoned them toward him with one long, tattooed finger. Larka had found his hands disturbing at first, too many of them and too many joints for a human, yet she had gotten used to them more quickly than she'd thought. Like his bone-white coloring and the black runes scrawled across every inch of his exposed skin, his fingers were just another part of him. An inhuman part, yes, but he wasn't human.

Larka obeyed the beckoning finger and crossed the throne room floor with the rest of her sisters. With each step, she thought of a new horror that Death might consider amusement, and with each step she had to force herself not to look afraid.

The princesses halted at the bottom of the steps leading to the throne and looked up at Sol.

"Before the War of the Gods," he said softly, his eyes looking somewhere far away, "before the argument that split us all, before brother killed sister and wife killed husband, before the ruin of the world, we would hold dances here that mortals could never imagine. Here, in this realm where no one living has ever walked." *Until us*, thought Larka. "Here, the goddess of war danced with the god of beauty. The Moon Sisters visited and filled the halls with laughter and light. And I oversaw it all. I know that nothing can bring back those days, not now that they are gone and I am the only one left. But I will see these halls alive once more, even for a brief time. So, dance for me, princesses, and pay your debt."

"Dance for you?" Larka said in disbelief. Of all the things she'd thought the death god would ask them to do, dancing was not something she had considered. Dancing was something done in the living world, at balls, before her father drowned at sea, filled with vibrant courtiers dressed in rich colors and brilliant jewels, laughing and moving together in time to the music. Dancing was not something she associated with death and decay.

"Yes. Dance for me, and pay your debt," Sol repeated. "What, did you think I wished you to die, to become shades here?"

"I—I—" she stammered. That had been what she'd thought, in moments of fear that she barely admitted even to herself: that he had saved their lives only so he could kill them himself in whatever way he wished.

"I have seen enough shades here," Sol interrupted. "All the dead who have ever been have passed through my lands at one point or another. I do not need more death. What I do not have is laughter. What I do not have—" and here he looked straight at Larka, "is beauty. What I do not have is life, not in this land. I might once have been content to rule a land of dead things, but that was before I lost almost everything. I may be King of the Dead, but I wish for more than watching shades travel to the afterlife that lies beyond my palace. Now I wish for life. I wish for warmth. I wish for a brief reminder that the world still goes on even though all I love is gone."

There was a strange sort of logic to Sol's words. Larka supposed that if she ruled a land of the dead, she would become weary of it, too, and long for something that was still living.

"Alright," Larka said. "We will dance for you, Lord of Death. We will dance until our debt to you is paid."

His smile was knife-sharp as he clapped his hands. The dull *crack* was loud in the silence of the room. At first there seemed to be no difference at all, and Larka wondered if perhaps his clap had been pure melodrama, but then Auri glanced over her shoulder, stiffened, and whispered to Larka, "Look behind you."

She turned, wondering what had given Auri such a fright, and had to stifle a yelp of surprise. Where there had previously been only Galen, there now stood eleven more figures in a line, ranging in age from children who looked about the same age as Alannah and Etain to young men not much older than Larka. Clustered in a corner was a group of musicians holding instruments that hung limply at their sides: a violin, a flute, and a small harp. All stared ahead with their eyes fixed on the wall. Or no—not on the wall, on Sol.

Dead. A shiver ran down Larka's spine at the thought. The boys and the musicians were dead. They all had the same oddly insubstantial look that Galen had, hollow husks drained of something vital.

"Your partners," said Sol. "I hope you don't mind that they are shades; living beings are, of course, rather scarce in this realm. Don't worry. They may be dead, but they are still men."

Larka said, "No, we don't mind. We'll dance." She hesitated and then asked the question she had been wondering: "Will you dance with us?" She held out a hand to him, the bandages gone after a week of Albin's salves. Sol had only summoned eleven shades; did that mean he was going to dance with one of her sisters? With her? Did she want him to dance with her?

Instead of descending the dais to accept the dance, Sol settled back on his throne. "No, I would rather watch. I am… rather out of practice. Galen will be a willing partner, I am sure."

"Of course." Larka made herself sound perfectly polite, yet she felt a hint of disappointment that she couldn't quite explain.

Despite the circumstances, Larka did want to dance, even if it wasn't with Sol. She had been only fourteen when her father died, old enough to have dancing lessons but too young actually to attend many balls, though she had watched from the doors and dreamed of being one of the graceful court ladies. Still, she'd loved dancing. All her sisters had—it didn't matter whether it was stepping stiffly in time with their instructor or twirling around their room or fumbling the steps and throwing back their heads to laugh. But then King Eldric had died, and it was unseemly to dance when there was a king drowned.

They'd still practiced, of course, and danced with each other when there were no other partners, but true balls had been scarce.

"Then, dance," Sol said. "Dance, and let there be

life in these halls once more.”

Chapter Thirteen

The shade musicians in the corner lifted their instruments and began to play. It was a song that Larka recognized, a country dance meant to be played with an energetic fiddle and a few small pipes. It was a dance meant to be full of leaping and swirling skirts and celebration, but down here in the dark, played by dead hands and ghostly instruments, the song seemed as sad and haunting as a funeral dirge.

Still, Larka's feet itched to dance to the song, for she remembered the steps, though it had been years since she'd learned them. Nevertheless, she hesitated. The girls' eerily strange dancing partners made her pause. Would the shades really dance with them?

Then, Galen stepped forward and offered Larka his hand. And so began her first dance in the halls of the dead. Her feet were clumsy at first, since it had been a long time since she'd danced, and she stepped on Galen's foot. "Sorry," she said automatically, before considering whether he felt pain. Galen smiled kindly and answered, "It's fine. I've felt worse."

Larka let Galen lead her in the dance, and her feet soon remembered the steps, how to step just so and have her skirt swirl around her ankles, how to match the rhythm of her feet with her partner's movements. By the second song, slower and more sorrowful, the rest of her sisters also seemed to remember the years of dancing lessons they'd had. Rhiannon moved gracefully with her partner, and Gwynna had quickly taken control of the dance as she always did. Even the younger girls were managing the steps well enough, although Larka was fairly sure that Mel was just copying what everyone else was doing, since she and her partner were several paces behind. Alannah and Etain twirled clumsily with their partners, giggling.

The princesses danced, and Larka found herself beginning to relax. There was nothing strange or monstrous about this, unless you counted the fact that she was dancing with a dead man.

Still, the entire time Larka danced, she kept finding herself looking at Sol out of the corner of her eye. It wasn't a conscious thing—she would miss one of the steps and then realize her attention hadn't been on the dance but on the god overseeing them from his throne. She couldn't help it.

Larka had read of the idea of meeting someone's gaze across a crowded room, of looking at them the same moment they happened to be looking at you. The novels she'd read when she was younger had always sold that moment of unexpected connection as the beginnings of fiery, passionate romance. But it wasn't really like that, Larka thought. There was no coincidence, no moment where her gaze simply wandered to him and he was looking back. It was just that she found herself searching unconsciously through the crowd of dancers until she found him, and then it was as if some part of her thought, Oh, it's you, and was satisfied with her search.

Larka looked away immediately whenever she realized she was looking for Sol again, but he was always in the corner of her eye. She had never thought that Death might be someone strangely human. She had certainly never thought Death might be a long-haired, handsome man with a proud tilt to his head and gentle hands. She'd never thought Death might have sorrow in his quartz-gray eyes. The thought embarrassed Larka enough—since when was she thinking of Death as *handsome*?—that she pushed it away and focused instead on the dance. It was easier to lose herself in that than she'd thought it would be. The music and the steps and her partner swinging her around with easy grace was enough to make her forget that she was in the underworld.

"Galen," Larked asked as they danced a pavane, a slow, processional dance that she'd always found boring, "Why are you so comfortable with Sol?"

"What do you mean?" he asked, guiding her through a turn of the dance.

"I mean that he's a god. Death Himself, no less. Why aren't you afraid of him? And why does he let you speak to him in such a familiar way?"

Galen considered the question. "I suppose it's because I've been down here for such a long time. It's hard to fear someone you know, and we've gotten to know each other very well over the years."

"Oh?" said Larka, hoping that he might tell her something interesting.

Galen nodded. "He's lonely, you know. He has his duties, but that's not enough to keep someone satisfied for all of eternity. I think he doesn't mind my familiarity because I give him company, which he misses, and I remind him that he's more than just a silent ruler of the underworld.

"But why are you here?"

Galen blinked and missed a step of the dance, the first time he had. "Because I'm dead, Little Queen. I thought you already knew that."

"No, I mean, why are you in Sol's palace? He said

on the first night that his duty is to guide the dead to the afterlife. Why haven't you gone with the rest of them?" The pavane was an easy enough dance that Larka could keep step even as she talked. It took barely any effort.

Galen sighed. "I don't want to. I… I suppose I feel that I don't deserve it. To be at peace with the rest of them."

"Why not?"

"It's a long story."

From Larka's court experience, a "long story" usually meant "a complicated story I don't want to tell." She wouldn't have pressed Galen for more details, but he continued, "I was an arcanist when I was alive."

"I guessed that for myself, considering you have the tattoos," said Larka drily, and Galen laughed.

"Yes, I suppose that is rather obvious. My point is that arcanists have very specific ideas about how to use our magic. We don't interfere in any business without payment, and especially not if it doesn't benefit the Citadel of Ink. If we use magic outside of studying on Drekkaria, special permission has to be granted."

Larka nodded and stepped backward in the dance. "Yes, the Citadel is still like that. I'm guessing you used your magic without permission?"

"Oh, yes. But not in the way you're guessing. I didn't try to save a sick child or heal someone I loved. I used it badly—and cruelly." Galen's voice was filled with guilt, and his steps were suddenly heavy. "Arcanists renounce any citizenship of the country we formerly belonged to and become purely students of magic. We don't have attachments to the outside world. At least, we're not supposed to. I was born and raised in Dalbrast, and I found it difficult to put aside my loyalty to the place I had known my entire life."

Larka couldn't imagine this, to live in another place, to renounce Belmarros, to not care about its people and land with every breath… it was impossible to her.

Galen continued, the notes of the pavane as quiet as his voice. "I had just passed my tests to become a full arcanist when Dalbrast went to war with the Crescent Islands."

"Which war?" asked Larka. Dalbrast hadn't only warred with Belmarros; over its long history, Dalbrasti soldiers had spilled blood on nearly every land across the ocean. The two northern islands of Limmar and Mareth were the least of it.

"The one under Kaiser Johann the Second," said Galen, naming a brief, bloody conflict about two hundred years earlier. "I was brave and foolish, and so I ignored the orders of my masters not to interfere. I went to the kaiser and offered my services. He accepted."

Larka had a nasty feeling where this story was going, but she could do nothing but dance and listen. She felt that she had to let Galen tell the whole ugly history.

"It was a slaughter." Galen's voice hitched, and she saw him force himself to continue. "The Isles had no defenses against magical fire that burned without end, arrows that sought out their targets until they found them, or plagues that swept through their soldiers and left the Dalbrasti untouched. They were helpless." He shook his head. "I have no idea how many I killed. I was almost glad when the master arcanists found me."

"And then?" asked Larka. Galen turned in the dance, and she almost forgot to turn with him.

He lifted his free hand and traced the two silver scars on his cheeks, scars that were shaped very much like crescents. "The master arcanists gave me these scars. They said they wanted me to see a reminder of all the deaths I had caused every time I looked in a mirror. They likely would have killed me, too, but I escaped before they could. I kept fighting for the kaiser because I didn't know what else to do, until someone got lucky and shot an arrow in my back a few months later." Galen paused and laughed a choked little laugh. "You know, the funny thing is, I don't even blame them for doing it. I would have done the same in their position. So here I am."

"Here you are," agreed Larka. The pavane was

reaching an end, to her relief.

"I help Sol with his duties," finished Galen. "I keep him company. We guide the dead together, and I suppose I hope that someday it'll feel like I've helped enough of them that I can rest myself. I know he gets lonely, though I had no idea he was planning to strike a deal with you princesses. Not that I can blame him; it gets unbearably dark down here."

A shiver went down Larka spine at the shade's words. She hadn't entirely realized until that moment that, no matter if their debt was paid out, she and her sisters would someday come there to stay. That might be decades in the future, but it would happen. And someday, when she had spent enough years down here, she too would forget the color of sunlight.

The last notes of the pavane faded away, echoing through the throne room, and Larka and Galen finally halted.

"Do you think I'm a monster?" he asked her, something raw and afraid in his gaze.

"I think," said Larka slowly, "that the mere fact you're still here shows you aren't."

The notes of another song struck up, this one more cheerful—or at least as cheerful as a song played by dead musicians could be. Galen stood, uncertain, until Larka offered him her hand again: a silent invitation. Galen took it, and they began again.

One more dance turned into two, then three, and by the time the last song ended, Larka had lost track of how many songs there had been. When they stopped at last, her feet ached, yet the music had filled some part of her that had been empty too long. Her sisters looked similarly tired but exhilarated.

Galen let go of her—despite how long they'd been dancing together, his hands remained frigid as ice—and bowed to her. "Well done," he said. "I have not had a dance with such a fine partner in an age."

"I suspect I'll be seeing you again soon enough. At

least, if Sol has his way."

Galen bowed and filed out of the throne room along with the rest of the shades, until only the living and the godly were left.

"You danced well tonight," said Sol from where he sat upon his throne, fingers curled like claws around the armrests.

Larka curtsied like the proper princess she had been brought up to be. "Thank you, Sol."

"I am glad you call me by my name and not my title," he mused. "I like the sound of it on your lips."

"Sol," said Larka again, softly. It felt more intimate than simply speaking a name should.

His smile was like flint catching at tinder, and she looked away, feeling a spark flare to life in her chest.

Sol sighed. "I believe it is nearly time for you to return to the world of daylight. I will see you again tomorrow, I suppose."

"We'll come back," Larka promised. She was surprised at how soon Sol wanted them to come back, but a debt was a debt. She beckoned to the younger girls, who were leaning on each other out of exhaustion, and they all left the ballroom and the underworld behind them.

It was a shock to Larka when the princesses reached the top of the endless staircase on the other side of the forest and found themselves in their familiar bedchamber once again. She had almost forgotten that there was a world outside of endless darkness and golden trees.

"Oh, thank the ancestors," Gwynna said and immediately went to her bed and sat down on it with a sigh of relief. Larka sat on her own bed and went to remove her dancing slippers from her aching feet. Instead, she let out a tired little laugh.

"What?" asked Kath.

"My shoes, they're worn through." Larka slipped off a shoe and held it up, poking a finger through a hole in the silk. "I danced so much they've got holes."

"Me, too," said Kath in dismay, looking down at her feet. They soon found it was the same for all the girls, even the youngest ones. Mel's shoes were so worn down it was a miracle they'd stayed on her feet during the climb up from the underworld.

"What should we do?" asked Auri, collecting the shoes into a pile in the middle of the floor and looking down at them.

"Let's deal with it tomorrow," suggested Karo, yawning.

None of the girls protested the idea, so Larka tapped the arcanist globes on the walls to shut them off and they all climbed into their beds.

Larka had two thoughts before she slept. First, she recalled the way Sol's name had tasted on her tongue and flinched away from it. She was not sure what lay down that path and wasn't prepared to find out. Then she thought of the weary look on the face of Galen as he spoke of long centuries in the underworld. Finally, sleep pulled her under like a tide, and she thought no more about death or fallen arcanists.

Chapter Fourteen

Larka's feet hurt. In hindsight, this should not have surprised her. As it was, she was still half-asleep when she first twitched her foot and winced at the ache. For a moment, she simply lay there, wondering what she'd done to make herself hurt like this, and then everything about the previous night came rushing back.

She'd danced for hours in the underworld, danced with a dead man and all the while felt the gaze of Death Himself following her every move. Now that she was back in the daylight world with her sisters around her and a new day beginning, some part of her felt as if it had all been a particularly strange dream. Except for the sore feet. No dream ever gave her sore feet.

Larka wanted desperately to lie in bed until she went back to sleep, but she could see that the clock across the room already read the time she usually got up. Someone would surely be suspicious if she lay in bed for hours more than she usually did. Besides, she felt nowhere near as tired as she should have felt. Perhaps that was the trace of death magic inside her.

With a groan of annoyance, Larka pushed aside the covers and got to her feet. The rest of her sisters were still asleep. Kath was snoring faintly, all the blankets on her bed kicked to the ground. Auri was wrapped so securely in her sheets that only the tips of her feet could be seen.

It took awhile to wake her sisters—Rhiannon was particularly resistant—and even longer to chivvy them out of bed and into getting dressed. Even then, everyone still looked sleep-rumpled. Larka expected that she was no better.

Stefan was sitting at the breakfast table reading over a pile of official-looking documents when his twelve nieces finally traipsed in. He took one look at them, all yawning and blinking sleepily, and raised an eyebrow.

"Late night?" he asked, putting down the papers.

"Yes," Larka admitted, reaching up to adjust the handful of hasty pins she'd inserted to keep her hair up and her small coronet in place. "We didn't sleep well."

"All of you?" Stefan said dubiously. She couldn't blame him. One or two people having a bad night's sleep was believable, but not twelve.

"Yes, all of us," Auri replied, sounding so uncharacteristically grumpy that Stefan took the hint and went back to reading his papers. Larka wasn't hungry, but she made herself fill a plate of food and sit down next to Stefan so she could read over his shoulder.

"What's the schedule for today?" she asked.

Stefan shuffled through the papers until he found a schedule and handed it to her. "Another council session," he said, and she inwardly winced at the memory of the endless debate that had happened during the last one. "A meeting with a few of the ambassadors, a cursory appearance at court to show that you haven't cracked under the strain of being ruler yet, and the usual weekly petitions at court."

The damned pins she'd put in her hair wouldn't stay

in. Larka wrestled with them, one ear on Stefan, before finally giving up trying to make them look good. She sighed. That was a lot to do in a day, and she'd have to do all of it without yawning every three seconds. "Anything else?"

"Oh! Yes, actually. I nearly forgot, but Duke Miron Brandt has requested to see you. I suppose he wants to jump straight into courting you."

Never mind another endless council meeting full of debates that went only in circles, meeting one of her suitors would be a thousand times worse. Especially the Duke, with his clever eyes and polished court charm.

"Is Larka going to marry the Duke?" asked Alannah in her clear, little-girl voice as she scooped more fruit than was probably wise onto her plate.

"No!" Larka said too loudly. She tried to soften her tone. "I mean, I don't know. Maybe. I'll meet a lot of other men in a few months, and then I'll decide which one of them I like the most and whom it would be best for me to marry."

"Oh." Alannah sounded disappointed. The other girls had probably been telling her stories about when Stefan had married Dario, making her excited for another royal wedding. "Is the Duke nice?"

"I don't know," Larka admitted. "I didn't see him for very long when we first met. I suppose I'll get to know him better if he's going to be at court now."

It was at that moment that Auri tactfully changed the topic, something for which Larka would be eternally grateful, and the rest of the girls' breakfast passed without another mention of marriage, suitors, or Duke Miron Brandt.

Larka just barely managed to survive the rest of the day. Thankfully, both the council session and the meeting with ambassadors were done sitting down, so she didn't give away the fact that both of her feet ached and had blisters, and the appearance at court was mercifully short. There were no shouting matches at the council sessions, the ambassadors didn't threaten war on behalf of their countries, and she thought she did rather well with small talk at court.

The only problem was her exhaustion, which caused her to pinch herself a few times during particularly boring parts of the council session and to swear that she would try some of Stefan's disgusting coffee the next day. She even managed to make it all the way back to the royal study, which she was still having trouble not thinking of as her father's, before semi-collapsing.

"I think that went rather well," said Larka to Stefan. She wondered if she was undignified enough to put her face down on the oak desk and decided she was. "But, my gods, am I tired." Her voice came out muffled.

"I hate to interrupt whatever intimate moment you're having with that desk, but you have a meeting with Duke Brandt in twenty minutes," said Stefan from where he was sitting across from her, drinking tea and staring out the window.

"Dammit," said Larka. She didn't swear much, having spent her childhood being lectured by various governesses about how it wasn't appropriate for a future queen, but she made an exception right then. The day had been feeling like a success until Stefan had reminded her of her unwanted suitor, at which point it all came crashing down like a house of cards.

She almost asked, "Do I have to?" before realizing those were the words of a tired child, not a queen. Instead, she allowed herself one truly exhausted sigh before heaving herself to her feet and saying, "Where are we meeting?"

"The Portrait Hall. I believe your advisors are hoping to encourage him by showing him what an illustrious line he could potentially be marrying into, or something like that." Stefan sounded amused.

"More like intimidate him by showing the sheer number of ancestors I have," Larka muttered. She looked down at herself and sighed again. Her dark blue dress was modestly appropriate for meeting ambassadors and trying not to doze off during council meetings but not for meeting potential suitors. "I should go change. Any chance you'll come along for moral support?"

"None at all. Dario and I are having an early dinner together. He's going to be gone for a month visiting his sister and her new baby, so I refuse to have that interrupted unless it's a matter of dire importance. Besides, you're the one who might be marrying Duke Brandt, not me." There was a hint of a smile playing around the edges of Stefan's lips at the mere mention of his husband, and Larka took a quick moment to think wistfully that she would probably never be as in love with her own spouse as Stefan was with Dario.

"I don't want to go alone," Larka complained.

"Bring Rhiannon, then, if you really need someone," suggested Stefan. "You can claim she's your chaperone."

"Good idea," said Larka, brightening. She thought she might be able to survive the meeting if she had Rhiannon's calm presence at her side to keep her grounded.

Fifteen minutes later, Larka was she was meeting Miron in the Portrait Hall because it was such a familiar place to her, hands clasped in front of her and hoping she didn't look nervous. Rhiannon stood beside her in plain dove gray, and Larka couldn't help feeling overdressed compared to her sister. She'd changed into a much fancier lavender silk dress, the short sleeves edged with lace and the neckline of her bodice a bit lower than her previous outfit. It made her a little self-conscious, and she kept resisting the urge to tug it up higher. Still, with her golden coronet, she felt almost queenly, or at least that she was doing a good job of pretending to be queenly.

Echoing footsteps jolted Larka out of her reverie, and she looked up to see Duke Miron Brandt coming toward her, his boots loud on the stone. An unfamiliar girl about Larka's own age followed him with quieter footsteps. She had the Duke's red-brown hair and pale skin, and Larka thought this must be the sister he had mentioned at their first meeting. Both siblings had shed their heavy, salt-stained wools and furs for lighter cotton and silk Belmarrian-style clothing. The Duke was in a green tunic, his sister in a purple dress several shades darker than Larka's own. There was a symbol of a diving hunting bird embroidered in gold on the front of their clothing, likely the Brandt family crest.

Miron Brandt halted in front of Larka and bowed at the waist to her, low enough that she could see the golden bird pin holding back his reddish hair. "Your Majesty," he said, rising. "It is an honor to see you again."

"Likewise, Duke Brandt." She was proud that her voice displayed no fear, or even anything at all except a cool politeness.

He smiled in a charming way that had obviously been practiced in front of a mirror many times. "If I am to be your suitor, you must call me Miron. I insist."

Larka thought about pointing out that he was the duke and she was the princess, and therefore, he really couldn't be doing any insisting about what she called him, but she decided it wasn't worth the effort. He was, after all, supposed to be courting her. "Very well then. Miron it will be."

Miron gestured for the girl behind him to come forward. "Speaking of names, I would like to introduce my sister, Janna Brandt. She was ill from sea travel when we first arrived in Belmarros, as I told you, but she's doing much better now."

The girl came forward and gave Larka a short curtsy. Besides the hair, she and her brother had enough of a family resemblance that Larka would have known they were related even without the introductions, though the lines of her face were softer than those of her brother and she had far more freckles. "An honor," Janna Brandt said softly. She, like her brother, had only a hint of a Dalbrasti accent.

"This is my younger sister, Rhiannon," said Larka, stepping aside so that Rhiannon could curtsy politely.

A spark of surprise flashed across the Duke's face. "Oh, this is your sister. I didn't realize. My apologies, Princess." He gave Rhiannon another one of his perfectly practiced bows, and Larka bit back a sigh. She should have been expecting this reaction since she knew Miron was a stranger to court and thus a stranger to her father's multiple marriages. Still, she disliked it whenever someone assumed that she and Rhiannon weren't sisters because of how different they looked. It didn't matter if Rhiannon had dark curls and brown skin while Larka was fair-haired and blue-eyed. They were still sisters.

Miron offered Larka his arm, and she took it, hoping he couldn't tell how nervous he made her. It wasn't just that he was a complete stranger with whom she was expected to talk, it was also that he was a complete stranger whom had been introduced to her as a possible husband. Every time she looked at him, she was reminded that she might marry him someday, as impossible as the idea seemed.

Larka tried to calm her racing heart as she walked into the Portrait Hall. She could do this as long as she took it one step at a time. She had to.

Janna and Rhiannon strolled a few paces behind Larka and Miron to give the couple some space as they walked through the hall. The sisters were supposed to be chaperoning; instead, Larka saw them fall into an easy, uncomplicated conversation almost as soon as they began to walk together. The Portrait Hall was a high-ceilinged room with a glass roof to let in plenty of summer sunlight. The long walls were painted white and hung with dozens of portraits of Larka's esteemed ancestors. Each king and queen had a gold border around his or her portrait, other members of their families merely silver.

Larka and Miron managed to make polite small talk as they strolled down the long hall, stopping to look at portraits of particularly famous rulers: the first queen of Belmarros, Ysobel, her painting dark and dusty with time; King Arn, who had been the first to establish an alliance with Astraia; beautiful Princess Vyta, who had been tragically murdered on her wedding day; Queen Lotta, who had changed the marriage laws of Belmarros so that she might marry two of her suitors. There was a dramatic play about the last that

Larka's mother had supposedly performed back in the days she had been a Gallow's Dance actress and not a queen. Farther down the hall were the namesakes of several of Larka's sisters. Queen Rhiannon, Larka's grandmother, gazed down the Portrait Hall with a disapproving, steely gaze. Princess Gwynna, a wild-spirited great-aunt, posed next to the fierce warhorse that she would later fall from and die.

Larka had chosen to meet Miron in the Portrait Hall because it was such a familiar place to her. She had spent a lot of time in the hall when she was younger, peering at the carefully painted eyes and solemn faces of her ancestors as she wondered if any of them had felt the same weight of expectations on their shoulders as she did.

Larka was proud of how composed she stayed during her walk with the Duke. She inquired of how Miron and his sister found Belmarros (hot but lovely), of the state of their rooms in the city (quite good), and of their estates at home (mostly farmland).

"The Brandt family is an old one," said Miron proudly. Polite as he was, it didn't escape Larka's attention that he enjoyed talking about himself much more than asking questions about her. "We are descended from a man who helped the first kaiser of Dalbrast take his throne. As a reward for loyal service, our family was granted a sizeable estate, which I now rule. The first Brandt, Friedrich Brandt, owned a cloak woven from the hair of a goddess and enchanted by the arcanists to give him invisibility. He used it to collect information on the enemies of Dalbrast, and we still keep it safe to this day."

"Please, tell me more," Larka murmured politely. She directed the conversation as smoothly as she could toward Dalbrast, until she felt it would be appropriate to ask, "If it's not too personal, could I ask why you decided to court me?"

Immediately she knew the question had been too forthright; Miron leaned back and blinked.

"I was only wondering," she added hastily, "because

Belmarros is such a long distance from Dalbrast. Surely you'd be able to find a bride in your own land? Not that I'm not flattered by your decision."

Miron paused with his hands laced behind his back. "I suppose I could marry within my country, but I find Dalbrast… restrictive."

"Restrictive?" said Larka cautiously.

Miron kept his eyes fixed firmly on the portrait before him. "The kaiser of Dalbrast can be… uncompromising. He sees the world in a single way and dislikes anyone who disagrees with that view. I am loyal to him, of course, yet I find myself curious to see the world beyond Dalbrast. And when I heard that the lovely new queen of Belmarros was seeking a husband, how could I not..." Miron ducked his head slightly and looked up at Larka through his lashes, a move which likely would have worked on her had she not spent entire life surrounded by scheming courtiers.

"I see," said Larka. "I appreciate the truth."

"I would give nothing less." Miron bowed again and offered his arm. She took it.

Miron was charming with an easy manner, but Larka couldn't quite forget that every one of his smiles had a purpose, and that purpose was to make his way into her heart.

At one point, when Janna and Rhiannon paused to look more closely at another painting, Miron turned to Larka and lowered his voice. "I wish to apologize to you, Your Majesty. The first day we met, I spoke rather badly of my sister. This is no excuse, but we had been at sea for a very long time and had become so sick of each other we quarreled at the smallest thing. I'm afraid I was still angry at her when I spoke to you. Again, I must apologize."

"I see," said Larka again, feeling a bit better. The dismissive way he had talked of his sister previously had left her uncomfortable. "I have eleven sisters myself, so I'm no stranger to arguments with siblings."

Miron smiled another one of his clearly well-practiced smiles. "Good. I am very sorry I gave you the wrong impression of my sister and me."

"It's alright," said Larka awkwardly. She wasn't used to very attractive dukes paying attention to her, or at least in the manner suitors were supposed to pay attention. Then she added, "Oh, look, we've gotten to the end of the hall! This is where they put the pictures of the current reigning monarch and his or her family."

"So, you?" said Miron.

"Er, no," replied Larka, remembering that he was from Dalbrast and they had different ruling customs there. She explained: "Technically, I'm not queen yet. I'm just of age to be queen. It's called being the Little Queen or Little King. I won't be officially crowned until closer to the end of the year. It's supposed to give the new ruler time to settle into her role without being overwhelmed by preparations for the coronation, unless it's urgent that she's crowned as soon as possible."

Miron looked a little puzzled, but he said, "I see. It is just that at home in Dalbrast, rulers are crowned as soon as the previous one dies, whether or not they are of age. I did not know it was different here."

Well, why did you come here to court me if you know nothing of my country or its ways? The question curled around Larka's tongue. She shoved it away. There would be time to ask him later, when it wouldn't come off as rude.

Eager to turn the conversation away from traditions and her ever-nearer coronation, Larka pointed at the end of the hall and said, "Look, this one is of my father, King Eldric."

Miron followed her gaze to the portrait of the last king of Belmarros, dead for four years since the ship he had set sail in toward the possibility of new trade agreements had been dashed to pieces in a storm. There was no sign of his impending death in the portrait, however; Eldric regarded the viewer with a look of amusement, as if he was laughing at a joke that no one else could hope to understand. His elaborate gold crown—not the same one Larka would be wearing soon, for that was lost at the bottom of the sea—was settled on his dark blonde curls at a rakish angle. He had always seemed too carefree to Larka, both in real life and in this painting. Too carefree to be a king. He had, after all, nearly ruined Belmarros with his parties and disinterest in politics.

Looking at Eldric's portrait always gave her a bad feeling in the pit of her stomach, so Larka moved on to the next one. This one was of Stefan and Dario, painted shortly after their marriage six years ago. They were sitting together in Eldric's study, arms around each other, and even through the long hours the painting had taken to make, there was still a hint of a smile crinkling Dario's eyes and a tender way Stefan was looking up at his husband. The biggest difference between the portrait-Stefan and the current-Stefan was that he seemed freer without the regent's pin on his collar, not yet burdened by a dead brother or a country to run.

Miron studied the portrait for a moment and then said, "I confess, I don't entirely understand the relationship between you and your uncle, Your Majesty. He is your uncle, yet he carries no royal blood? And is only ten years older than you?"

Larka, who was no stranger to people being confused over the generations of her family, launched into an explanation. "Don't worry. Half the people at court don't really understand it, either. My grandmother, Queen Rhiannon, married into my family by way of the old king, my grandfather, and had my father, King Eldric, with him. After my grandfather died, she remarried to an earl from the north and had Stefan. Eldric, being much older than his brother, got married and then had me when Stefan was only ten. So, Stefan is my uncle and brother to the old king, but he himself carries no royal blood. It's one of the reasons he was chosen as regent—besides being a close relation to me, he has no actual claim on the throne and wouldn't be able to keep ruling after I came of age even if he wanted to."

Miron had a slightly dazed expression by the time

she was done. “I see. I suppose that makes sense.”

Larka couldn’t help it; she laughed. “If you think that’s confusing, wait until we get to my sisters.” She paced along the wall toward the paintings of Eldric’s wives, each of them edged in silver. These portraits had always had a slightly sad quality to them, as if their subjects had all realized that marrying a king was a bad idea when it was far too late to back out.

“I would appreciate an explanation, actually,” said Miron, a hint of self-deprecation in his voice. “No offense intended, but your family tree can be a little… complicated.”

Larka sighed. “My father married five different women in fourteen years, so I can imagine it would be confusing to an outsider.” Obviously that’s why Queen Lotta allowed polyamory in Belmarros, she thought sarcastically. So the king could marry as many beautiful women as he wanted and discard them as soon as he got bored with them.

“Five?” Miron sounded startled despite himself.

“Yes, five.” Larka moved to stand in front of the row of paintings depicting Eldric’s wives. “His first wife was my mother, Marion, an actress from the lower class. Not approved of by the council at all.” She touched the edge of her mother’s portrait. Marion was only a few years older than Larka in the portrait, with the same silver-fair hair and delicate build, though there was a smattering of freckles on her cheekbones that her daughter had not inherited. A lump lodged in Larka’s throat as she said, “She died when I was a little over two. She miscarried and lost too much blood.”

“I’m sorry,” Miron said softly. “I lost my own parents when I was quite young as well, not long after Janna was born.”

“It’s alright,” Larka lied. “I hardly remember her anyway.” She moved on to the next portrait, desperate not to talk about her mother. “I do remember my father’s second wife much better. Asha. She was from Astraia, part of an alliance. She was the mother of Rhiannon and Gwynna, who are closest to me in age, as well as the triplets, Krista and

Kath and Karo. I expect you'll meet them all at some point."

Asha's portrait looked more regal than that of the actual king. It was easy to tell she had been high nobility in Astraia, the daughter of a general, the king's nephew. Her skin was a darker brown than the five daughters she had borne, her hair a little curler, but the resemblance was still clear. In this painting, there was no sign of the lingering illness that had caught hold of her after the birth of the triplets and pulled her away from her daughters slowly and inevitably.

Miron moved on to study the third portrait. "She looks sort of… unhappy," he said hesitantly, as if trying not to offend Larka. She sighed. It was true—though the painter had tried his best to flatter his subject, with careful detail to her golden curls and slim figure, there was still a sad line to her full mouth, and her hazel eyes were downcast.

"That's Auriana, my sister Auri's mother. She died not long after Auri was born in an accident. I don't think she ever wanted to be queen-consort. My father got her pregnant when she came to court, so he did the honorable thing and married her." *After all, what's three wives when you already have two? Especially when they keep dying and you can just replace them.* Auriana had died a horribly preventable death by slipping on the icy castle steps and cracking her head open.

Miron looked vaguely scandalized. Too late, Larka remembered learning in her lessons that the Dalbrasti were more traditional about marriage and that such a thing never would have happened in the Duke's homeland. Auri probably would have been born in a country estate and ignored by all her relatives as much as possible, as if that could negate the shame of an unfaithful husband.

Larka cleared her throat and moved onto the next painting. She told herself it didn't matter if Miron was scandalized by her family. After all, he was trying to marry into it, and if he couldn't handle it, he would likely leave and she'd never see him again.

Larka shook away the thought—she shouldn't be

trying to drive away her suitors, not when she'd have to marry one of them—and moved on to the second-to-last portrait.

"This is Iris, the mother of three of some of my younger sisters, Yara, Talia, and Melina," said Larka. "You haven't met them yet since they're not old enough to be part of court." Miron studied the portrait of Iris with the same intensity as the others, as if memorizing them was part of a test that he didn't want to fail. Iris had her daughters' plain brown hair and straightforward brown eyes, though she lacked the glint of mischief that was ever-present in them. Larka had been only five when Iris married Eldric, though that had been old enough to tell that the councilors had arranged the marriage as a way to try and erase the scandal of the affair between Eldric and Auri's mother. Iris had lasted almost seven years as Eldric's wife, until a creeping tumor in her breast had appeared.

The final portrait was of Eithne, married to King Eldric for only a few years before his ship had gone down. A lesser princess of the Crescent Islands, the match had been ill-suited in almost every way; the loudest thing about her was red curls she'd given to her daughters, and she'd been practically crushed underfoot by her overwhelming whirlwind of a husband. She hadn't been on the ship that had killed her husband but had died eight months later delivering Alannah. Larka still remembered that day: standing in the hall outside Eithne's rooms with Alannah in her arms, listening to Eithne's cries, watching the servants hurry back and forth with bloodied linens. That final, horrible moment when Eithne's screams had fallen silent, replaced only by the wailing of a new baby. This was when Larka had known that the last of their mothers was gone. This was when she had known they were going to be alone except for Stefan.

Larka stepped back and looked at the long wall of portraits, the long row of dead queens of Belmarros. Some people said that her father must have been cursed to have married so many times and lost every one of his brides within a few years. Larka always thought that was a foolish belief. Still, looking at the portraits sent a shiver down her spine.

She forgot, often, how much her father had twisted the laws of their lands so that he could marry whomever he wished. But it was a hard thing to forget when confronted with all the women who'd wed him and died.

Larka cleared her throat and stepped back. "Anyway, that's enough of that. The Portrait Hall can be boring, especially on such a nice day. Would you like to take a walk in the gardens?"

Miron gave her a smile that if clearly practiced was no less attractive. "Of course, Your Majesty," he said, offering her his arm. They stepped out of the hall into the sunlight, leaving behind the row of portraits and Larka's memories of the dead women.

Chapter Fifteen

Several weeks after her walk through the Portrait Hall and nearly a month after her coming-of-age, Larka once again found herself in the Temple of the Fallen Gods. It wasn't for another ceremony, however, but rather for a Remembrance Day. Once a month, the court—or at least the members of court who cared—gathered in the temple to commemorate the gods who had died so that humanity might live.

For most of Larka's life, the War of the Gods had been an undeniable truth: the gods had fought, and the gods had died. Their battles had raged in the seas and in the skies, and one by one they had been cut down, falling from the heavens to land on the world they had fought over, their skulls becoming hills and their spines mountain ranges. Larka couldn't remember a time when she hadn't known the history of her world.

Larka sat alone in her seat at the temple. On Remembrance Days, all in attendance were supposed to be equal, but she was still the Little Queen, and apparently that meant she was no longer allowed to sit with her family. It did give her plenty of time to think, though.

If she hadn't seen Death with her own eyes, hadn't felt his touch and his power divine flowing through her, she never would have believed that one god still lived. But Larka had held the proof in her hands, and as she sat alone in the vast temple, she wondered what else had been left out of the histories. She thought of Sol, of the loneliness and grief etched on his face, and wondered exactly how he had managed to survive. The other gods had supposedly been immortal, too, and they were dead anyway. So how had Sol managed to live?

Larka fiddled with the seed pearls stitched on the cuffs of her red mourning gown. The whispers of the courtiers filing into the temple were growing loud enough to distract her from her thoughts. She was certain she could feel the gaze of every person in the temple on the back of her neck, pricking her like needles. How many of the whispers behind her were people assessing her and finding her wanting, no better than her father?

Larka resisted the urge as long as she could and then finally turned to look at the seats behind her. They were unusually full, crowded with row upon row of nobles dressed in their best red clothing. She'd always thought it was a strange thing to do—people wore red when a mother or a brother or a dear friend died, not gods who'd been gone a thousand years—but she thought she understood the impulse better now that she'd met Sol. She'd seen how he still mourned the gods' war, and that grief had made it more real to her. Now it was more than old history to her.

The living world had a vast, echoing space where the gods should have been. Each land had its substitute: Belmarros threw itself into traditions, Veanara into debauchery, and Dalbrast into a strict moral code, but there was nothing that could be done to fill that emptiness. The world had become used to living without its gods, and only on days like this one did it even really acknowledge that things had once been different.

Larka saw plenty of familiar faces in the crowd—the devout families who came every month to pay their respects and mourn what their world had lost—but there were plenty of unfamiliar faces as well. She had no doubt they weren't here because they actually wanted to remember the gods who'd died to save their ancestors. They were here to take another look at the girl who would be their queen by the end of the year. She could feel their eyes upon her, though they'd all looked away when she'd turned around. The sensation made her stomach do a slow roll. This was how it was always going to be: a life lived as the person everyone looked toward and judged.

Larka had never minded being the center of attention when she was younger and participating in the plays the younger courtiers had put on. Then, she had been reciting words that had been recited a thousand times, sinking into the skin of whatever warrior queen or brave peasant girl she'd been cast as. When she was queen, there would be no script, no rehearsals. All of her words would be her own.

Larka turned back around in her seat, but even when she focused her gaze on the mosaic of warring gods at the front of the temple, she couldn't forget the hundreds of eyes looking at her.

A priestess dressed in a robe the color of blood climbed the steps to the podium at the front of the temple. Records said that, before the War of the Gods, priests wore pure white. Now they only wore red, mourning everything that had been lost.

The red-robed priestess folded her hands before her and bowed her shaved head. Larka did the same and knew from the rustle of cloth behind her that everyone else was also bowing.

"We gather here today," said the priestess in a voice as clear and calm as a mountain stream, "to remember those who fought for us and died for us. We gather here to remem ber the dark days when some of the gods looked down upon us and believed that what they had created were weak, corrupt creatures who had to be cleansed away in order for this world to be made pure. Others, though, looked down upon us and saw that we were flawed, yes, but that did not mean we were beyond saving. They fought their own brothers and sisters for that belief, fought to save us, the children made in their image. We must believe ourselves to be worthy of that honor. We must be the people they believed we could be."

The priestess launched into a speech about virtue and kindness and how humanity must always strive to be as good as its saviors thought it was. Larka tried hard to pay attention, but it was a long, rambling speech, and she became lost within a few minutes. With Remembrance Day only once a month, it was as if the priests saved up everything they'd thought to say since the last speech and then dumped it on their congregation all at once.

She'd always felt a little sorry for the priests and priestesses, who had almost nothing to do except clean the temple and recite the sermons. Back when the gods were still alive, there had been offerings to give, messages to deliver, and omens to interpret. Perhaps even a visit from a patron god if one was lucky enough. Now all the priests did was call out into the emptiness knowing that no one would ever reply.

At last, the priestess's speech ground to a halt and the court was free. The gathered nobility filed out of the temple's main room toward the traditional lunch held in the antechamber. Larka lingered in the protection of the temple as long as she could, knowing that the moment she stepped through the door to the lunch, the small talk would begin. It was ridiculous to dread something so tiny, but she couldn't help it. It would be her first after-temple lunch since becoming Little Queen, and that meant dozens of people trying to meet her at once.

She wasn't wrong. All of her gathered courage threatened to abandon her once she stepped through the door and was pelted with questions.

"A lovely service, don't you think, Your Majesty?"

"Your Majesty, I was wondering if you'd like to meet my son? He's away hunting in the south, but he'll be back in time for the next Remembrance Day, and I know he—"

"Little Queen, Little Queen! This is my cousin. He's visiting court and would love to have a private lunch with you soon."

"Majesty, what do you think of the new fashion of forest green with embroidered flowers? I think it's tacky myself, but—"

"Oh, Highness—I mean Majesty—I was wondering if I could have a word about your plans for the coronation—"

Larka blundered her way through the crowd as best as she could, barely able to answer one question before being bombarded with another. She twisted away from one extremely persistent courtier asking her to go on a private carriage ride and decided that perhaps people would leave her alone if she sat down to eat.

Larka wanted to sit next to her sisters, but the empty seat at the head of the table was clearly meant for her, and she didn't think she could avoid it, so she sat down on the gilded chair and adjusted her skirts for a long moment. When she dared to look up, she saw Duke Miron Brandt hovering at her shoulder, holding a rectangular package wrapped in brown paper and twine. He wore scarlet from head to toe, his reddish hair looking faded against the violent color.

"Duke Brandt," she said in surprise. "I didn't see you at temple with us earlier. Did you attend?"

"No, I didn't come," he said. "We Dalbrasti prefer to honor the sacrifice of the gods through fasting and contemplation, not gatherings and speech. I—well, I came here because I wanted to speak to you and give you a gift." He held out the wrapped package. "I thought you might enjoy it."

Larka took the package and began to pick at the sturdy knots holding it closed. There was an awkward silence between Miron and her as she untied the twine, and she found herself unable to fill it with some inane question. At least everyone around them had the decency to continue on with their own conversations and pretend they weren't spying on her.

After what felt like an agonizingly long time, Larka got the knots undone and folded back the paper to reveal a slim printed volume. The front cover was a plain brown, emblazoned in gold with the title, *The Autumn Bride: A Play in Three Parts.*

Larka looked up in surprise and not just because she hadn't thought a man like Duke Miron would read such a play. *The Autumn Bride* was a tragedy about a young woman forced to choose between marrying her lower-class, childhood love, a soldier, and marrying a rich, cold man to save her family from debtor's prison. It contained a great deal of melodramatic declarations of love, duels, and more elaborate metaphors than Larka cared to keep track of.

It was also the play her mother was starring in when she met her father. Eldric, it was said, had attended a performance at the suggestion of one of his friends. He'd been entranced by Marion from her first line; by her closing bow, it was said, he'd been in love. They had married six months later and named Larka after the lead character. Three years later, Marion was dead.

The Autumn Bride had never been a play that Larka loved, yet she kept coming back to it over and over again. She was fascinated with tragedies, the way they could be read countless times and always end the same way. Her namesake would always die tragically young while the soldier wept at her grave, and there was no choice that could make a different ending. Rather like life, she supposed. Like the story of her parents, which started out as two people in love and ended with a neglectful king and a dead consort.

Larka swallowed past the lump in her throat.

"How kind of you," she said at last. "I didn't know you read plays."

Miron duck his head, suddenly looking shy. "I don't, really. Theater is out of favor in Dalbrast. I asked around court about what kind of present you might favor."

Larka knew that was the proper behavior of any suitor. Still, she couldn't help feeling a little touched. Perhaps it was a coincidence, but perhaps he really did know how much this play meant to her.

"I know I missed your coming-of-age, but I wanted to give you something," continued Miron. "You and your sisters have seemed very distracted and tired lately, and I thought a play might cheer you up."

Larka shoved down her sudden panic at his words. She told herself that Miron's observation meant nothing; he was hardly going to conclude that they were sneaking to the underworld at night to dance for a god. To distract herself, she ran a finger across the raised golden title of the book and asked, "Was there any particular reason you picked *The Autumn Bride?"*

"I'd like to say it was my idea," said Miron with a kind of ruefulness that she suspected was far more cultivated than it appeared, "but I had some help. I was speaking to one of the councilors about you, and he happened to mention that you liked plays."

"Which councilor?" asked Larka. The idea of Miron speaking to the council about her without her knowledge was uncomfortable; she shoved it away. She was going to be queen soon and would have to get used to that sort of thing.

"Oh, Lord Aengus Braddock," said Miron offhandedly.

Larka winced before she could remember to control her expression.

"What is it?" said Miron.

"Lord Braddock and I don't, ah, entirely see eye-to-eye," said Larka with reluctance. "He was not… not fond of my father."

"Forgive me for speaking bluntly," said Miron, "but from what I can tell, most people in Belmarros weren't fond of your father."

Larka sighed. She wasn't in the mood to get into the particulars of Braddock's condescension and lack of faith in her ability to be queen, so she just said, "It's complicated. Let me just say that Lord Braddock isn't exactly my dearest friend in the world."

"He didn't seem so bad to me," said Miron. "A little stern, perhaps, but he was quite willing to help me out. He said that, as long as I remain at court, I'm free to count him as a friend and ally."

Of course he would say that to one of my suitors and not me, thought Larka sourly.

Miron, ever the courtier, clearly sensed that his praise of Braddock wasn't winning him any favors and swiftly changed the subject. "Anyway, I hope that you enjoy the gift."

"It was very kind of you," assured Larka. "I can only hope the rest of my suitors will give such lovely gifts."

"I'm glad you like it." Miron bowed again and left her. Larka found herself relieved when his too-knowing eyes were no longer directed her way.

Chapter Sixteen

"Everyone ready?" asked Larka. She and her sisters had been dancing for Sol for weeks, long enough now that it had nearly become routine. That night they were late; there had been a court dinner full of gossip and backhanded compliments that they had not been able to escape from early. Larka hoped that Sol wouldn't be offended that they were arriving later than usual.

"Almost done," chorused the triplets. Kath was buttoning up the back of Karo's rose-pink dress while Krista braided Kath's curly hair.

"I'm all done," said Auri, hooking in the last of her small silver earrings and adjusting the folds of her midnight blue dress. "So are the younger girls."

"Right, then. I suppose we'd better go," said Larka. She smoothed her hands over the folds of her royal purple dress, unaccountably nervous. No matter how many times they opened the portal, she always feared that perhaps this time their connection to the underworld wouldn't work.

Not long after they had begun dancing, Larka had discreetly ordered the silver, gold, and diamond leaves bound together with wire into a pendant so that she could wear them as a necklace. Now she pulled the necklace over her head and knelt down to press it to the floor, an act that was quickly becoming a habit.

She didn't have to wait long for the portal to open. Within a few minutes, the princesses were descending the now-familiar spiraling metal steps down into the dark, with their skirts clutched in their hands.

No matter how many times they walked this path, Larka thought she would always find it as strange as the first. The staircase descending from the sky, the shining forests of metal, the black waters of the lake that lapped against the shore with a sound like whispering… it was beautiful, yet in a way that made it clear it was not part of the world Larka knew so well.

Sol was waiting for them at the entrance of the ballroom when they arrived, pale as ever and still dressed in his long black robes. Larka wondered if he ever wore any other clothing.

"You are late," he said, a note of accusation in his voice that was, however, almost swallowed up by worry. "I feared you would not come tonight. Galen insists on guiding the dead again, and so I have no other company."

"I'm sorry, my lord," said Larka, dropping into a hasty curtsy and seeing her sisters follow suit. "I had responsibilities at court that I couldn't escape easily."

Sol walked forward and took Larka's hands, pulling her up from her curtsy. "I told you to call me Sol," he said, but there was humor in his voice, not anger. "There is no need to call me 'my lord.' I am not angry with you. I understand duties very well myself."

Larka could feel herself blushing and cursed her fair coloring. "Of course."

"Now come, dance for me," said Sol. He dropped Larka's hand—her stomach dropped with an odd kind of disappointment at the loss of his touch—and went to sit on his tall, stark throne to watch with his chin propped on one hand.

There was already a row of silent shades waiting to dance with Larka and her sisters.

These nighttime dances might have been the strangest balls she'd ever attended and probably would attend, but Larka couldn't squash the tiny spark of excitement she felt when the ghostly musicians struck up and her partner led her into the first steps of the song. She hardly ever had an opportunity to dance in her daily life.

After a few songs, her feet sluggish with exhaustion, Larka heard Sol call a halt to the music. Surely it hadn't been a full night of dancing already? She looked up at Sol, who was lounging on his throne watching them with an intense, almost hungry, look.

What I do not have is laughter and beauty and life, she remembered him saying, and felt a twinge of pity for him. God or no, it couldn't have been easy to spend all of those centuries since the War of the Gods down there alone but for the shades.

"Rest awhile, princesses. You look tired." Sol hesitated and then continued, "Larka, I would be honored if you would walk with me while your sisters rest, if you do not mind."

"Yes, of course," said Larka. When Sol descended his dais and offered Larka his black-clad arm, she took it despite Rhiannon sending her a desperate look. Larka ignored her sister. She knew very well that Rhiannon distrusted Sol and his motivations, but she didn't think that he had any terrible, secret intentions toward her. He was lonely and sorrowful, and Larka could understand that easily.

And she was curious. That much she could admit to herself. Though her feet ached from dancing, Larka didn't hesitate to take Sol's arm. Why with her, out of all of her sisters, did he wish to walk? Was it simply because she was the eldest, or was there another reason?

"We will not be gone too long," promised Sol. Rhiannon made another face that Larka ignored as she let Sol lead her away through one of the many doors lining the walls of the ballroom. Larka's sisters sat down on the steps to Sol's throne as they rubbed their feet and complained about the holes in their shoes.

The door clicked shut behind them, and Larka was alone with the god of death. She kept pace with Sol until they were so far away from the ballroom that she didn't think she'd ever be able to find her way back on her own. Sol finally stopped then, before a massive set of double doors. They were black as night, engraved with writhing vines and scenes of a hunt riding through a forest. A large padlock kept the doors locked firmly.

Larka shot Sol a quizzical look. "You brought me all the way here to see a door?"

He smiled faintly. "Not the door. What is beyond it." He held out his free hand and crooked a finger. The lock fell to the floor with a clunk, and the doors smoothly slid open.

Beyond was the night. A chilly breeze blew through the open doors, and she could hear the lake slapping against the nearby shore. But it wasn't the same part of the lake that Larka and her sisters had traveled through to get to the palace—the door was different, and a path lined in tiny arcanist globes curved away into the distance.

"Where is this?" she asked. "I don't remember seeing any of this when I walked here with my sisters."

Sol closed his eyes and tilted his face up slightly, seeming to relish the cold breeze that blew across his face. She wondered how much time he spent within the maze-like confines of his palace. "This is the back of my island," he said. "A place where no mortal being has ever set foot. Walk with me here, Little Queen, and you will see."

They stepped out of the palace and onto the island.

The arcanist globes were small, but the light they cast was strong enough to illuminate all of their surroundings. Larka saw that the land around them was flat and empty but for the palace that lay behind. The path followed the very edge of the island, which dropped off steeply into cliffs with the quiet waters below. She thought it might be beautiful by daylight. At night, it was merely somber.

"Is it always dark here?" she asked. "Or is it only because we come at night?"

Sol shook his head. "No, it is always night here. The other gods used to visit, to bring light and laughter here for a time, but it has been like this since they died. I cannot make it bright enough on my own to drive away the darkness forever, no matter how hard I try, no matter how many captured globes of light I make."

Larka frowned at that; she'd always thought arcanist globes were only made by arcanists, hence the name. Then again, who was she to question a god's magic? Especially when it made the night a little less dark?

She looked up at the sky, instinctively searching for the moon or stars but finding nothing but night. It made her feel as if the darkness was pressing down upon her. The night four years ago when she had held vigil over her father's drowned body before his burial had felt endless, as if each second were stretched into hours. She could not imagine bearing two thousand years of such a feeling. It would have driven her mad.

But would Sol have been alone? "What about the dead, like Galen? Don't they keep you company?" Larka asked. She wanted to understand the rules of the underworld.

Sol shook his head. "No. They linger awhile, sometimes, but always leave in the end. Even Galen will someday. That has to do with what I wished to show you, actually. You will see soon."

Sure enough, they had reached a staircase of dark, time-smoothed wood with arcanist globes set into it. It was wide enough that Larka and Sol could descend together, and they did. At the bottom of it was a beach covered in fine white sand that glowed faintly. Sol held up his robe with one hand and stepped onto the beach, his bare toes curling into the sand. Larka bent to take off her thin slippers, not wanting to ruin them, and followed him.

The sand shed enough light to show Larka the round

entrance of a tunnel hewn out of the cliffs and a stream of people walking out of it. With each step, they became more solid, becoming people instead of scraps of ghostly mist. The people were of every age and gender and race, but they all walked in the same steady, exhausted way. All had the same faded appearance, and none of them seemed to notice the two visitors watching.

Looking closer, Larka saw Galen standing next to a cluster of hardened warriors in plate armor. He looked up briefly, nodded at Sol and Larka, and then went back to the warriors. She saw that he was speaking quietly with the dead, guiding them out toward the lake with a pointing hand and a gentle push on the back. Those whom he spoke to walked with more purpose, though plenty still wandered dazed and uncertain.

"Are these all the dead?" Larka whispered. Watching them walk silently, she felt as if she had to keep her voice in a hush, though their eyes did not so much as turn to her when she spoke. The figures passed her and Sol and continued down the beach, out along a sandbar that went farther than she could see. There were many of them, and more arriving every minute, but nowhere near the vast numbers that she'd expected.

"Some of them," confirmed Sol. "Those who do not get lost. Those who can find their way here. They must come on their own, now that I am not powerful enough to bring them myself. All I can do is hope that the dead make their way here eventually, even though I can no longer guide them." He gazed out over the dead, but Larka thought he didn't really see them.

"Do you remember my father?" Larka asked softly.

Sol kept his eyes upon the row of shades emerging from the tunnel. "I think so. A little."

"Was he afraid? Were any of the others on the ship afraid? Or in pain?"

Sol closed his eyes. "I do not remember," he said, his words rough. "I am so much less than I was. I feel that

I am forgetting things that I should remember, important things, and all the dead are beginning to blend together. But death does not come easily to most. I think they would have been afraid. You, though… I remember you."

She caught her breath. "Me? But I wasn't even there. My father died far from home."

Sol shook his head. "Not when he died. After. I told you once that the hopes and dreams for a ruler's reign die as well. The strongest hopes follow the dead to the underworld, and I remember seeing you. It was just for an instant, but I remember you were holding vigil over your father's body in a temple as all your thoughts of his future died along with him. You wore a dress the color of blood and gold in your hair, and you did not run when your light flickered out and left you in the dark."

He was telling the truth; Larka had worn a gold circlet on the night of the vigil and a red mourning dress, and she remembered watching the candles flicker out hours before dawn. That was the night she had been forced to accept that her father was gone, ripped away from her, and that she would be ascending the throne far sooner than she'd thought. "I didn't know you had seen me before," she said at last. "I thought midsummer was the first time we met."

"So did I. I did not remember, not until now, but that must have been why your soul seemed familiar when I felt you dying. You were brave to hold that vigil. Grown men cower at the thought of spending a night in the dark with the dead."

"Is that why you saved me? Because you saw me and thought I was brave?" Larka wanted, so badly, to understand the god before her. To know his mind and history and why he made the choices he did.

Sol opened his eyes and turned to her. His pale gray gaze was piercing. "I think it was. I recognized something in you, and I could not bear the thought of watching you and your sisters walk down this path when you had hardly lived. So I… I saved you."

She took his hand in hers. His skin was colder than a human's, yet she found she didn't mind. After a moment of hesitation, he twined his twelve fingers through hers and held on tightly.

It felt right to hold his hand in this endless darkness. It felt right to leave him a little less lonely, even if it was just for this moment as they watched the dead walk past them in a slow, endless stream.

Chapter Seventeen

At last, Sol stirred. “Come. I would show you where the dead go once they come down here.” His hand still in hers, they began to walk along the beach, following the dead. Larka thought the sand would be trampled down and stirred by hundreds of feet, but it was untouched and pristine. The only marks in the sand were left by them. It was a stark reminder that they were the only real people on the whole beach.

Larka followed Sol and the dead out onto the long sandbar jutting from the beach. It was wide enough for two or three people to walk abreast, but she still felt uneasy once they had walked far enough that the glowing sand behind them was lost in darkness. It made her think that perhaps the dark water would come rushing up, eating away at the sandbar until there was nothing left, and she would be pulled under into the waters of the underworld. Larka forced the thought out of her head and focused on putting one foot after another in front of her.

The sandbar stretched straight ahead for longer than

Larka thought was possible. She wondered what was at the end. What waited for the dead there? She and Sol passed more kinds of dead than she'd ever imagined before: orphans in ragged clothing, mercenaries with axes at their hips, noblemen in silk and fur. On and on the line of spirits went.

"Where are they going?" asked Larka. "What's across the lake?"

"That I cannot say," said Sol. "Not when you are still alive. The mysteries of the dead are not for the living, nor even for me, to know before our time comes. I believe it to be a place where the dead may find peace—and oblivion, if they wish it."

"So, you've never been there?"

Sol looked out across the vast expanse of the lake.

"No, not even when I was young and the world newly made."

"Why not?"

Sol shrugged, a pained little smile on his face. "Because I am not dead. That is my blessing and my curse, to be the last of the surviving gods. To live when all others have died. I sometimes wish I could have gone with them." He gazed out across the lake, as if he could see something beautiful and unreachable on the other side.

Larka looked at him, startled. "You do? But don't the dead need you to guide them on the path from the living world to the afterlife?"

Sol sighed. His shoulders sank as if carrying an incredibly heavy burden. "They do, and so I cannot leave them even if I wish to. All that I knew and loved is gone and has been gone for many years. Sometimes it feels as if there is nothing left for me in this world, and I am only a remnant of a time long past."

Larka didn't know what words could comfort him. He had lived through things she could never imagine, through the rise and fall of empires, through the ruin of the War of the Gods, through the dark centuries afterward. What words could offer him solace? All she could do was hold his hand and walk next to him as they looked out across the expanse of the lake and toward the unknowable other side.

Sol halted abruptly when they passed one small group of dead. A woman with light brown skin and a many-colored skirt held two infants in her arms as two more older children staggered after her. Exhaustion and grief were etched on every line of the woman's face, though Larka thought she was only six or seven years older than herself.

"My lady," said Sol respectfully as he stopped in front of the woman and her children. "What is your name?"

"Aelia," she said shortly, barely glancing up at him as she struggled to hold her two infants while guiding the older children before her.

"My lady, Aelia, I see you are tired," said Sol. "May I carry your children for you to ease some of your burden?"

Aelia looked up at him with tired, wary eyes. "Do we have much farther to go?"

Sol's voice was kind and quiet as he said, "A ways yet, Lady, though we are more than halfway there."

"Who are you?" she asked suspiciously. Her two older children clutched her bright skirts and peered at Sol with big brown eyes.

"The lord of this land," Sol replied. "In your tongue, I would be called Death."

"So, it's your fault that my children will never grow older, and that my husband is left with an empty house and five graves to pay for?" Aelia asked, a touch of anger in her voice.

Sol shook his head. "No. I do not control the fate of humankind or when death comes to each one. Lady, it is a long walk until you may rest, so I ask again, do you wish for me to help carry your children?"

"Alright," Aelia said at last, clearly exhausted beyond measure. Sol untangled his hand from Larka's and knelt down to let one of the older children climb up to sit on his shoulders. He carefully took the infant held out to him into his arms, and they continued on.

Larka could not help marveling at his kindness. Two thousand years he had been alone in the dark, and yet he did not hesitate to reach and help one who needed it. Two thousand years, and there was still enough kindness in him that he would carry a strange woman's children on his shoulders and in his arms. People were wrong when they said death was cruel. He was inevitable. But he was not cruel.

They continued on along the sandbar. Sol had not lied; it was a long journey until they reached the end of it, long enough that Larka began to wonder if it would ever end. As they walked, Larka also wondered what had caused the death of the woman and all four of her children at once. She had heard of no war, no plague, no disaster in Belmarros that might cause such a tragedy. And the woman was Belmarrian; she had the light brown skin of someone with Astraian ancestry, though she spoke with the distinctive rolling accent of southern Belmarros, and Larka recognized her bright skirt as a style commonly worn in her homeland.

Sol stopped suddenly, pulling Larka out of her puzzled thoughts. He handed the infant back to his mother and gently set down the older child on the soft sand. Larka looked around to see where they had ended. The glowing sand beneath their feet seemed to be the only light in the whole world. All around them she saw only impenetrable darkness and the silent waters of the lake, lapping gently at the sandbar. Behind her was the way back to the palace where her sisters waited, but it all was so impossibly far away, and the daylight world ever further. The only real things in this moment were the expanse of pitch-black sky above her and the equally dark lake stretching off into the distance.

At the end of the sandbar waited a fleet of boats no larger than the ones Larka and her sisters had paddled in when they visited summer estates, only large enough for one or two people. With their black paint, the boats would have nearly disappeared in the night except for the gold and silver adorning their bows. Each shade stepped into a boat and sat calmly as it pulled away into the darkness. Empty ones floated back across the black mirror of the lake and toward those who waited at the shore.

As Larka watched, Aelia helped her children into a waiting boat and then climbed into it herself. Sol stepped away from them and began to talk gently to a group of bewildered-looking soldiers still clutching their weapons.

"Wait!" Larka blurted out before Aelia could push off from the shore, her worry pushing the words out of her mouth. "I—I know it might be rude to ask such a question, but how did you die?"

Aelia turned back to her wearily. "What do you care? My children and I are only five of many people who have walked this path."

"I'm from Belmarros," Larka said. "I can tell by your clothing that you are, too, and I was wondering if… if something happened. Something bad. What happened to you for death to take you and all of your children at the same time?"

The grief in Aelia's eyes was sudden and piercing. "Drought," she said softly. "I lived in the south, where the vineyards grow. It's always been hot, but this summer the rains did not come as they should have. The rivers dried up. The wells were drained. Within a month, what water was left was dirty, not fit to drink, and yet we were desperate enough to drink it anyway. And so, we died."

"But the governors of your lands!" Larka protested. "Surely they could have given you aid—that's what they're for, to rule over their people and give them aid."

Aelia looked at Larka with a kind of sorrow in her eyes that the princess could barely begin to understand. "Death came quickly for the five of us. If the governor of our lands sent any aid, then it was too late for us."

"But—" Larka stopped, biting her lip.

Aelia raised an eyebrow. "Yes?"

"But I—I didn't know there was a drought in Belmarros severe enough to kill."

Aelia shrugged, an elegant gesture despite the child she held in her arms. "Perhaps you know less about Belmarros than you think."

I am the queen, or will be, thought Larka. *Who else should know the most about Belmarros than me? How is it that I am queen-to-be but don't even know when people are dying in the land I am supposed to rule?*

Larka started to speak again, to try and think of the question that would clear her confusion. Aelia raised a hand to stop her.

"I'm tired," she said. "More tired than I have ever been, in my blood and in my bones and in my soul. I can't give you answers to your questions, and I only want to rest. So, please, let me and my children leave."

Larka bit her lip again. "Of course. I'm sorry. I—I just wanted to understand what happened."

Aelia sighed and shifted the weight of the child in her arms. "It's alright. I just can't give you any of the answers you want." She cocked her head to one side. "What does a dead girl care about Belmarros, anyway?"

"I'm not dead," admitted Larka awkwardly. "I owe Sol—Lord Death—a debt that I must pay. I don't belong here, and when I go home, I go to Belmarros."

"You owe a debt to Death Himself? That must be a complicated story."

"Very," said Larka, not in the mood to get into all the lies and secrets she and her sisters were keeping. "The point is that Belmarros is my home. I want the best for it."

"Then go back to it. No one living belongs down here, and anyway, you can't save Belmarros from the underworld."

"No," said Larka quietly. "No, I can't."

Sol, who had finished gently ushering the dead soldiers into their own boats, walked back down the sandbar, to where Larka stood with Aelia and her children.

He inclined his head slightly and said, "My lady, are you ready to leave?"

Aelia clutched her youngest child tighter to her chest and glanced out across the still, black lake. The expression on her face wasn't fear; it was anticipation and acceptance. Larka wondered if she would feel the same when it was her turn to cross this lake for the final time. Would she would have welcomed this final journey if she had walked it on Midsummer with her sisters?

"Yes," Aelia said. Her brightly colored skirts swirled around her in a cold underworld breeze. "I am ready."

Sol reached down and pushed the boat off the sandbar with a single strong gesture. A current pulled it along swiftly, and soon Aelia and her four children were entirely out of sight, swallowed up in the depths of the underworld along with so many other boats traveling in the same direction. She did not look back once.

Even long after the boat was gone, Larka and Sol stood side-by-side on the sandbar. Larka dug her toes into the shining sand and watched the endless trail of dead as they sailed to whatever final destination awaited them.

Finally, she asked, "Why did you show me this?"

Sol, who had similarly been gazing out across the water, turned to her. Strands of his waist-length braid had come loose and fallen across his face. She found the effect oddly endearing.

"I suppose I wanted you to understand it," he said at last.

"Understand what?"

"What death is really like down here." Sol folded and unfolded his arms, seemingly nervous. "I… I wished you to understand that my realm—that death—is not some frightening unknown."

Larka frowned. "You brought me down here as a moral lesson? So I wouldn't be afraid to die?"

"I did not want you to be afraid of me," Sol admitted. "I thought if I showed you that there can be beauty down here, beauty in the sand and the water and in how people do not fear what is on the other side, then you would not fear me."

"It didn't work," said Larka.

Hurt flashed across Sol's face. "So, you fear me?"

"No!" she rushed to amend. "I mean, you didn't need to do this. I'm not afraid of you."

"You are not?" The hurt smoothed away from Sol's face to be replaced by astonishment. The fact that the sudden light in his eyes was because of *her* sent a jolt through Larka that was somehow pleasant and painful at the same time.

"No," answered Larka, surprising herself with her boldness. "You don't frighten me, Sol." It was the truth. He was strange, yes, and sometimes inhuman, but he wasn't human. And no matter what he was, it was impossible for Larka to fear him after she had seen the grief and kindness that still lingered inside him even after everything he had lost.

Larka held out a hand toward Sol, and after a startled moment, he took it. His skin was cold yet not unpleasantly so. Larka squeezed his fingers lightly, and after a hesitant moment, he squeezed back.

You can't save Belmarros from the underworld. The dead woman's words echoed in Larka's skull. She was right; the underworld wasn't the place where Larka could find answers about the drought or why she hadn't known of it. She could only do that in the living world.

She still had a debt to pay, though, and the night was not over. So, for a few minutes at least, Death and the Little Queen stood at the edge of the lake and gazed across at the unknowable other side. Larka found herself surprised to realize that she would miss this moment when she had to return to her real life. She would miss the comfortable silence between Sol and her that she felt no need to fill. In a few hours, she would go back to Belmarros and the weight of the duties that awaited her there. But, for now, Larka was content to stand on the shining beach, hand-in-hand with Death, and listen to the whisper of the waves against the sand.

Chapter Eighteen

Although Larka sat in her gilded chair in the Council Room like any other day, she wasn't thinking about her own boredom or calculating how many minutes were left until she could go free. She wasn't even half-dozing after a long night of dancing, which had become a bad habit over the last few months. Instead, Larka was thinking about the grimly exhausted way the dead woman, Aelia, had said the word "drought."

How could there be a drought in Belmarros severe enough to kill? How was it possible that Larka hadn't heard of it before? She supposed court was so filled with excitement over her impending coronation that any other news was drowned out. The council should have known about it, though, and if they had not mentioned it to her, they likely weren't aware of it.

So, Larka sat in her council seat, tapping her foot with impatience, and waited for an opening in the debate so she could speak. Unfortunately, Councilor Eugenio and Councilor Davin were making it rather more difficult than she'd predicted. Ever antagonistic toward each other, the two men had been arguing back and forth for ten minutes about whether or not to raise the tariff on goods imported from the Crescent Islands of Limmar and Mareth. Larka had attempted to follow the argument and gotten entirely lost; by this point, she wasn't even sure who was arguing for which side.

Davin finally pinned Eugenio down with an argument about how Alannah and Etain's mother was from Limmar and so Belmarros should respect the trade agreements negotiated as part of Queen-Consort Eithne's marriage, even though she was now dead. Eugenio had risen from his seat during the debate. Now he stood there, sweating and fumbling for a reply, and Larka seized her chance.

"Councilors," she said, doing her best to sound diplomatic but firm, "while I'm sure we all appreciate your dedication to the small details of our trade affairs, I'm afraid I'm going to have to ask that we move on in the agenda."

Eugenio gaped like a fish in air—less because he desperately believed the issue was important, Larka thought, and more because he liked the sound of his own voice enough that he couldn't believe someone was asking him to be quiet. Or maybe most of the shock was that it was Larka, of all people, who was asking him. She could admit to herself at least that she'd never spoken as much in council meetings as was expected of her.

Councilor Davin, by contrast, looked relieved. He swept some of his light brown hair out of his eyes and said, "Of course, Majesty. I apologize for getting so caught up in the discussion." He sat. After a moment, and a pointed glare from Davin, Eugenio did the same.

Eugenio coughed and said, "Majesty, was there another item on our agenda you wanted to discuss?"

Larka braced herself. Holy gods, she hated speaking in front of the council. Without doing anything at all, they somehow managed to make her feel very small and young.

"No, actually. I want to introduce a new topic. I am wondering if any of you could confirm a report I heard?"

"A report?" asked Councilor Mariana, leaning forward slightly so she could see Larka better.

"Yes. I've heard that there is a drought in the south. I wonder if any of you have heard that it is happening, and if so, what has been done about it."

Silence fell through the Council Room, the kind of panicked silence that Larka associated with her younger sisters when they were caught misbehaving and were frantically trying to think of a lie. Not the kind of silence she associated with the councilors.

"Who gave you this report?" asked Councilor Mariana at last. For the first time that Larka could remember, there was a crack in the councilor's steely mask. She had not seen this coming.

"It doesn't matter," said Larka. She could hardly tell the council that a dead woman in the underworld had told her. "All that matters is that I know it was the truth. So, have any of you heard of this drought?"

Again, there was silence. Larka resisted the urge to fill it; it was the councilors' turn to speak. She wanted to hear what answers they had to give, why they were behaving so oddly.

Eventually, Councilor Trajan—an old, rail-thin man with steel-colored hair who had once commanded the armies of Belmarros and now spent his days hashing out tax problems—cleared his throat. "Your Majesty," he began, a distinctly guilty note in his voice, "please believe me when I say that we do not disrespect you or believe you lack the capability to be a good ruler."

Unease danced its fingers down Larka's spine. "But?" she prompted.

Trajan cleared his throat again. "But… we felt that with your illness—and your upcoming coronation and arrival of suitors—it wasn't necessary to, ah, burden you with all of the issues concerning our country…." Trajan trailed off as if he wasn't quite sure how to keep defending himself when every word made him and the council look worse.

Larka thought she knew what he was dancing around saying. To confirm it, and to make him say it out loud, she said, "Please explain what you mean clearly, Councilor."

Trajan looked as if he might start squirming in his seat. He was a respected member of the council and a feared general in his day, yet Larka didn't think she'd ever seen him look so uncomfortable in her entire life. Then again, she'd never caught him keeping a secret before, let alone one of this magnitude. "Your Majesty, we didn't think you needed to worry about another drought, so we as a council decided to handle the matter on our own. To, ah, inform you only if it felt, ah, necessary."

A spark of anger flared in the pit of Larka's stomach and quickly became an inferno. Yes, she was worried she wouldn't be the kind of queen this country deserved. And, yes, the council knew she was a quiet, nervous kind of person who often didn't speak up as much as she should. But that was no excuse to keep this kind of information from her.

"Councilor," said Larka, surprised at the icy anger of her own voice, "that is not an excuse. I am your queen, descended directly from Queen Ysobel the Founder. By the laws of this land, I am a grown woman. You cannot decide to keep information from me purely because you don't wish to bother me."

Trajan began to stumble through apologies, but Larka didn't let him finish. "Again, I remind you that I am your queen, sworn to this country in blood and word. I deserve to know what is going on in Belmarros, especially when it's something so serious as a drought. People have died, and yet you still didn't think I needed to know?"

Councilor Mariana coughed delicately, interrupting Larka. "My dear—"

"Don't call me dear," Larka snapped. "I give you the respect you deserve by calling you Councilor, not Mariana. I'm not a child anymore. The least you can do is give me the same courtesy." Larka had been called 'dear' so many times over the years, but it was only at that moment that she started to hate it. Every time she was called 'dear,' she was a child again, not a young woman forced to grow up faster than she ever would have chosen.

"My apologies, Your Majesty," said Councilor Mariana.

That matter settled, Larka turned to Trajan. "And you. Was it your idea to keep from me the fact that my own subjects are dying? How long were you planning to keep this a secret from me?"

Trajan winced. "Your Majesty, I must offer my sincerest apologies for our misjudgment of the situation."

"I will accept your apology only if you swear to change your behavior," said Larka with dignity and a touch of scorn. I sound like a queen, she thought in surprise, and I don't even think I'm acting. This is me, angry. "Harmless as you clearly thought the decision not to inform me of the drought was, it was anything but. I don't care if you had doubts about my ability to balance all of my duties; you still should have told me."

"We really didn't think it was necessary," said Mariana stiffly. "It was only one matter, and you are still so very young. There's plenty of time yet for you to learn how to be a good queen."

Larka threw her hands up in the air in exasperation. "I can't learn how to be a good queen if you won't let me!"

"With all due respect, Your Majesty, you haven't always been willing to learn."

Mariana's words cut straight to Larka's core. As much as she wanted to deny them, it was true. She had dragged her feet when it came to her duties, shut her eyes against being queen, barely paid attention to the ruling of her own country. She had spent more council meetings than she cared to admit counting the minutes until it was time for her to leave instead of paying attention to the issues at hand. She had been no better than her own father. Despite all her vows that she would be better than him, that she would care more and make the right decisions, she hadn't been.

When Larka had been younger, her behavior had been excusable. What fourteen-year-old wants to be forced to listen to debates over raising tariffs when she could be wandering through the castle gardens? But Larka had no excuse now. She was considered a grown woman by the laws of Belmarros, and grown queens-to-be weren't allowed to be children anymore. Queens-to-be weren't allowed to sit by while people died from drinking dirty water and their ghosts wandered the underworld. Queens-to-be could not be so frightened of doing wrong that they did nothing at all, for that meant they could do no good either. If Larka didn't behave like a queen, then no one would treat her like one.

"Majesty?" said Mariana. "If I have overstepped—"

Larka shook her head. "No, Councilor. I know that I haven't been the Little Queen that I am expected to be. I—I haven't cared about my duties as much as I should have. I understand." She traced her fingers across the golden patterns of vines on the armrests of her chair. It was still ridiculously large, her feet not even reaching the floor, but for the first time she thought of it not as something that swallowed her up and made her feel small but perhaps as something that she could someday feel comfortable sitting in. "I will do better in the future. All of us will have to, for the more you try to protect me from the realities of ruling Belmarros, the less I learn."

"She's right, you know," said Councilor Davin, drawing startled looks from the rest of the council. "We thought dealing with matters on our own was the best thing to do, but one can only learn how to rule when given experience. This council works because we all sort out of the matters of state together."

"Thank you," Larka said to him, and she meant it. She was grateful to discover that there was one other person on the council, at least, who was willing to admit when he was wrong.

Davin ducked his head. "Your Majesty, don't thank me just because I know we did wrong. You would be well within your rights to dismiss all of us from the council entirely."

Larka hadn't even considered that action until he pointed out it out. "I won't," she said. "Each one of you has far more experience than I do when it comes to ruling Belmarros. I won't dismiss any of you, as long as you promise that none of you will ever go behind my back like this again."

Visible relief swept through the Council Room at her words, and she remembered that dismissal had been a common threat, often followed through on, when her father was king. Many dismissed councilors had been reinstated as soon as Stefan had become regent, but they still likely feared losing their power again.

"It won't happen again, Majesty," said Councilor Mariana. "I swear on the Crown, we will not knowingly keep information from you again." Trajan and the rest of the council echoed her, sounding so sheepish that Larka couldn't help but be amazed.

Larka settled back into her seat. "What have you done to help with the drought?"

"We sent some food and water a few weeks ago using what funds could be spared from the treasury," said Davin helpfully.

"You should send more," said Larka, thinking of the story the ghost woman had told her of how there had been no water to spare. "From what I heard, the only water left is unfit to drink. How much more can we take from the treasury?"

"Some." Mariana shuffled through the stack of papers on the table before her. "There are, of course, other drains on the treasury that must be accounted for, such as preparations for your coronation."

"Use any money that can be spared for the drought instead," ordered Larka. "I would rather dance at my coronation ball in rags knowing my people are taken care off than wear silks while they starve."

Mariana nodded. "My Queen, it will be done. If you don't mind extending this council a little longer, we can begin to go over the expenses immediately."

"Yes, please," said Larka, and she found that she truly meant it. She didn't long to leave the stuffy, formal confines of the Council Room for fresh air and a breeze, not if there was important work to be done.

The council was in session for another hour after that, and it was worth every minute. By the time they dispersed, Larka's back ached from her uncomfortable chair, she was desperately thirsty, and she felt that she had actually accomplished something in a council meeting for the first time in her life.

When she looked up from reorganizing the papers before her and finishing her notes, Larka discovered that Stefan had snuck into the Council Room at some point and was leaning against one of the pillars. He was smiling, and the look of pride on his face made her smile back so widely her face hurt.

As the rest of the council filtered out, Stefan made his way up the long table to where Larka still sat in her throne-like chair at the head.

"That was well-handled," he commented. He sat down in the chair to her right and put his boots up on the table, something he wouldn't have dared do when he was regent and the whole kingdom looked to him for guidance. "The council will think twice about going behind your back now that they've seen you have a voice of your own."

"You were there for all of that?"

"Only the tail end. It was very impressive, though, from what I saw. You have more of a bite than any of them gave you credit for."

Larka snorted. "You think? Honestly, I'm not even sure where it came from. I suppose I was just… so angry that they thought I didn't need to know what was going on in my own kingdom."

"I'm glad," Stefan said. "A queen needs backbone, and you've always had trouble standing up for yourself when it comes to the council."

Larka ducked her head. "I know, Stef. You don't need to lecture me. I'm trying to be better. It's just that my father ruined this country. He absolutely ruined it, and I'm afraid that no matter what I do, it won't be enough to make up for his failures." She hadn't been able to say this to the council, for fear that they'd see it as weakness, but now it all came pouring out.

Stefan's expression turned grim, and Larka immediately felt bad for bringing it up. He was, after all, the one who had been responsible for dealing with the aftermath of Eldric's rule and the disasters that had come from the former king's inattention and careless spending. Stefan had been forced to find ways to pay the royal debt at the same time he was arranging the funeral of his brother.

At last her uncle said, "My brother wasn't a good king, Larka. I don't think you could find a single person in this kingdom who'd disagree with that statement. But you're not your father, and you never will be."

The euphoria from Larka's earlier triumph was starting to drain away. "I… I'm just worried that I won't be enough. That I'll make the wrong decisions and make things worse. I mean, I just read the accounts of all the kings and queens who guided Belmarros through harder times, and I don't understand how they knew what to do."

"Darling," said Stefan gently, "you're eighteen. Besides Eldric, no one has taken the throne at such a young age for decades. Most rulers have years of experience governing provinces or cities as practice for when they're crowned. Don't compare yourself to others who had things you didn't."

"That's just the problem," said Larka. She knew how self-pitying she sounded, but she was unable to stop herself from talking this way. "Other rulers have experience. I don't. If they made mistakes when they were governing those cities or provinces, it only affected part of the country, and the real king and queen could step into make this right. If I make a mistake, it affects the whole country, and then I have to figure out how to fix it."

"You might not have experience, but you have heart. You care about this country and the people in it, and you want to do right by them. I think that's the biggest difference between you and Eldric: He never cared about more than his own comfort, and you care about everyone's. And as long as you do want to make the right decisions, I guarantee you will."

Larka shifted in her big, gilded chair, putting her chin on her hands. "You really think I could be a good queen?" she asked. It was one thing to feel that she finally knew what she was doing but another for people to agree with it. Stefan's opinion was one she trusted when it came to ruling.

"I do," promised Stefan. "Just give yourself time. And, well, hopefully you can rely on the council more in the future. You won't be solving problems alone."

Larka sighed. "I hope so. I think they won't keep things from me anymore, and they understand that I'll involve myself more." Larka made to hop off the chair and stopped. "Thank you, Stef. It's good to know that some people think I can be queen."

"I only told you the truth," Stefan demurred. Larka got up to leave, and he suddenly raised a hand, saying, "Wait, please." Larka looked back at him, concerned at the terribly serious note in his voice, even more so than the way he'd just been talking.

Larka sat back down, wincing at the uncomfortable gilded knobs digging into her shoulder blades. "What? Is something wrong?"

Stefan took his boots off the table and arranged his face into the carefully calm expression that she'd seen him use on so many people. What was going on that made Stefan treat her the same as an unruly diplomat or overly arrogant courtier?

"I wanted to ask if everything is alright," said Stefan

"With you and your sisters, I mean. Things have been… different lately, ever since your illness and the approaching coronation. I just want to let you know that you can talk to me."

"About what?" Larka had an uneasy feeling about where this conversation was going. She wanted to get up and leave, but that would only make Stefan more confused—and more certain that she was hiding something. No, she just had to get through this.

"About whatever is going on!" A note of frustration entered Stefan's voice. "You look so tired lately. I thought it might be the upcoming coronation and the stress, but it's all of you, even the younger girls. You go to bed early but walk around the next day like you've barely slept. And I could be imagining things, but you all seem as if you're keeping secrets. You're always talking to each other and stop as soon as I come near, as if you don't want me to hear what you're talking about."

"We're not keeping secrets," Larka said. The lie tasted bitter in her mouth.

Stefan didn't look convinced. "Aren't you? I don't understand why else you all would be acting so differently lately."

"We're not doing anything," said Larka, hoping the lie sounded convincing. "Stefan, we've all been under a lot of pressure lately. The illness, the coronation, the suitors, everyone who doubts the transfer of power… I think you're seeing a conspiracy where there isn't one. There is *nothing* going on."

She knew he would keep asking questions, because he was Stefan and he loved her and he sensed that something was wrong. He would keep asking questions and would not understand that she would not—*could not*—answer them. He wanted the truth because he loved her and didn't want her to suffer alone, but he didn't understand that the truth was the one thing that she could not give him.

She saw in his eyes that Stefan was forming another

question. Before he could ask it, and before she could deny him answers, Larka stood and left.

Chapter Nineteen

The rest of Larka's suitors arrived just as summer was crawling leisurely into its last few weeks, like a cat reluctant to leave the sun. After so long with only the company of Duke Brandt and the members of the summer court, it was an avalanche of unfamiliar faces and foreign tongues and new arrivals underfoot wherever Larka turned. One moment she had one suitor, and the next there were strangers from across the world stuffing themselves and their servants into whatever spare rooms could be found at the palace.

Larka had known it was coming—after all, the Royal Council had long ago fixed the date by which suitors must declare themselves—and yet the end of summer rushed up faster than she could believe. The days of court business and the nights of dancing bled together so quickly it seemed impossible that so much time had passed.

The day after the last suitor arrived, the whole court gathered in the throne room to watch them all officially declare their intention to try and win Larka's hand. Being in the throne room was odd; it had been used only sparingly while Stefan was regent, and Larka kept expecting to see Eldric stride across the gray-streaked white marble tiles to lounge across the heavy gold throne as if he didn't have a care in the world. This was the place that he had most loved to hold court, this high-ceilinged room with a skylight beaming sun directly down onto his throne, a long, red carpet running down the length of the room to show someone the minute he stepped inside where the center of attention was.

But Eldric wasn't here. He would never again reign over this hall or boast to the people clustered between the high, white pillars or sit with his legs tossed over the side of the throne while he pretended to pay attention to the business at hand. It was Larka who was seated there instead, feeling the spirals and etchings of gold digging into her back despite cushions piled there. She wore a heavy dress of indigo velvet edged with gold, which she was already regretting wearing; the weather had been cooler lately, but the throne room was currently filled with the heat and bustle of hundreds of curious courtiers.

Larka had barely settled down onto the throne when the big double doors at the far end of the hall, engraved with trees and leaping deer, slid open thanks to the determined efforts of half-a-dozen court pages.

One by one, the suitors marched in. Miron Brandt was the first to enter, having somehow secured the coveted place at the front of the line even though he was a foreigner. He walked the length of the long, red carpet and bowed before Larka. She thought that he very much enjoyed the whispers that followed him as he took her hand and kissed it in a rather possessive way. Miron was smiling as he stepped back and the page recited his titles.

Another suitor came, and another, and another. Larka began to wonder if half the world had come to court her. Though she'd memorized the list of suitors the council had sent her, it was only now that she began to put faces to that long, impersonal list of names.

Fergal MacKay. A prince of the Crescent Islands—the sixth son, so not as important as the title implied. He was a cousin of Alannah and Etain, although he was closer to Larka's age, and his hair was brown instead of red.

Varian Valonos. An Astraian merchant so bedecked with gold that Larka wasn't sure how he didn't stagger to the ground under its weight. The red- and black-striped robe he wore reminded Larka of the clothing Queen-Consort Maria had worn in the hotter summers.

Aubrey Allard. A preening peacock of a count with gleaming black hair and more brocade than Larka had ever seen in her entire life. She was not surprised to learn he was from Veanara, the country that had given itself entirely over to the pursuit of pleasure and wealth.

On and on the introductions went. There were dukes and princes and warlords from countries across the world, men who commanded vast shipping fleets or were heir to staggering wealth and power. Those were the interesting ones, the suitors from foreign lands who were strangers to the court. Miron Brandt, Larka noted with interest, was the only Dalbrasti suitor.

After that, there were several suitors from Belmarros. Larka knew them all, for their names had been tossed around for years as possible matches for her. There was the governor of the largest port city in the south, the heir to a vast merchant company, the earl of the northern plains, a baron who'd made his fortune through mining the eastern mountains, and more minor lords than she cared to count who wished to increase their power by marrying royalty.

It didn't escape Larka's attention that, except for the earl, who was twelve, all of her suitors were older than she was. Miron, who was twenty-three, was one of the youngest suitors. The Crescent Island prince was twenty-nine, the Astraian merchant nearly fifty, the Veanaran nobleman in his late thirties. The Belmarrian baron had granddaughters Larka's age. Perhaps if Larka had taken the throne at a more normal age, she wouldn't have found it odd, but as it was, her suitors made her feel even more like a child than she normally did.

Power and wealth, she reminded herself. *That's what's important. Not their age, not their temperament, and not my opinion of them, not truly. This is what comes of ascending the throne at a younger age than most.*

Larka cast an eye down the long line of suitors beside her and wondered if any of them had the potential to make her feel anything other than vague dread and boredom. Because it was boring—the whole affair was a carefully constructed ritual of bowing and hand-kissing and title recitation. There was nothing real about it. There was no way to learn anything about the men who came before her, and no way for them to learn anything about her. It was difficult to care when everything was so staged.

After all of the suitors had been officially announced, the court retired to the nearby drawing rooms for refreshments. Supposedly, the occasion was for everyone to get to know the suitors in a less official capacity, but Larka knew that it was really just an opportunity to gossip and analyze the men who had come to seek her hand.

Larka glided through one of the drawing rooms, decorated in shades of blue, silver, and white, like the winter storms that would be becoming once she was crowned. She waved away a servant at her side offering food and drink; her stomach was still unpleasantly knotted from the presentation of suitors, and she didn't think she could force anything down.

She went from group to group of courtiers clustered throughout the room. She'd accept a few compliments on finally receiving her suitors, offer a few polite phrases in return, and move on to the next group. A queen had to make her subjects feel seen; Larka had learned that much from her tutors over the years. And small talk she could do, so she circled around the groups of courtiers, smiling and pretending to be interested in their outrageous gossip.

Larka saw her sisters scattered in the crowd: Rhiannon standing with her head bent toward Janna Brandt, who was smiling and blushing; Gwynna flirting with a pair of visiting Veanaran nobles, Giovanni and Faustina Acconci; Auri holding court with a cluster of infatuated boys and girls around her age; the triplets, dressed in three shades of pink and wide-eyed at one of their first official court gatherings, though still probably plotting mischief.

Larka saw her suitors on the other side of the room as well, talking to members of the Royal Council. Her feet refused to carry her over to them even though she knew the purpose of this entire gathering was to speak to them, to get to know them as men instead of titles. If that was even possible.

Instead, Larka made her way over to where Stefan and Dario stood with a group of Belmarrian merchants, hoping that they wouldn't notice she was avoiding her duties.

"Hello, Larka," said Stefan. He was holding a glass of ruby-red wine in one hand, his other arm wrapped around Dario's shoulder as his husband conversed animatedly with the merchants. "Aren't you supposed to be talking to your suitors?"

Larka bit back a sigh. It was impossible to fool someone when they'd known you all your life and raised you for the last four years. "Yes, but I'm… intimidated." That was putting it mildly. "I mean, how do I start a conversation with someone knowing they want to marry me? And that people want me to marry *them*?"

"You'll never get to know them if you never talk to them," replied Dario, turning away from the conversation with the merchants. His dark curls had been wrestled into braids, each tipped with gold beads, which knocked against each other when he turned his head. "Besides, they won't bite if you say something wrong. They're men, not wolves."

"Sometimes those two things are closer than you'd think," muttered Larka.

"Just talk to them," suggested Stefan. "They're

here because they want to marry you, Larka. Give them a chance."

No, they want to marry my crown, thought Larka, but she went. If Stefan had noticed she was avoiding her own suitors, then surely other people would start to.

It was easier than she'd expected, even if every conversation began to blend into the next one as she talked. All she had to do was ask how the journey to Belmarros was and if the rooms they had been offered were suitable. As long as she forgot that people were expecting her to marry one of them, it was almost tolerable.

Larka's face ached from smiling, and she was desperately craving a cold drink by the time she had made her way through the crowd of courtiers and suitors in the drawing rooms. Still, she had done her duty and entertained her court, so Larka decided she could have a minute to herself before she braved the circuit again. Besides, it wasn't as if stiff court etiquette was difficult, as long as you'd memorized the curtsies and titles and trite, polite phrases.

Rhiannon passed by Larka, discreetly leaning against the wall and drinking a glass of water. The former paused in front of a nearby table of food and began to pile late-summer fruit on two plates. Larka watched as Rhiannon glanced toward Janna Brandt. She saw a sparkle in her sister's eye and a smile on her lips that hadn't been present since Rhiannon was jilted by a merchant's daughter the previous winter.

"You like her, don't you?" asked Larka, making her way over to Rhiannon. "Janna Brandt, I mean."

Rhiannon jumped. "Larka, you scared me! You walk so quietly."

"Do you like her?" prodded Larka.

Rhiannon bit her lip and looked back at Janna, red hair spilling over her shoulder as she laughed at some clever comment a courtier had made. There was something open and sweet about Janna's face that her brother's was missing. "I do," Rhiannon admitted. "Miron is… well, I always get the impression that the side of him I'm seeing isn't real. But Janna's not like that. She's genuine. And kind and gentle and… Well, yes. I like her very much."

"Is she a good kisser?" teased Larka.

Rhiannon's blush told Larka all she needed to know. "You're not angry about it? I mean, she's the sister of your suitor."

"No, of course not," said Larka, patting Rhiannon's arm. "You're happy. That's what matters the most to me. Besides, now at least one of us can be glad that the Brandts came to court."

Rhiannon went on her way with the plates of fruit. There was a little pinch in Larka's heart when she saw the way her sister and Janna leaned toward each other and laughed; Larka doubted that she would ever be so comfortable with her suitors. One could only have that kind of easy familiarity with someone when one chose them for oneself, as opposed to having them thrust upon you by others.

Larka lingered by the food table to rest a moment longer, though her reprieve didn't last long; Miron Brandt and Aengus Braddock ambushed her as she drank her third glass of ice water.

"A lovely gathering, Little Queen, don't you think?" said Lord Braddock, coming up to Larka on her left. For such a large man, he walked cat-quiet, and Larka jumped when she realized how close he'd come without her noticing.

"Very lovely," said Larka automatically. She snuck a look to her right to see if there was an escape route in that direction, only to see Miron Brandt coming up to her as well. Before she could properly formulate some sort of excuse to flee, both men were before her and she was well and truly pinned. There was no way to leave now without looking rude.

"Miron," said Larka. She hoped he didn't hear the wariness in her voice. "How good to see you. I don't think we've had a chance to speak much lately. You look well." It was true; after enough time in the Belmarrian sun, Miron had a golden tan that suited his red hair much more than the sunlight-starved skin of most Dalbrasti.

Miron bowed. "Thank you, Your Majesty. It's a pleasure to see you. I've been busy getting to know the city of Vaelkarra a bit more over the past few weeks."

"Please, tell me all about it," said Larka. She turned toward him more firmly and hoped that Lord Braddock would leave now that she was clearly engaged in another conversation.

To her confusion, Miron replied, "Perhaps another time. There is something else I would like to talk to you about."

"That we would both like to talk to you about," interjected Braddock. Larka's stomach dropped unpleasantly at his cool tone.

"Yes?" she said, treading cautiously.

"Miron and I," continued Lord Braddock, "are both concerned about you, Little Queen."

"Concerned how?" asked Larka. She wasn't even really playing innocent; she wasn't sure what they were talking about. Concerned about her suitors? Her upcoming coronation? Her fear that she would be like her father? There were so many things to worry about.

Braddock stepped a little closer, until Larka's back was flat against the wall in an attempt to stay far away from him. "Miron mentioned a few weeks ago that he thought you seemed out-of-sorts. He said you seemed tired and distracted and wondered if this was normal for a young queen preparing to start her reign. He wanted me to keep an eye on you."

"I don't need anyone to keep an eye on me!" said Larka indignantly, to hide her mounting fear. "I'm not a child."

"I know," said Braddock, sounding as if he was humoring her. "Nevertheless, I agreed to watch over you and your sisters for Miron. And imagine my surprise when he turned out to be on to something."

"I really don't understand what you're talking

about," said Larka. She fought the urge to run. Running would only make her look guilty. Running would only confirm that she really did have something to hide—that she and her sisters danced for Death at night.

Braddock took her elbow in a grip that would have looked courtly and polite to anyone who couldn't feel the pressure of his thick fingers. "Why is it, Your Majesty, that you and your sisters have seemed so tired these last few months, and that you dismiss your servants and retire so early to bed with your door locked? Why does the court cobbler report making twelve new pairs of dancing shoes every few days? What possible use could you have for so many dancing slippers?"

Larka tried to pull away from Braddock's hand and failed. "I don't know. Why don't you tell me?" She glanced desperately at Miron, hoping that he might rescue her from the interrogation. He merely stood at her side and watched. There would be no help from him.

"I think, Little Queen, that you and your sisters are hiding something," said Braddock, pulling her attention away from Miron. "Perhaps you're locking your bedroom door only to sneak out to the Gallow's Dance and cavort the night away. Perhaps you have a lower-class lover and are forcing your sisters to cover for you. I can't say what you're doing, only that your behavior is shocking for a queen-to-be and that I intend to get to the bottom of it."

Larka jerked her arm, hard, and succeeded in pulling it away from Braddock. She fixed him with her best steely gaze and said, "Your behavior, Lord Braddock, is shocking for someone who claims to have my best interests at heart. My sisters and I are hiding nothing, and even if we were, it would be none of your business unless it interfered with my ability to rule Belmarros. We may use our allotted funds from the treasury for whatever we wish, and I promise you that ordering extra dancing slippers for our lessons is nothing sinister. If you keep throwing wild speculation around, then I will have no choice but to inform the council and have you dismissed from court."

Braddock stepped back, clearly shocked by the force of her words. "My queen—"

Larka shook her head. "Don't try to apologize. You overstepped your boundaries and you know it." She started to walk away, then stopped and turned to where Miron was lurking sheepishly against the wall.

"I don't need protecting," Larka told him. She realized her fists were clenched by her side and forced her fingers to relax. "I don't need people to keep an eye on me, especially if they start outlandish rumors and accuse me of abandoning my duties."

"You're young," Miron protested. He looked deeply uncomfortable; Larka guessed that public confrontations weren't exactly his favorite past time.

Larka snorted. "That's rich, coming from someone only a few years older than I am. I may be younger than you, but I'm still a queen. I can take care of myself. If you don't believe that, then perhaps you shouldn't have decided to court me."

"Your Majesty—" Miron had gone sickly pale under his tan, clearly realizing that picking Braddock over Larka had been a mistake.

"I am done here," said Larka shortly, brushing past him. "Either respect me or withdraw your suit." She left Miron gaping behind her, her head held high even though fear rushed through her body. The longer this lie went on, she knew, the more people would see through it.

Chapter Twenty

Larka couldn't quite shake the veil of apprehension that fell over her in the next few days, even though she was busier than she had ever been before. Her suitors were everywhere: in the gardens when she wished to walk alone, in the library when she tried to have a moment of peace, at meals that were normally only for family. The Astraian merchant, Varian, pestered her about new trade relations at every turn, even though she firmly told him that kind of business was for council meetings. Aubrey Allard bombarded her with questions about what the coronation ball would be like. Fergal MacKay sat beside Larka at every meal but flirted with other court women the moment the dessert course was over, and he completely ignored Alannah and Etain, even though they had shyly told Larka they wanted to get to know their cousin.

Her suitors were inescapable—except for Miron Brandt. He was clearly wise enough to know that an apology wasn't enough to get him back into Larka's good graces. He stayed away from her as much as possible.

The first night after her suitors arrived, Larka found herself genuinely looking forward to the underworld dancing. It might have been suffocatingly dark there, and she might have danced with the dead, but at least she didn't have to endure the constant attention of men who only wanted her crown.

That night, dancing slippers on and hair tied back, Larka knelt in the center of the princess' bedroom and pressed the glittering leaves to the floor. The rest of her sisters knelt beside her in a circle, as they had done so many times, clasping hands.

Instinctively, Larka ran an eye over her sisters to check that they were all there. *Rhiannon, Gwynna, Auriana, Katharine, Kristina, Karolina, Yara, Talia, Melina—*

She stopped. Where Melina normally should have been, dirt on her face and wildflowers woven into her hair, was only empty space.

"Where's Mel?" asked Larka.

Auri frowned and blew a strand of blonde hair out of her eyes. "She was just here a minute ago…."

A covert yet panicked search ensued. After only a few minutes, Rhiannon marched back to the room holding Mel by the arm. The younger princess had escaped to the garden, apparently, and had been playing among the shrubs with no sense of urgency to return. Though she hadn't been gone long, there was already mud on the hem of her dress and grass speckled in her brown hair. She looked up at Larka with wide-eyed false innocence.

"Mel, you know we're supposed to go dancing tonight!" scolded Larka as soon as Rhiannon had locked the door to keep them safe from anyone listening.

"I don't want to go dancing," muttered Mel, dropping her innocent act as soon as it became clear it wouldn't fool anyone. "I don't want to anymore, Larka." She fiddled with her hair, and Larka sighed at how tangled it had become in only a few minutes.

"It doesn't matter what you want," replied Larka wearily. "We promised Sol that we'd dance for him, and so we will."

"Dancing is damn stupid," said Mel, a sullen edge to her voice.

"Don't swear," Larka admonished.

"Talia does it."

"Well, Talia shouldn't either," replied Larka, shooting an accusatory look at Talia, who ducked her head guiltily. Honestly, sometimes Larka felt more like a mother than a sister when it came to the younger girls. Then again, none of them had mothers anyone. "We have a promise to keep and a debt to fulfill, so we *have* to dance."

Larka led Melina back to where the rest of their sisters knelt in a circle. They opened the portal as they had so many times before, and for the next few hours, Larka glided across the stark white floor of Sol's palace with a quick-footed shade. Yet even as she danced, her worries didn't entirely leave her.

Larka might have threatened Aengus Braddock into silence, but the fact remained that he had noticed something was different about her and her sisters. Miron had noticed there was something odd going on, and he hadn't even known Larka or her sisters before the illness. Stefan, too, had inquired about the changes in their behavior. The girls' mask of normalcy wasn't perfect, and it couldn't last forever.

Even as Larka danced to the tune of a lively song made hollow and haunting by the ghostly musicians, she kept worrying. Mel, childish as her complaint had been, had a point: She didn't want to keep dancing. And they *couldn't,* not forever. Sooner or later, the arrangement had to end—and before someone became suspicious enough to try and force the truth out of Larka and her sisters.

Back in Belmarros, Braddock didn't confront her again and Miron stayed away, but Larka stayed uneasy. Every time one of the men entered the same room as her, she feared that they had somehow discovered her secret. And, again in the underworld, walking through its glittering forests, hearing a branch snap was enough to make Larka jump and look behind her. The impulse was ridiculous, she knew, yet Larka couldn't stop fearing that someone might discover the secret she and her sisters kept. She was terrified someone might crack open the delicate shell of lies they had built around the truth.

And then, only a few days later, Larka's worst fears came true.

It started as a normal night of dancing: the journey across the dark lake with Sol waiting for them, ball gowns and hole-filled slippers that the princesses hoped to make last one more night. Larka's partner that evening was a nobleman dressed in an extremely ugly gold coat that had been the height of fashion some two hundred years ago. He had a graceful enough step that Larka looked forward to dancing with him, yet not even one song into the night, Sol raised his hand and cut the music with a screech of ghostly strings. He flicked his hand carelessly, and the dancing shades froze mid-step. Sol climbed off his throne and down the steps of the dais until he stood in the midst of the unmoving dancers.

Larka untangled her hands from the shade she had been dancing with and stepped toward Sol, confused. "Sol—" she started.

"Wait," he said. "I feel something… strange."

"What kind of something?" replied Larka. Her confusion began to morph into fear. If the lord of the underworld said he felt something strange, then it must be truly strange.

Sol swept a look across the ballroom. "I feel magic that should not be here. Arcanist magic. *Human* magic."

"Are you sure?" asked Larka.

Sol turned a searching gaze on Larka's sisters, who flinched back under the intensity. "I know arcanist magic as well as I know the magic of death. And I know it is here tonight. I have sensed it for the last few nights, but only now am I sure it is not my imagination."

"Well, none of us have magic," said Auri, who

wasn't cowed by Sol's sudden severity.

"Could you have brought something enchanted with you?" asked Sol.

Auri shook her head. Wisps of hair that had escaped from their elaborate knots blew around her face. "Not a chance. Before you, we'd barely encountered magic except for arcanist globes."

"Well, then," said Sol. He began to pace the floor in a way that reminded Larka of a hunter stalking prey. "If none of *you* carry magic, then someone else must." He made his way around the perimeter of the room, peering intently at corners that seemed entirely empty.

Larka felt as if she had swallowed stones and they now sat heavily in her stomach. "You think someone else is here? That someone… followed us?"

"No," said Sol. He stopped at the edge of the room, near the door the girls had come through. "I *know* someone has." He reached out one hand, grasped at what seemed to Larka like a handful of empty air, and *pulled*.

There was the sound of cloth ripping, and the air split open to reveal Miron Brandt standing in the middle of the throne room. Where Sol had been holding empty air, now he clutched a shredded gray cloak embroidered with black arcanist runes.

Larka froze in shock. She was stone, she was ice, she was only the thought *This can't be happening* repeated over and over.

Miron made a feeble attempt to grab for the cloak. Sol gave him a fierce glare and held the garment out of reach, leaving Miron to flinch and stumble backward onto his knees. There was a clattering sound, and something fell out of the cloak's pocket: twigs of silver, gold, and diamond from the forest that Larka and her sisters had just walked through.

The scene before her made Larka dizzy. Her mind couldn't reconcile seeing the two men before her at the same time: Miron, who belonged in the daylight world of court and gossip and banquets, and Sol, a creature of the darkness and silence and death. Only a terrible tangling of the threads of fate could make their paths cross.

Miron shifted as if to stand, and Sol said, "None of that now." He waved his free hand, and tendrils of darkness crawled from the corner of the room like snakes. Larka shivered and stepped away, but the writhing shadows weren't aimed at her. They made their way toward Miron and wrapped around his hands and feet until he was bound securely in his kneeling position.

The sight of Miron dressed in court silks and tied with shadows, his normally charming face full of fear, was so very out-of-place that Larka resisted the hysterical urge to laugh. The urge was broken when Sol held up the tattered remains of Miron's cloak—Larka remembered suddenly that Miron had once told her his family owned an invisibility cloak—and spat out, "Who is this man?"

"One of my suitors," admitted Larka. She crossed the floor on unsteady legs to stand beside Sol. Up close, she could see the runes on the cloak shifting as if they were alive and the rip had upset them.

"Your suitor?" repeated Sol, raising an eyebrow. He looked back at Miron. "How did you come to the underworld, then?"

"I followed the princesses," said Miron reluctantly from where he knelt on the ground.

"Why?" asked Sol, smoothing a finger over the embroidered runes on the cloak. "This debt is between the princesses and myself only. It does not concern you, so why follow them?"

Miron said nothing. He only scowled up at Larka and Sol like a cornered animal that knows it cannot escape its fate yet still attempts to. His silence was the only defiance he had, caught as he was now.

Sol took another step closer to Miron until he was looming over him. The god's eyes flashed, dark and inhuman, and for the briefest of moments, Larka saw his face turn from man to skull. The shadows binding Miron tightened for a second, enough that he grunted in pain.

"Why did you come to the land of the dead?" Sol asked again.

Miron swallowed hard in the face of Sol's overwhelming presence—Larka couldn't blame him; she was used to Sol by now, yet a primal kind of fear had thrilled through her at the sight of Sol's skull-face—and the wall holding back his words fell.

"Because I knew there was something strange going on. Everyone in the court of Belmarros says that the princesses have been more secretive since their illness, that they go to bed early yet still seem tired. When I confronted Larka, along with another member of court, I knew that there was something more going on."

"I didn't tell you anything!" protested Larka.

A shadow of Miron's usually clever, self-satisfied smile slipped across his face. "You didn't have to. I know a liar when I see one, Your Majesty."

Larka closed her eyes briefly. Hadn't she feared this? That Miron might discover their lies? Still, not even in her nightmares had she dreamed that he would be bold enough to follow them to the underworld.

"So, you decided to spy on us?" Gwynna broke away from her dance partner and strode over to Miron with an outraged look on her face. "On the person that you hoped to marry?"

"I only wanted to help," said Miron, though Larka wasn't convinced. Miron was not the kind of person to do things out of the goodness of his own heart. When one grew up in court, every move was calculated.

"Really?" said Gwynna skeptically.

"Does Janna know about this?" blurted Rhiannon from where she stood with the younger girls. There was pain in her voice, and Larka remembered the way she had seen her laughing with Miron's sister only a few nights ago. Larka didn't even like Miron, and she was still upset by his actions—

it couldn't be pleasant for Rhiannon to consider that Janna might have been spying on them as well.

"Janna knows nothing about this," said Miron, and Rhiannon's shoulders fell in relief.

A terrible thought occurred to Larka. "Does Braddock know about this? Did he put you up to it?"

"No," Miron said. There was a touch of pride in his voice when he replied, "It was all my idea. Braddock was put off investigating further in case the council heard about it, but I wasn't. I wanted to know what was happening. My family owns a cloak sewn with runes of invisibility, so it was a simple enough thing to put it on at night and get into your rooms when you left the door open."

Larka thought of how they'd been forced to search for Melina a few nights before and resisted the urge to groan. They had left Miron the perfect opening for him to follow them.

"I didn't entirely understand what was happening," Miron continued, "but I followed you down the staircase and jumped into one of your boats as you crossed the lake."

"That's why my boat felt so heavy the last few nights," said Auri indignantly, putting her hands on her hips. "I thought it was different."

"Different?" Miron shook his head in amazement. "This whole world is different. I never… I never could have believed that this was your secret. Midnight balls in another world with a god who should be dead."

So, he knows all of it, thought Larka, resigned. She wasn't surprised; Miron was clever enough to piece things together. He would have quickly been able to figure out the truth, no matter how impossible it seemed.

"How many nights have you done this?" Sol shook the cloak at Miron. "How many nights have you tried to learn secrets that are not yours to know?"

Miron looked away from Sol's furiously gleaming eyes. "Tonight is the third night," he admitted.

Larka crossed her arms over her chest protectively.

"And what were you planning to do after this?"

"Yes, what?" challenged Gwynna. "What was your plan, exactly? Were you going to tell the council and have Larka removed from the throne, if you're such good friends with Braddock?"

Miron winced. Clearly there was some truth to her accusations. "I hadn't decided yet. I—I took twigs from the forest as proof of what I'd seen, but I hadn't decided what to do quite yet. I thought, maybe, I would marry Larka—"

"Oh, so you were going to rescue us all like one of the heroes of old and hope that Larka would be grateful enough to marry you? Or did you want to learn our secrets and use it as blackmail to force her marriage?"

"I hadn't decided yet," Miron mumbled again. He did not deny Gwynna's accusations.

Sol laughed, cold and sharp as a sliver of ice. "So, you're a spy and a fool." He let the invisibility cloak drop to the ground, and Miron was wise enough to let it fall without grabbing for it again. "Now that we've found you, foolish little spy, the question is what to do with you."

Miron paled, though he did not beg. Larka was, despite herself, impressed. She knew—or hoped, at least—that Sol wouldn't do anything terrible, but Miron didn't know that.

"There was a promise made that this agreement would remain between myself and the princesses only. No one else would know of it. So, something must be done."

"Don't kill him!" blurted Gwynna. "Please! He might be a spy, but he doesn't deserve to die."

"I was not going to kill him," said Sol crossly. "I may be Death, but I am not a murderer. Still, surely you know he cannot be allowed to go free, not if he was never supposed to know of this bargain and if he would truly use it against you."

"I think he would," said Larka. She didn't trust Miron not to.

It was at that exact moment, all of them crowded

around Miron Brandt and trying to figure out what to do with him, that Galen came into the throne room. Larka had seen Galen only a handful of times over the past few weeks. Still, he was as unchanged as all of the dead, still sporting short brown hair standing up in spikes, runes on his exposed skin, and a silver scar on each cheek.

The only thing different about Galen was the expression of worry on his face, which now morphed into confusion. He stopped short before Larka and gawked at the tableau before him. "What," he said at last, "in the name of all that's holy and dead, is going on here? I only wanted to talk to Sol, and now there's a living man down here?"

Larka and her sisters stumbled over an explanation of Miron's spying. Larka couldn't help feeling that this was her fault. If she had been a better liar, if she had realized that Miron wasn't convinced by her, then none of this ever would have happened.

When everything had been explained, Galen glanced over at Miron and said in a low voice, "Why don't I just take his memories away?"

"How?" asked Larka, exasperated.

Galen shrugged. "When I was an arcanist, there was a spell to take a man's memories and trap them in glass. It was a simple enough spell, and I think I could probably still do it."

Gwynna cast a distasteful look at Miron. "Do it. He'll never keep this a secret, not if he remembers."

"Do what?" asked Miron from where he knelt. "Please, please don't kill me! I only wanted—"

Sol rolled his eyes. "I have told you once already, I do not intend to kill you. Galen, come perform the spell you spoke of."

"Of course." Galen went to stand next to Sol. Miron was trying to pull himself out of the shadow bindings, with little success. Galen looked at him severely. "Please hold still. You have nothing to be afraid of; this shouldn't hurt. At least, I don't think so."

Galen rolled up his sleeve and traced a rune on his forearm with the tip of one finger. It reminded Larka of a rose if the petals were jagged, tooth-like spikes.

In one swift movement, Galen stretched out his hands until they hovered over Miron's head. He held them out, utterly still, so long that Larka started to wonder if he had any idea what he was doing. There was absolute silence except for his harsh breathing. Then runes on Galen's arm began to shiver, then twitch, then move as if they were living creatures. Larka stared in fascination as the rune that Galen had pointed at glowed with silver light.

Galen began to chant in a low, soft voice in what Larka recognized as the Divine Tongue. Individual words jumped out at her but not enough to fully grasp the spell. The rest was just a long, sing-song rush of sound like water racing over rocks.

Finally, a silver-white cloud began to build under Galen's outstretched hands. Larka saw flickers of memories in it—Miron's memories: the Duke pulling the invisibility cloak out of a trunk, her own frightened face, twelve silhouettes walking through a gleaming gold forest, the cold white halls of Sol's palace.

Galen was still chanting, his face twisted in concentration and his hands thrust out. The cloud built and built. Larka could tell by the tension crackling in the air that he was nearing the climax of the spell.

And then Galen cut off with a gasp and a ragged curse. The silver cloud faded and vanished back into Miron's head.

"What?" asked Larka, leaping forward. "What's happened?"

"I can't remember," said Galen, frustration lending his words an edge. "It's been too long since I cast any magic, and I… I can't remember what comes next." He began the ending of the chant again, his voice harsher this time. He was nearing the part where he had stopped, and by the annoyance on his face, Larka knew that he still couldn't remember.

Suddenly, another voice joined the chant. Sol. The words slipped out of his mouth naturally. Of course they would; this was his birth tongue, words he had spoken before any human language was dreamt of.

Galen broke off again, this time in astonishment. "You know this spell? Why didn't you say so?"

Sol's face creased in an uncertain frown. "I… do not know. You spoke the beginning, and suddenly I knew the ending. It was as if I had always known it but the words had buried themselves inside me."

"Why wouldn't he know it?" asked Larka. "I mean, it's in the Divine Tongue."

Galen shook his head. "It's not god-magic, though. We arcanists took the tongue and twisted it to our own purposes, made new spells in it. It might use the Divine Tongue, but it's human magic."

"I had forgotten I could do such a thing. How could I forget my own abilities?" Sol shook his head in bafflement. "Nevermind that now. I have forgotten so much already that one thing is not much more, and we need to complete the spell."

Sol found a rune on the underside of his wrist and lifted his hands up alongside Galen's. This time the chant came from both of them, with strength and confidence, and the cloud forming over Miron's head didn't evaporate. Miron's eyes rolled back in his head, and Sol and Galen's arms shook as if they carried a heavy burden. Finally, Sol and Galen sang out the last line of the chant and lowered their arms with a gasp of relief. The ropes of shadow around Miron disappeared, and he fell to the floor as if he had no bones, his eyes shut.

"Is he dead?" cried Larka. Just because she didn't like Miron didn't mean she wanted him killed.

"No," said Galen wearily, "just unconscious. He'll wake eventually."

Galen twitched his fingers, and the ball of Miron's memories floated to his fingers. It solidified in his grip until it looked like glass, the Duke's missing memories, tiny and distorted, still playing out in the depths of it. Galen slid the ball into his pocket, and it was gone.

"It's done," said Sol, looking down expressionlessly at Miron's body.

"What now?" asked Rhiannon. She drew forward and knelt beside Miron to arrange his limbs in a more comfortable manner. He did not wake, but Larka saw his eyes moving restlessly under their lids.

"You should go back to the living world, I suppose," said Sol. "Take the cloak with you; it is useless now, but he will notice if it is missing."

"What about the dancing?" said Gwynna as she tucked the scraps of cloak into one of her pockets.

"I will let you go free tonight. I think it best to get this suitor back to your world before someone notices he is gone."

"Do we have to carry him all that way?" Gwynna sounded dismayed, and Larka couldn't blame her. Just the idea of carrying Miron through the forest and up the staircase made her back hurt.

"I'll help," volunteered Galen. "It was my idea, anyway. I should be able to carry him at least to the staircase."

They hoisted Miron's unconscious bulk up into the air, Galen carrying his feet, Larka his middle, and Rhiannon his head. The rest of the sisters clustered around, helping or, in the case of Talia and Melina, tickling Miron to see if he would wake. Larka pushed them away. It would be a disaster if Miron woke before they reached Belmarros.

Before the party turned to leave, Galen glanced back to where Sol sat on his throne. "I think we should talk when I come back. Please."

"About what?" Sol asked.

There was a touch of grimness in Galen's voice as he replied, "Matters of the underworld."

"We will talk later, Galen" said Sol wearily. "Good night, princesses."

The princesses and Galen carried Miron out of the hall and into the night. But no matter how heavy the body was, it wasn't as heavy as all of the secrets weighing Larka down.

Chapter Twenty-One

The next afternoon, Larka ate lunch with a group of female courtiers around her own age. The council had taken pity on the Little Queen and given her a break from her suitors after three days of bombardment. The young women ate a picnic by the reflecting pools, enjoying the warm stones of the courtyard and relishing the summer sun that would be gone all too soon. Larka could hardly believe autumn would arrive shortly; the days of court and nights of dancing had rushed by.

The other courtiers may have been there to eat lunch and relax, but Larka was there to learn whether or not Miron remembered anything. As soon as she was able, she asked, "Has anyone seen Miron Brandt today?" She popped a grape into her mouth and tried to appear casual.

"I have!" said one girl, Etta, tilting her parasol to keep the sun off her porcelain skin and perfectly curled brown hair.

“Oh? I feel as if I haven’t seen much of him since the rest of my suitors arrived.” Larka tilted her face toward the sun. Unlike Etta, she didn’t care about getting freckles. Spending so much time in darkness made her hungry for the light. Even the touch of death magic inside her wasn’t enough to banish her craving for the sun.

Etta shifted the folds of her daffodil-yellow dress and slid closer to Larka. She dropped her tone into the dramatic whisper that all courtiers used for gossip. “He was found passed out in the gardens last night with a flagon of wine spilled all over his fine court clothes. He drank so much he can’t remember the night at all. People say he’s heartbroken because he thinks he’s fallen out of your favor. Look, there he is!”

Etta pointed one slim finger to the edge of the courtyard, where, indeed, Miron stood framed by an ivy-covered archway. Larka could see that he looked more disheveled than usual, his reddish hair a mess and his green coat buttoned awkwardly.

Miron looked toward Larka, and vague confusion crossed his face. He was someone grasping for a memory only to find it missing. Truly, he didn’t remember any of the previous night, and judging by Etta’s story, the set-up Larka and her sisters had left him in had worked perfectly. After all, what courtier hadn’t had a little too much to drink at some point or another and lost some memories?

Miron stood in the entrance of the courtyard for a second longer, then pivoted away and left. Larka breathed a silent sigh of relief. “Poor Miron,” she said, just to keep up appearances.

“So, have you decided yet?” asked Etta slyly.

“Decided what?” said Larka, still thinking of the night before and just how badly things could have gone if Miron had made it back to Belmarros with her secret. He could have been forcing her into marriage at that very moment if Sol hadn’t caught him.

Etta laughed one of the perfectly cultured court

laughs that Larka had never managed to learn and stretched out on her side across the warm cream stones of the courtyard. "Which suitor you're going to marry, of course," she said, as if it had been a silly question.

"No!" said Larka, startled. "How could I? I barely know any of them."

"Well, you'll have to make a choice soon enough, won't you? If I were you, I'd get to know them quickly. There's only another month until your coronation."

Larka grimaced. *Don't remind me of that.* How in the name of every dead god was she supposed to decide which suitor was going to be her husband in such a short period of time? And she really *did* have to make the right choice. Only by choosing the best suitor and making the best alliance could she compensate for her father's disastrous marriages.

Larka stood abruptly, not able to stand this conversation for another minute, and said to the courtiers, "I'm going to see what my sisters are up to. It was lovely speaking to you all."

"The pleasure is all ours, Your Majesty," said Etta. Larka suspected Etta was telling the truth—she had, after all, learned that Larka had no idea which suitor she would choose as her husband. It would probably be about three minutes before the rest of court knew it, too.

Larka found Gwynna sitting with her feet in the reflecting pool as she watched Kath and Auri unsuccessfully try to sail toy boats. Gwynna held Alannah on her lap and was reading the five-year-old stories from an ancient volume no doubt stolen from the library.

"If you drop that in the pool, the librarians will probably kill you," said Larka. She slid off her shoes and sat down beside her sisters with her feet in the water. It was deliciously cool on her tired feet.

"I took it for a good cause," said Gwynna cheerfully.

"Oh? Reading to Alannah?"

"Reading is always a good cause," replied Gwynna

and then winced as Alannah accidentally elbowed her in the stomach by accident. "Lannah, sweetheart, why don't you go play with Kath and Auri for a minute?" she suggested.

"Okay," said Alannah cheerfully. She waded into the reflecting pool and immediately swamped one of Kath's boats, prompting a squawk of alarm.

"So, this book," said Larka. "What's it for that's so important you'd risk the wrath of the librarians?" This felt almost normal: teasing Gwynna about her love of reading, watching her younger sisters enjoy some time away from the stiff etiquette of court. Then Gwynna said, "I was doing research on arcanists, actually," and the illusion was broken. Nothing could be entirely normal when Sol still waited for them in the darkness.

"I thought you'd already done research on arcanists, back when we thought Sol was one." Larka resisted the urge to look around; that would only make it obvious she was discussing something guilty and private.

"I've done some, but I was curious about the spell that Sol and Galen cast, so I decided to do more."

"Did you find anything interesting?"

Gwynna frowned and kicked idly at the water. "Yes, actually. There's this old story about the arcanists and the gods that I found. They say Lady Truth would weave people's memories into a tapestry after they died to create a picture of what the world was truly like. When the arcanists made a spell to take someone's memories and turn them into glass, she was angry because she couldn't use those memories anymore to make her tapestry."

"And?" said Larka, not understanding the importance of the story. "That's very interesting, I suppose."

"It made me wonder why Sol used that spell if the gods hated it so much. And if it was arcanist magic and not god-magic, then how did Sol even know how to do it?"

"Galen showed him," Larka pointed out in a low voice. Talking about this in open air, surrounded by people, felt dangerous even if no one else was close enough to hear.

Gwynna shook her head. "Galen *reminded* him. And why did he have the rune to perform the spell?"

"I don't know!" Larka threw up her hands. "He's a god, Gwyn. He doesn't have to explain himself to us. You're overthinking this."

Gwynna sounded unconvinced when she said, "Maybe. I just… I think that there's something else going on. Something that Sol hasn't told us, or something that he's forgotten, even." She probably would have gone on theorizing if Rhiannon hadn't sat down between the two of them with an unhappy thump and put her head in her hands.

"Rhee?" said Gwynna, going instantly from scholar to concerned sister. "What is it?"

Rhiannon lifted her head from her hands and burst out, "I hate this!"

"Hate what?" asked Gwynna.

"All this lying! I hate that we have to keep so many secrets and that we can't tell the truth even if we want to. I'm grateful to Sol for saving our lives, I truly am, but I'm so tired of having to lie to everyone. I've had enough of it!"

Larka frowned and put a hand on Rhiannon's shoulder to try and comfort her. "Did something happen?"

"Yes," said Rhiannon unhappily. "We took Miron Brandt's memories from him. I know we didn't think we had much choice about it. Did we really, though? We could have convinced Sol to let us go, to end the dancing. We could have convinced Miron not to tell. But instead we let Sol and Galen reach into his mind and tear out his memories and convince him he never spied on us at all."

Rhiannon was distraught, but more so than Larka thought someone like Miron deserved. "Is this entirely about Miron?" she asked.

Rhiannon slumped. "I suppose not."

"Is this about Janna, too?"

Rhiannon sighed and raked her fingers through her hair. "How can I look Janna in the eyes when I have to lie to her? How can I kiss her when I'm hiding something about her brother? She asked me if I knew why Miron got so drunk he can't remember last night, and I had to lie to her. It's not *fair.*"

Gwynna pulled her feet out of the pond and looked across the courtyard contemplatively. "Larka, how much longer do you think we're going to dance for Sol anyway?"

"I don't know," she admitted. "I hadn't really thought about it."

"We can't keep doing this forever. Sooner or later, it has to end." Rhiannon stared out glumly across the reflecting pool. "It's not only that I have to lie to Janna. It's eating me up inside that we can't talk to Stefan about this. That we can't talk to anyone about this."

Rhiannon had a point. Secrets were heavy things to carry. Lies, too. Combined, the weight was almost more than Larka could bear. With each secret came another lie, and at the rate things were going, they would keep piling up. A few more people as suspicious as Miron Brandt could be their ruin. Yet Larka found that a part of her would miss the eerie beauty of the underworld, the freedom she found in the midnight dances—and the god who awaited her there.

"You should talk to Sol," suggested Gwynna. "He likes you best."

"He does not!" Larka protested, feeling her cheeks flush red.

Gwynna rolled her eyes. "It's just a fact, Larka. Don't bother denying it. If you tell Sol that we have to stop dancing at some point, he'll listen to you."

"Fine," she agreed, nerves churning in her stomach like eels at the thought of talking to Sol about ending their bargain. How would he react? Did she even want the bargain to end? Without it, there would be no dancing and no Sol. "I'll talk to him as soon as possible. Tonight, even."

Rhiannon sighed. "And then this can all be over. We can go back to normal and forget it ever happened."

Larka wasn't sure that was possible. How could she remain unchanged when she had walked in the forests of another world and been so close to dying that Death Himself had to step forward and drag her back into the living? How could any of them remain unchanged after that?

Chapter Twenty-Two

Larka thought about ways to ask Sol to end their bargain the entire time they traveled to the underworld that night. In fact, she was so wrapped up in her own thoughts that she didn't hear the arguing voices coming from the throne room until she was right before the doors. Uncharacteristically, the doors were firmly shut when the princesses arrived, but that wasn't enough to disguise the sound of raised, angry voices on the other side. Larka froze immediately. She had spent a great deal of her childhood listening to people argue in other rooms, usually her father and his councilors, and the reaction was instinctual. The rest of her sisters crashed to a halt behind her.

"Who is it?" whispered Yara.

"Sol and Galen, I think," replied Kath. Her voice was equally hushed as she put her ear to the door. There was really no need. The argument going on in the throne room was loud enough to be heard even through the heavy door. Normally Larka would have dragged her younger sister away from eavesdropping, but it was impossible *not* to hear the argument in progress.

"Avoiding my duties?" This was Sol, the first time Larka had ever heard him shout. "How dare you accuse me of that? I am Lord Death. I am nothing but my duties."

"Not when the princesses are around." Galen's voice was muffled but still clear. "Don't try to deny it. When they're around—when *she* is around—I see you forgetting yourself. You sit here and watch them dance, and all the while the dead have no one to guide them. They become lost, they walk into the darkness and never come back, all because you don't care about them!"

Larka exchanged wide-eyed looks with her sisters. She had seen Sol guiding the dead when she walked with him along the edge of the lake, seen him gently urge them along to where they needed to go, but she hadn't dreamed that his absence meant they could no longer make the journey properly. She tried to picture what it might be like if she had died and come here searching for rest and oblivion, only to become lost in the endless night. The idea made her recoil. Judging from the expressions on her sisters' faces, they were thinking the same thing.

Inside the throne room, the argument raged on. "The dead can go a few hours without someone to show them the way!" Sol spat. "I have given them two thousand years; surely, I can take a few hours for myself!"

"Can you?" asked Galen calmly. His voice faded back and forth. Larka could picture him pacing furiously across the floor as he argued.

Sol made an inarticulate, angry noise that Larka recognized from countless arguments with her sisters: the sound of someone who doesn't want to admit their opponent has a point. "You guide them, then, if you are so concerned."

"I've tried." There was a desperate, pained note in Galen's voice. "Every night while you watch those girls dance and try to remember what it's like to live, I am out there trying to guide the dead. But they won't listen to me. I'm just another ghost; I'm not a god. I don't have your power. They need you, Sol."

Sol was silent. If he had a reply to Galen, then Larka couldn't hear it. Then he said, in a much calmer voice, "They're here."

Larka jumped guiltily, feeling very much like she had when people caught her eavesdropping as a child.

The doors groaned open without anyone touching them. From inside, Sol called, "Come in." There was no anger left in his voice, only weariness deeper than Larka could imagine.

Sol was seated on his throne as he always was, though there was still an angry flush on his cheeks that lent his bone-pale face some color, and Galen stood resolutely in the middle of the room. Galen's hands hung at his sides in a way that made Larka think he was resisting the urge to clench them into fists. The anger traced across his face made him look more alive than Larka had ever seen him.

"Princesses, it is good to see you, although I suppose you heard all of that," said Sol. Exhaustion and apathy dripped from his words.

Larka swallowed. "Yes. I'm sorry—"

Sol waved a hand. "Do not bother apologizing. Half the underworld likely heard that argument."

"Good," said Galen harshly. "They deserve to know their ruler is abandoning them."

"I am not abandoning them," snapped Sol, anger flaring back to life in his voice.

"Oh? Then what else would you call it?"

"I do not require your judgment right now," said Sol, pointedly not replying to Galen's challenge. "Leave us."

Galen did, although with reluctance. Larka wondered if being a shade meant that Galen had to obey Sol's orders even if he disagreed with them. It certainly didn't keep him from voicing his opinion.

Larka waited until Galen was gone to say, "Sol,

could I talk to you for a minute before we dance tonight? Or—maybe more than a minute?" The argument with Galen had only emphasized what she already knew, that she and her sisters couldn't continue paying their debt for much longer. The more they danced, the more they disrupted things, both in the underworld and in Belmarros.

"Of course," said Sol, although there was a hint of wariness in his voice. He slid off his throne and descended the steps, offering his hand to Larka once he reached her. "Little Queen, it is good to see you. Come with me, and we will talk." The words were polite, expected, and yet Larka liked hearing them more than she wanted to admit.

Larka took Sol's arm, and he escorted her out of the throne room. After they turned a few corners, Larka found herself in front of an alcove seat cut into the wall and softened with black cushions. Sol sat, and after a pause, she sat next to him. They did not touch, but the hem of Sol's black robe brushed the skirt of her gray dress.

"Now tell me," he said. "What is wrong, Larka?"

Larka took a breath and spoke before she could lose her nerve. "Galen's right, you know. We can't keep dancing for you. This has to end, and soon."

"Oh," said Sol faintly. He looked taken aback.

"Miron was only the first person to try and discover our secrets," said Larka. "There will be more. People are going to want to know what's going on. They'll want to know what has changed. Where we are going. Why we refuse to tell our secrets."

Sol looked down at his twelve-fingered hands. He said, "I do not regret saving you. I do not regret the agreement I made with you and your sisters. Do you regret it?"

"No." Larka said it as firmly and quickly as she could, in case he got ideas about reversing the bargain. Who really knew how the minds of gods worked? "No, I don't regret it. I will always be grateful that you saved us. But this needs to end. The dancing has to end before more people find out."

Sol turned to her. The expression on his face was pleading, helpless. He looked raw in a way that she had seen only twice before: when he showed her the dark beaches of his realm and when he spoke of all he had lost in the War of the Gods. "I thought dancing at night would be a small-enough thing that it would not disrupt your lives too much. I thought you would dance for me and you would live, and I would be a little less lonely while it lasted."

"I know." Larka really did. It was impossible to look at him and not see the loneliness that had burrowed under his skin. "But we can't keep dancing for you always; we have to go back to our real lives. A queen can't spend her nights in the underworld."

"So, you want to leave," he said. "You will be crowned queen, and you will marry another, and you will never think of me or this place again."

Larka bit her lip at the pain his voice. It wasn't jealousy, not really—it was more of the same terrible loneliness, and she hated knowing that it was because of her. "Sol, I—"

"No, I understand what you mean. I know what it is like to be confined to this world. I understand why you would not want to dance here forever."

"I didn't mean it like that," said Larka desperately. "It's just… my sisters and I, we really can't spend our whole lives dancing at night in the underworld. There's too much going on in our lives already. Besides, none of us knew that you were abandoning your duties while we danced for you, not until tonight."

"Can I not take a few hours for myself? A few hours in which I do not have to be a guide standing and pointing the way for the dead?" There was a pleading note in Sol's voice, but Larka thought he wasn't pleading with her. He was pleading more with himself and with the unshakable facts with which Galen had presented him.

"The dead need you, Sol. And Belmarros needs me," Larka said firmly. "I see it, and so do you. Neither of us can afford to abandon our duties."

"You will be queen for a few decades. I will be king forever, stretching on and on until the bones of the world are crumbled to dust. It is not the same thing." Something ancient flickered in Sol's eyes, overriding the loneliness and reminding Larka that no matter how human he seemed at times, he wasn't.

"The dead will need you forever," said Larka stubbornly. "As long as humanity exists, we will need you to show us through the dark."

Sol sighed. "I understand. I could not close my eyes against the cost of your visits forever anyway."

"So, you'll release us from our debt?" As much as Larka looked forward to not owing a massive debt, a part of her was conflicted about the idea that she would never come there again, down into the dark to dance before a god who watched her with a hunger for life in his eyes.

"I will release you," said Sol. "Dance for me until you are crowned queen, and then you and your sisters will be free. Your debt will be paid."

Larka was stunned by the ease with which she and her sisters were released. A few words, and the end of their dancing as in sight.

"Thank you," she said, an odd mix of giddiness and sadness soaring in her chest. "Sol, thank you." She almost leaned over and hugged him, but she stopped herself at the last moment, unsure of how she would respond. Instead, she took his hand. He held it tightly, like a drowning man clutching at his last hope of survival.

They sat in silence for a minute. Larka knew she should probably get up and go back to the dancing. She also knew that she did not want to.

After awhile, Sol asked, "Will you forget me, when you are queen?"

Startled, Larka could only say, "No. No, I won't."

"You probably should. Do they still tell stories of what happens when maidens and gods meet, or has all of humankind forgotten that particular kind of tragedy?"

"I am not a maiden," said Larka. "I am a queen, or I will be. And story or no, I would not like to forget you."

There was real surprise etched on Sol's face this time. "You wouldn't?"

"I hope not," she said. "You saved my life, after all, and the lives of my sisters. I could never forget that. And—" She stopped, embarrassed, once she realized what words were about to come out of her mouth. She stared hard at the black-and-white checkered wall across from the alcove and could feel a hot blush crawling up her cheeks.

"And?" prompted Sol with kindness in his voice. It was that kindness that convinced her to finish the sentence.

"Sometimes I think you're one of the only people who looks at me and sees me," Larka said in a rush. "I mean, everyone else besides my family looks at me and sees a crown first and me second. You see… you see *me*. And that makes me feel—at least *feel*, even if it's not true—beautiful. Or not beautiful but *wanted*, as myself instead of just as a queen. And it sounds foolish, but—"

Sol stopped her with one gentle finger on her lips. Larka halted mid-sentence, acutely aware of the feeling of his skin on hers. It was just for a second and then he lowered his hand, yet her lips burned with that one brief touch.

"I look at you like that because it is the truth," Sol said quietly. "You are beautiful, and you are yourself, and anyone who looks at you and sees only the crown and not the person who wears it is a great fool."

Larka said faintly, "Oh." It was the only thing she could really think of to say. Her thoughts seemed to come from very far away, and it look a long time until she could continue, "I will not forget you, Sol, even when I am queen."

"Good," said Sol. "I would hate to be forgotten by you." And then he leaned down and took her face in his free hand. Larka froze in surprise at the touch.

"I feel brighter when you are around," he whispered. "I do not feel the dark pressing upon me as it usually does."

He was so close that his words stirred the hair that had fallen from her braid. There was a tiny part of her that thought she might have to redo her hair sometime that evening. The rest of her was focusing on the feeling of Sol's hand on her cheek, his cold, godly flesh against her hot, mortal blood and the way his thumb rested on her cheekbone. She knew she should have been bothered by the eerie chill of his skin, and yet she was not. She wanted him to touch her, to see if his mouth was as cold as the rest of him. But the next second he had drawn away, the pressure of his hand gone, and he was standing, smoothing his black robe in an oddly normal gesture. "Come," he said. "I wouldn't want you to miss the dancing."

"Of course not," said Larka, shoving all thoughts of touching Sol into some deep recess of her mind where she put truly embarrassing thoughts and impulses. What had she been *thinking*? Sol was not some normal, human sweetheart who would bring her flowers and kiss her under the starlight. These little looks and touches meant nothing at all. He was a god, and a would-be queen and a god were not the same thing. He was untouchable by the likes of her.

Wasn't he?

Chapter Twenty-Three

For the next month, Larka and her sisters continued to dance every night. Each evening, they performed the routine that had become almost normal: opening the portal in their room, descending the staircase, walking through the shining forests filled with a beauty which had once been strange and glorious and was now merely familiar.

Miron Brandt never showed the slightest indication of remembering his excursion into the underworld, and Larka's threat to Braddock had quieted him enough that she didn't think he would confront her again, at least not publicly. Stefan, too, kept quiet, though no doubt he thought Larka or one of her sisters would come to him eventually with whatever problem plagued them.

Still, the secrets Larka and her sisters carried were an uncomfortable weight, and she was glad that she could look forward and see the day when they could set down their burden for good. Even so, Larka felt conflicted. In the be ginning of their arrangement, when the invisible musicians struck up a tune and she took the cold shade hand of her partner, Larka had felt that she'd spent her entire life dancing in the underworld and would spend the rest of it this way, too. Now she heard a little clock in her head ticking down the days: *One month until I am crowned and we dance no longer. Twenty days. Ten. Five. One.* It would all be over soon, and Larka wasn't sure if she was excited or filled with regret to see that day come.

In preparation for her coronation, Larka also moved into the Royal Apartments. She had put the move off as long as she could, but the court had finally determined that it wouldn't be appropriate for its future queen to continue sleeping in a room made cramped and busy by eleven other sisters. Larka could hardly tell the court that she needed to stay with her sisters so they could continue opening a portal in the floor to the underworld at night. So, although she'd been reluctant, Larka had slowly allowed her possessions to be moved from the battered, old wardrobes she shared with her sisters to the vast, unfamiliar closets of the Royal Apartments.

Even before her father died, Larka hadn't been in the Royal Apartments for years. Eldric had never been the kind of father with whom she talked at the end of a long day, or who sat with her and puzzled out the mathematics her tutor had given her. He'd been like a star in the night sky; somewhere he had been blazing brightly, but for Larka he'd only been distant and cold. His personal apartments were reserved for himself and whomever was sharing his bed at the time—whether or not he was married to them. Larka's last memory of being in the apartments was a vague and fuzzy snippet of sitting on a lush, red carpet stacking blocks while Eldric and Queen-Consort Asha argued in the background. Larka guessed she'd been about three.

The night before her coronation, Larka stepped out of a last-minute council meeting only to be confronted with a pair of servant girls.

"Your Majesty?" said one of the girls after she had given a long, low curtsy to Larka. "The preparation of the apartments is done. Would you like to see them?"

There was only one answer Larka could give. "Of course," she said, smiling tightly, and followed the girls through the palace to the wing that had been closed for four years. Inside, she was cursing; now that her new apartments were ready, there was no way she could insist on staying in her childhood room for one more night.

For the first time since Eldric's funeral, the gilded double doors of the apartment were propped open. It was as if someone had dragged open the doors of a tomb, and when Larka stepped through the doors, she felt as if she was walking on someone's grave.

It had been four years since Eldric died with water in his lungs and seaweed twining through his crown, and Larka still half-expected her father to stroll out of the receiving room or poke his head from the closet. The rooms were so very *Eldric* that it was impossible to imagine they might someday be hers. Everything was decorated in his favored shades of red and gold, instead of Belmarrian blue and green, and the walls were lined with elaborate tapestries depicting boar hunts and feasting nobles. A massive canopied bed, easily the size of a small room, lay against one wall and a mirror twice Larka's height against the opposite. Each door to another room was painted with a golden crown. From what Larka could see, one door led to a series of receiving rooms decorated much the same as the bedroom, another to a private garden, a third to a private library, and a fourth to the closets. Everything was gilded and opulent, and Larka shuddered to think of how much it must have cost the royal treasury.

"What do you think, my queen?" asked the maid standing at Larka's elbow.

"It's very… clean," said Larka, looking around at the spotless windows and fresh sheets on the beds. Four years of dusty neglect had been wiped away without a trace.

"You did an excellent job of restoring it."

The other maid twisted her hands. "Thank you, my queen. Is there anything you would like changed? It's traditional for each ruler to redecorate in the style he or she prefers."

As much as Larka hated these rooms, it felt too soon to start reworking them to her own preferences. To start now would have felt like desecrating a tomb.

"Perhaps later," Larka said to the maid. "When I've had a chance to look around and think. Besides, my coronation will be soon. I'd rather focus on that instead. Thank you for your work, though."

The maids bowed. "Of course, my queen." Then they left, and Larka was alone.

She let out her breath in a long sigh and flung herself down on the bed. She half expected dust to puff up, but no, the maids had done their job well. It was softer than any place she'd ever slept and so big she could probably lie spread-eagled in the center and not reach the edges, certainly a far cry from the often-cramped quarters she shared with her sisters. She would be able to sleep here without hearing Gwynna talk in her sleep or Auri snore. She would have utter peace. Utter loneliness.

Larka was struck by a sudden, ridiculous pang of homesickness. This vast, cold room decorated by a dead man didn't feel like a place she could sleep in. And even if she did sleep, she would never again wake in the night and be comforted by the sounds of her sisters around her. She would sleep alone.

At least until she was married. Then she'd share this massive bed with her husband, whoever he ended up being.

Larka groaned and put her head in her hands. This was definitely one thing she didn't want to think about. She'd known her entire life that, although she would be the one to officially choose her husband, it would be based on how many armadas his father commanded or what country his mother ruled, not if her eyes sought him out in a crowded room or that she felt fire spark across her skin when he touched her.

To distract herself, Larka explored the rest of her new apartments. She investigated the armoire (thankfully empty of her father's clothing and now filled with hers), went into the private garden (only bare dirt waiting to be filled with her preferred flowers), wandered around the sitting room (years out of fashion), and discovered a portrait of her father on the wall (which she took down and hid in a closet with his face turned away).

Finally, though, she had exhausted all of the mysteries of the rooms, and the sun had completely set. A new king or queen's first night spent in the Royal Apartments might not have been a tradition written down in the history books of Belmarros, beside the palm-cutting and the coronation, but it might as well have been. Some of the more superstitious members of court thought that the first night was an omen for the ruler's reign—a peaceful slumber meant an uneventful reign, fitful sleep a turbulent one, a nightmare a war.

On his first night in the apartments, Eldric had hosted a party the likes of which Belmarros hadn't seen for years, using up a good portion of the treasury's monthly expenses. He had retired with the beautiful young actress Marion, scandalizing the whole court. So, perhaps there was some truth to that superstition.

Larka wondered what it meant if a new ruler couldn't sleep at all. She at first lay utterly still, watching moonlight filter through the windows. When that didn't work, she tossed and turned, and yet still failed to find a comfortable position. The pillow was too soft, the room too quiet, her head too full of churning thoughts.

At last—she thought it must be far past midnight—Larka gave up sleep entirely and sat up in bed. The braid that she'd done up before retiring had come undone, and her hair was a messy snarl that she began to comb out with her fingers.

Larka closed her eyes, both against the darkness, be

cause it seemed to press in on her, and because she thought she might start crying. It was foolish; she was on the verge of her coronation and then her wedding, the sort of thing any other girl would have been dreaming of for years. Yet all she did was worry: if she would be a good queen, if she would make the right choices, if she even knew who she wanted to be once she was crowned.

If she would love her husband.

It was selfish, Larka knew, but she wished she could be sure of that. She would never have to choose a husband she hated, of course—she had that much control over her future, at least—and many people at court said they preferred an advantageous and friendly match to a passionate courtship full of fire and poetry. Yet Larka still wanted more. She wanted someone who made her feel alive, someone who saw more than the crown on her head and the power she held.

Larka dragged a hand through her knotted hair in frustration and felt her knuckle brush against the slender chain she still wore around her neck, the chain that held the three leaves from the underworld. She skimmed her fingers down the length of the necklace until she felt the rough edges of the tiny leaves, warm from resting against her skin. The habit was so familiar that she didn't realize the significance for a full second, that if she had the leaves, her sisters did not. And if they didn't have the leaves, they could not travel to the underworld that night; they could not dance. The last night before Larka was to be crowned, and the princesses couldn't finish paying their debt. She had thought her sisters might dance their last night without her—an idea that made her feel oddly lonely—but without the leaves they couldn't do even that.

Larka flung herself back onto her pillows and sighed. Well, Sol would just have to understand. They had danced for him for months, after all, and coronation traditions had to take precedence if they wanted to keep their secret. Besides, Sol had told her he understood they could no longer dance when she was queen.

An idea occurred to Larka as she cupped one hand around the necklace. Her sisters couldn't go to the underworld, but she could. Perhaps she could travel there and explain to Sol why her sisters couldn't come to dance on their final night. Perhaps she might see him one last time before she bore the weight of a crown on her head and the doors of the underworld were closed to her forever. Relief flooded through her at the thought.

Larka closed her eyes and thought of the underworld as she had dozens of times before. This time, though, she thought not of glittering forests or the starless sky. This time she found her thoughts straying to Sol, to the sheen of his hair and the curve of his cheek, to the weight of his hand in hers as they walked with the dead, to the thrill that had gone through her when he kissed her bandaged palms.

"Sol." Larka said his name so quietly that it was more breath than name, so quietly that she herself barely heard it even in the nighttime stillness of her bedchamber.

Even after all the nights of summoning the portal, Larka didn't think anything would happen as she spoke his name. After all, there was a very large difference between opening a portal to death and summoning the god himself. So, when the shadows on the wall next to her stirred and a very familiar voice said, "Hello, Little Queen," Larka was so surprised that she yelped and nearly fell off the bed.

Chapter Twenty-Four

Once her shock had worn off, Larka turned to see Sol standing in the corner of her bedroom. The shadows behind him formed an arched doorway.

"My apologies," said Sol. "I thought you knew I was there."

"How would I know that?" said Larka. She was acutely aware that she was wearing a ridiculous lace nightgown and her hair looked as if it had been dragged through a hedge.

"Because you summoned me," said Sol, shrugging. He was, as ever, coolly put together, his white hair in a long braid and the lines of his black robe crisp. He was in darkness except for a strip of moonlight that fell across his face and illuminated his eyes. "You were thinking of me as you held a part of the underworld, and so I came."

"Can you read my mind, then?"

"Not exactly. I felt the touch of death magic inside

you reach out to call for me. I thought that meant it would be alright if I visited." Sol twisted his hands together, the first true sign of nervousness that she'd ever seen him exhibit. "If you like, I can leave—"

"No!" Larka blurted out, surprising herself with the intensity of her emotion. "No, you can stay. Come sit down."

"I cannot," said Sol awkwardly. "I'm, ah, not really here."

"What do you mean? You look real enough."

Sol lifted one bare foot to show her the expanse of shadows where he stood. "I am in a sort of… extension of the underworld. I connected the shadows in your room to the shadows of the underworld. The spell does not last long, and I cannot leave this one shadow."

"Oh," said Larka, disappointed. "So, you're just kind of… stuck there?"

"Yes," admitted Sol. "I do not think I thought this through very well."

"Then why come at all?" asked Larka, moving so that she faced Sol and her legs hung off the bed. It was so high that her feet didn't touch the floor and made her feel like a child.

"You did not come tonight, and I was worried," said Sol. He seemed a little taken aback by his own honesty; he blinked and stepped back, fiddling with his hair. The shadows drew a little tighter around him.

"Oh," said Larka. She'd been so distracted by the fact that her summoning had actually *worked* that she'd completely forgotten why she had called Sol in the first place. "Yes. About that, I'm really sorry that we didn't come dancing tonight. I moved to the Royal Apartments and I forgot to give my sisters the leaves from the underworld, so—"

Sol raised one hand, stopping her torrent of words. "I understand now. Besides," he added, "I wanted to see you, not your sisters."

"Oh," said Larka again. It was her turn to be taken

aback. "But you said it yourself, you can't come to our world for longer than a few minutes."

"No," agreed Sol, "but you may still come to mine." He held out a hand to Larka, and she saw that his power was already starting to dissolve. He was so faded that she could see through him.

"I…" she said hesitantly.

"Come to the underworld," he urged her. "One last night. You are not queen yet."

Sol stood, hand extended toward her. There were no worried sisters waiting for her to return. There were just Sol, Larka, and the darkness around them. The moment felt ripe with a potential that she couldn't quite name.

Larka made her decision. She walked toward Sol and took his hand. He was insubstantial, of course, his grip more like a cold pocket of air than anything else. Larka almost didn't expect anything to happen, but the moment she reached for him, she was somewhere else: an utterly dark void with no up or down, no left or right. A place between life and death that didn't truly exist. Larka tried to breathe and discovered she didn't have lungs. She simply hung in transition, in blackness that was more the absence of *anything* than the absence of light.

After what could have been seconds or hours or years, Larka felt a tight squeeze on her fingers. The touch reminded her that she had fingers—and a body and a mind. The touch pulled her forward, and there was a brief feeling of pressure, of everything contracting around her like a tunnel getting smaller and smaller, and the shadows spat her out in an unfamiliar darkened room in the underworld.

Larka gasped, getting used to the sensation of having lungs again, and straightened. "What *was* that?"

"Shadow-travel," said Sol, watching her with a concerned expression. "I can walk through one shadow to another. It is quicker than a portal."

"And stranger," Larka said, still trying to catch her breath. "I felt… I felt as if I didn't exist!"

Sol ducked his head. "I am sorry. I did not realize that shadow-travel would affect a human so much."

Larka waved him off. "I'm fine, really. It was just disorienting. And we're here now, wherever *here* is." She finally looked around and saw that they had appeared in a long, high-ceilinged room. Swirling patterns of small mirrors and arcanist globes were embedded in the wall, and Larka saw herself and Sol reflected jaggedly back through a thousand shining chips. The only thing in the room beside them was a high, dark dais against the far wall. Or no—not a dais but a bed, perfectly untouched as if no one had slept in it for years. A bedroom, then, but terribly stark and bare.

"My rooms," said Sol. "I did not think of a specific place when we traveled, and it is at the heart of my palace, so I suppose we ended up here."

Larka looked at the room again with new eyes. Of course his bedchamber would look like this, if he spent his days walking beside the dead and showing them the way to the afterlife. He would hardly have much need for it. "Do you sleep?" she asked. "I've never heard that gods have to sleep."

"I do not need to sleep, truly, but I like to. The years pass slowly down here. I sleep when I cannot bear to be awake."

Larka pictured the endless years down in the dark, forever guiding the dead, forever walking under a starless sky. No wonder the boredom and loneliness would become a heavy enough weight that he'd want to set it down for a few hours.

"Do you dream as well, then?"

"Sometimes. I dream of memories, I think, but I can never entirely recall them when I wake. Fire from the sky and gold blood and fear…" Sol shook his head, the rope of his hair swinging. "Nevermind that. It was a long time ago. I would rather not talk about the past, Larka, and you seem sad."

"I do?" she said, surprised.

"Yes," he said. "I know sadness well enough to see it in someone else. What is wrong?"

An embarrassed blush spread across Larka's cheeks, and she hoped that it was dark enough that he couldn't see it. "It's nothing. Just foolishness," she said. Sol was a god; he didn't need to be bothered with her silly mortal worries about coronations and husbands.

"Nothing that causes grief is foolish," said Sol patiently. "Sit and tell me about it. Simply speaking about something can often be enough to lessen the burden."

Larka wondered exactly how he would know that, alone in the dark as he was, but she sat stiffly with Sol on the edge of his empty bed. He sat beside her, feet tucked up comfortably. He was more relaxed than she had often seen him. Of course he would be more comfortable here, she thought. This was his home, the place where he slept and dreamed whatever dreams a god has.

Larka caught a glimpse of Sol and her in one of the mirrors: two fair-haired figures seated together but not touching. They looked very similar but for his black robe and her white nightgown—and her hair. Larka saw that her hair stuck up in wild tangles, and she put a hand to the back of her head.

Sol noticed her dismay. "Here," he said. "Let me. Turn around, and I can help you."

Larka did and soon felt the hesitant pressure of his fingers in her hair, oh-so-gently untangling the mess that she'd made of it. She leaned back and felt Sol shift so she could lean against his knees. Heat flickered across her skin when his fingers brushed the back of her neck, and she thought of distant heat-lightning dancing across the sky.

"Now, tell me what is on your mind," said Sol after long enough had passed that Larka had started to wonder if perhaps he'd forgotten about her worries and her entire night was going to be sitting here while a death god combed her hair.

"It's really nothing," Larka said. "Honestly."

"Is it?" said Sol doubtfully.

Larka sighed. "I just… I've been thinking about what it will be like when I'm ruling Belmarros. It feels as if everything is happening very fast. I have so many choices to make, and I don't know if I'm making the right ones."

"I know little of being a ruler," Sol said. He brushed his fingers through her hair one last time and then began to braid with gentle fingers. "Or the ruler of a land with living subjects, at least. But I think that even the fact that you are worried about what kind of queen you will be means you will be a good one. Better to worry that you are doing wrong than not care at all."

"My Uncle Stefan says the same thing to me. But just because I want to be a good queen doesn't mean I *will* be."

Sol sounded amused when he said, "No one is born knowing how to do something. Not even me."

"Not even you? You're a god. Shouldn't it be, I don't know, instinct for you?"

Sol's fingers faltered briefly—Larka wondered if having twelve made it easier or harder to braid hair—and then resumed their work. "No. Not even for me. After the War of the Gods, I felt as if I was a shadow of myself. I forgot almost everything I was and everything that I had to do. I felt torn in half, fragmented and incomplete. I had to learn how to be Death all over again. There are still… I think there may still be things I cannot remember. Important things." He was silent for long enough after this confession that Larka began to wonder if he regretted laying himself open to her. Then he said, "You remember who you are. You know who you are and who you want to be, even if you do not realize it yet. And that is, I think, all you truly need in order to be queen." She felt his fingers tug at the end of her braid, fastening it with something, and then he said, "It's done, Larka. Come, look at me."

She did. His eyes were solemn and tired. "Did that help?"

"I suppose so," said Larka cautiously. She had been caught up not in the way he tried to reassure her, but in the way he had spoken of being fragmented after the end of the gods' war. What would it have been like, to have your world so thoroughly destroyed that you no longer remembered who you were?

Sol said, "That is not all that is bothering you, is it? I hear it in your voice. And do not say that it is nothing. The things that upset us, they are never nothing."

Larka let out a long breath. Talking about this with Sol felt dangerous, like walking out onto ice that might break under her weight at any moment and send her somewhere else entirely. But then again, this whole meeting was unorthodox. He had never visited her before, and she had certainly never gone to the underworld without her sisters.

"I'm thinking about my husband," Larka said at last. "The country expects that I will marry soon. The suitors are already gathered. Belmarros needs to know that I will be a stable queen who can make good alliances, and my husband will be part of that. But I don't want to get married. Not yet. Not to any of the men who came to ask for my hand."

"Why not? Are they not good men?" She detected something she thought might be jealousy in Sol's voice. He might be a god, but he was so human in that moment, with his knees drawn up to his chest and his braid spilling over one shoulder.

"No, they're good men. Or most of them are, at least. It's just… I don't love any of my suitors. I could be friends with them, perhaps, but I don't really care about any of them. And every time I speak with one, I know that he's only courting me because I'll be queen and he wants to be king-consort. And I wish… I wish one of them could look at me and see a person instead of a crown."

"Is there anyone who makes you feel that way?" Sol asked. "Like they see you?" His eyes met hers, searching for an answer, searching for a confirmation.

Larka hesitated. This, then, was the final step; one

more and she would be too far out, surrounded only by black ice that might break and fall apart. And if it did break, where would it send her? What would happen, if she really acknowledged this unspoken thing between Sol and her, if she made it real and tangible?

"Yes," she said at last. "I think there is." Because she would be queen soon, because she would no longer dance in the world of night, and she would no longer hold the hand of a god as he showed her forgotten things, and she would soon lie in bed next to a man who shared her crown but not her heart.

Sol moved toward her. They were already very close, but not quite close enough, and he had to shift toward her just the tiniest bit in order properly to reach her. Larka felt as if that one moment lasted a lifetime. And then Sol was before her: a god of death, on his knees before her, his hood down and hands reaching for her. She let him cup her face in his hands, as if she was made of glass, and leaned her forehead against his.

Sol brought his cold mouth to hers, and Larka thought she might dissolve into the shadows around them. She felt tension in his body, which she'd never realized was there, fade the moment he kissed her. He had been afraid, she supposed, that this thing between them had been all imagination on his part. Larka had feared the very same thing, and together they had been cowardly enough that now they only had this one moment left.

They were completely still for a moment. Neither moved. She was afraid to, as if it would dislodge the moment, somehow make it unreal.

At last, Sol moved back from her. It was not so dark that she couldn't see him looking for some sign that he'd done the right thing. Larka gave him one. She grasped his hair, tugged him back down to her, and kissed him hard. The cold of his mouth was still a shock but a good kind of shock, like walking out in a late autumn rain and lifting your face to the sky. His tongue was like ice.

They kissed for a long time, seconds or minutes or hours—a more pleasant kind of limbo than the shadows she had walked through to come here. She lost herself, for a time, in the pleasant chill of his skin and the softness of his hair.

When they broke apart again, Sol rested his head in the curve of her neck and whispered, "I did not think you would come here tonight."

"Why not?" asked Larka. To hold the solid weight of Lord Death in her arms, and to stroke his hair and feel his breath upon her collarbone—she had never dreamed of such a thing. She'd certainly never dreamed that she could want such a thing.

"There is beauty in this realm," he said, his words soft as butterfly wings against her skin, "but few see it. There is a library of all the forgotten stories from the living world, and forests of metal that grow fruit containing the memories of the dead. But no one sees the beauty of it all; I myself forget it sometimes. Even the dead are afraid of the starless sky, and they worry that something is watching them from the shadows."

"And?" prompted Larka. She wasn't sure what this had to do with her visit.

"And then, when you took my hand, I saw that you do not fear the underworld, not like your sisters," said Sol. His breath tickled the skin of Larka's shoulder, and she shivered when he brushed one finger down the bare skin of her arm in an absent kind of way. "You see that its strangeness is also beauty, and you do not fear it. You do not fear *me*."

"Should I?"

He laughed, a soft huff. "I am Death. Most people would fear me. But you did not; you *called* for me." There was a kind of awe in his voice. "Why did you call for me?"

"The same reason you came," said Larka. "Because I wanted to see you. I will be queen tomorrow, Sol, and all of this will be over. I wanted to see you one last time before then."

Sol lifted his head from her shoulder and looked at her. "Tonight will not last forever. Day comes eventually, and you must go with it."

"Dawn hasn't come yet," she said firmly. He had only been gone from her arms for a moment, and already she itched to have him back. There was so little time until her coronation; she wanted to take something for herself for once. To have someone she wanted before she would have someone she didn't. "And tonight is not for talking about the dead."

"Then what is it for?" asked Sol.

"Tonight is for living," said Larka, and she drew him back to her. She did not flinch at the cold touch of his mouth and hands; already, it was familiar to her. Sol hesitated, though, when she untied the bow that kept the throat of her nightgown closed.

"Are you certain?" asked Sol. "I would not want you to be—"

"Yes," Larka interrupted. "I'm sure. There's a tea I've been drinking for the last few years so I won't get pregnant." Albin had given it to her when she turned sixteen, around the same time people had begun to talk about suitors and marriage. It had been drilled into her by tutors and doctors her entire life that, as the heir, she might take whomever she wished into her bed as long as she only had children by suitable men. And she did not think that a forgotten death god counted as "suitable" in any sense of the word, so she was grateful she'd taken their advice. The entire court would probably die of shock if she unexpectedly had a child.

"I did not mean about that, although I am glad," admitted Sol. "I am Death; I cannot create life. I cannot make you or anyone else with child."

"Then what is it?" Larka's nervousness began to creep back in.

"Do you truly want *me*?" Now it was Sol who sounded nervous. "I am a god, Larka. I will not be able to walk with you in the sunlight or openly court you, not like your suitors. I do not want you to make a choice that you will regret."

"I won't," said Larka firmly. She smoothed a hand over his hair. He closed his eyes and leaned into her touch. "You're right, I do have a castle full of suitors. But I'm not choosing one of them. I understand what you are, Sol, and I choose *you*."

Sol opened his eyes. He looked more vulnerable than she'd ever seen him.

"Do you believe me?" she asked.

"I do," he said.

"Well, in that case…" Larka leaned forward on the bedcovers and kissed Sol again, nearly falling over in her haste to get back to him. He laughed into her mouth, perhaps the first true laugh she'd ever heard from him, and kissed her back. He pulled her down on top of him, and Larka let herself forget that dawn would ever come.

Chapter Twenty-Five

Larka knew she was back in her own bed before she even opened her eyes. She could feel the warmth of soft morning sunlight against her skin, instead of the now-familiar constant chill of the underworld. She vaguely remembered falling asleep some time before dawn. Sol must have brought her back while she slept.

He hadn't even said goodbye. It shouldn't have hurt—they had said everything that needed to be said, everything that had been unspoken between them—but she still wished Sol had taken the time to say even a brief word of farewell. Larka couldn't summon him again; the necklace of underworld leaves was gone, her neck bare. She vaguely remembered Sol unclasping the necklace at some point, when it must have fallen to the ground and been lost.

There would be no more midnight visits from him.

Larka had known her relationship with Sol couldn't last. Of course it couldn't, not when Sol couldn't leave the underworld and she would no longer be able to go to him, with her new responsibilities as queen. She had known, even as she had taken his hand, that the previous night would be the first, last, and only time such a thing would happen. Still, there was a dull and persistent ache in Larka's heart that refused to leave her entirely, even as she sat up and smoothed the wrinkled blankets. She had never understood before that the word "heartache" could feel so real.

A knock on the door startled Larka out of her reverie. She pulled her thoughts away from the underworld and back to the world that was actually before her. Sol was gone. She couldn't afford to dwell on him right now.

"Yes?" Larka called. "Who is it?"

"Your maids, Majesty," replied the muffled voice of a young woman. "We're here to start dressing you for the coronation."

The word jolted Larka ever further away from the underworld. Coronation. Yes. She had known it would be today, but she hadn't thought preparations would start so early. It had still been at the back of her mind, overshadowed by the previous night. It was also, she remembered, All Hallows' Eve, a day of spirits and dead and mysteries. It seemed a fitting day for her to be crowned.

Larka smoothed her hands nervously over her dress and said, "Come in."

There were four maids, a number that seemed excessive until they dragged out her coronation dress. It was a deep royal blue, the color of the sky the moment before it turns to full night, and made of sleek silk that glided under her fingertips like water. The embroidered vines of deep green that twined across the skirt and sleeves reminded Larka of Sol's tattoos curving across his pale skin, a thought that she shoved away almost as soon as she had it. There was no point in thinking about Sol, not anymore.

Larka had spent weeks being fitted for her dress, but this was the first time she had seen the finished product. So much of it—the colors, the material, the cut—were determined by tradition that her own input on how it looked wasn't required. The first sight of her coronation gown was more overwhelming than she'd thought it would be.

"Do you like the dress, Your Majesty?" asked one of the maids holding it up. She was about Larka's own age, her light brown hair pinned back so tightly that Larka's own scalp practically ached in sympathy. When Larka put a hand to her hair, she found that it was still in a careful braid, the end tied off with a piece of black cloth that Sol must have used.

"Your Majesty?" prompted the maid.

Larka let out a breath and looked hard at her coronation dress. This was not the soft, silly dress of a child or the bright, pretty dress of a young woman or even the more grown-up, enticing dress of someone choosing her consort. This was the dress of a queen: regal and proud, meant for someone who walked with her shoulders thrown back and her stride long and confident. The skirt was full and heavy and the sleeves long, but the neckline dipped low. It was the dress of a woman, not a child.

A few months ago, Larka never would have thought she could wear such clothing. But now, after she had stood up to the council, after she had made her own decisions, after she had taken the hand of Death and followed him to the underworld, she wasn't a child anymore.

"Yes," Larka said at last. "I like it very much. Please, help me put it on."

The whole affair took such a long time that Larka understood why the maids had come so early. The dress had dozens of tiny pearl buttons, so many that it took even the most quick-fingered maid minutes until she was done. Then there was the matter of the box of jewelry the maids had brought and the decisions about what gems to wear. By the time they were done deciding, Larka was weighed down with jewelry: gold rings, a heavy necklace of twisted links, emerald-studded bracelets, and sapphire earrings like tiny drops of the sky. Soft shoes were slipped onto Larka's feet, and a slim leather belt was fastened around her waist, with an empty scabbard for the godbone knife she would soon carry there. Her hair was unbraided—Larka covertly slipped Sol's hair tie into her sleeve so as not to lose it—and combed, though it was left spilling free across her shoulders, pale as moonlight. Putting it up would only interfere with the crown she would wear by the day's end.

Larka had never thought that she'd regard the day of her coronation with anything but dread and horror. These were, after all, the feelings she'd had toward it for more than eighteen years. Yet with the day now before her, she found that those emotions had changed. There was apprehension, yes, but it was joined by excitement and a kind of impatience. She was no longer fearing the weight of the crown on her head and the choices she had to make. Rather, she'd become interested to see what kind of queen she would be, to test her will and ideas against the world.

Somehow, almost without thinking, she had gone from child to woman. Maybe it was nearly dying or learning how to keep a secret. Maybe it was holding the god of death in her arms while he whispered her name or finally being able to look Aengus Braddock in the eye or challenging the councilors who had tried to keep secrets from her.

Larka didn't know exactly what had made her go from child to queen. Yet she had. And she was not afraid.

"Your Majesty, we're done," said one of her maids. Larka blinked—she'd been so lost in her own thoughts that she hadn't realized the preparations were done. Two girls brought forward a mirror to show Larka her appearance. She pulled her thoughts away from the past and future and brought them back to the present to look at the queen in the mirror, dressed in her deep blue dress and glittering gems.

"What do you think?" asked one of the girls nervously.

Larka let out her breath. She'd expected to see a stranger looking back at her from the mirror. That wasn't the case. She saw only herself, perhaps a little older and wiser but still herself.

"I look like a queen," she said and meant it.

Shortly after Larka was finished dressing, Rhiannon, Gwynna, Auri, and the triplets arrived at the Royal Apartments. Allegedly, they were there to talk about last-minute adjustments to the coronation schedule, but Larka knew they must really be there to talk about the end of the bargain, something they couldn't do while the servants were present.

The triplets collapsed in a heap on the carpeted floor, while Gwynna and Auri hurled themselves onto Larka's bed. Gwynna was holding a slim leather book, which she placed carefully on the bedside table. Larka was certain that the previous night was spelled out on her face and wasn't sure if she wanted her sisters to know what had happened. She wasn't sure how they would react.

"More research, Gwyn?" asked Larka. She remained standing; she didn't want to risk wrinkling her dress when she'd just put it on.

Gwynna smiled ruefully. "Always."

"That's a book of children's stories," pointed out Auri.

"There can be truth even in children's books," said Gwynna. "There's a lead I'm chasing, something I'm trying to figure out. Anyway, that's not what we're here for. I'd rather talk about… the coronation." She glanced at the maids.

"Your dress looks lovely," said Rhiannon, seating herself neatly on one of the overstuffed chairs in the corner.

"Thanks," said Larka, plucking at her sleeve. "It looks nice, but I'm pretty sure it's part of an evil plot to smother me to death before my coronation."

"Not going to argue with you about that," murmured Auri. "It's a pity you couldn't have a say in your own dress. Sometimes I think Belmarros is a little too obsessed with the past."

The sisters maintained a steady stream of innocent complaints and gossip until the servants left. Then, finally, as the door was shut and any outsiders were gone, Rhiannon said, sobering, "Much as I love complaining about our ancestors, now isn't really the time. We need to talk about Sol."

Larka's stomach lurched. "What about him?"

"Well, we were supposed to go dancing for him last night, but we didn't have the leaves."

"I know," admitted Larka. "I didn't realize I had the necklace until I was in the apartments, and by then it was too late."

"The point is we didn't uphold our end of the bargain, and that can't be good," continued Rhiannon.

"What Rhee's trying to say," chimed Kath from where she lay sprawled on the floor, "is that she's wondering if Sol is going to ride up from the underworld on a horse of bone and harvest our souls for breaking our agreement. Or something like that."

Rhiannon glared at Kath. "That is not what I mean, and please don't joke about it. What I did mean is that Larka knows him best, and I want to know if she thinks Sol will be angry with us for not showing up."

"Will he want us to dance for him longer now?" chipped in Gwynna.

Larka hadn't been entirely certain how she would tell her sisters about Sol's visit, but now she knew she didn't have much of a choice. "Actually," she began slowly, trying to think of how she would say this, "actually, I saw him last night. He came to the Royal Apartments."

Rhiannon sat bolt upright. "He *what*?"

"I thought Sol couldn't leave the underworld," added Krista.

"He can't, not really," said Larka. She forced herself to stop twisting one of the heavy gold-and-sapphire rings she wore. "He only came for a minute, and then I… I followed him to the underworld."

"Why are you only telling us this *now*?" demanded Rhiannon. "Larka, you should have told us the moment we came in!"

"There were servants here! And, anyway, I wasn't sure how?" said Larka. It came out as more of a question than she wanted. The truth was she had wanted to keep it to herself, even for a little while.

"Well, what did Sol say about our debt? Is it paid? Are we released?" Rhiannon's voice was urgent, her eyes piercing.

"We're released from it, I think, but we didn't really talk about it that much." *Or talk that much at all, actually. At least later on.*

"Why not? You went back to the underworld with him, surely there was enough time to talk about the debt hanging over our heads!"

"Er…" Larka struggled to think of how she could frame this. "Rhee, Sol didn't actually visit me to talk about the end of our debt. It was for… personal reasons."

Larka saw the moment her sister understood what she was really talking about. A shocked expression crossed Rhiannon's face. "Tell me you aren't serious, Larka. Please, please tell me you and Sol didn't—"

Gwynna raised a hand, stopping Rhiannon mid-sentence. "Wait, wait. Larka, did you or did you not actually sleep with Sol last night? Or is Rhiannon just leaping to conclusions and you two just, I don't know, braided each other's hair while talking about your feelings?"

"Both, actually," admitted Larka.

Auri blinked. "Alright, I definitely wasn't expecting that answer."

"He has twelve fingers, Larka!" burst out Rhiannon. "Twelve!"

Larka bit the inside of her cheek in a wild attempt to keep from laughing; Rhiannon sounded so indignant that it was hard not to. "That's what you're choosing to focus on? That he doesn't have the right number of fingers?"

"Well, I suppose I could mention that he's the god of death, but I think you probably already know that!"

Karo, lying on the plush, red carpet, raised herself up on her elbows. "He is very handsome. I mean, you have to admit that much."

"Have you seen his hair?" agreed Krista. "He's really pretty for someone who's not human."

Rhiannon smacked her forehead in frustration. "Oh, gods! All of you are making me extremely glad I'm only attracted to women, if you consider the god of *death* handsome."

The only one of Larka's sisters who seemed to be taking the revelation with anything approaching calmness was Auri. She asked, "Really, though? Not to be as judgmental as Rhee—I think she's in shock, give her a bit—but why did you do it? Why take Sol, of all people, into your bed?"

"I just… I was tired of expectations," said Larka, struggling to articulate the emotions that had rushed through her the previous night. She wanted to explain, though. She wanted her sisters to understand. "I was tired of having everyone's eyes on me, and I wanted to be someone besides a queen-to-be for a night. Sol… he looks at me first and then my crown. That's more than I can say of most people at court. And last night, he was there, and he wanted me, and I wanted him, and in the end it was an easier choice than I'd ever thought it would be."

"What about your suitors? I mean, you have eligible bachelors from half a dozen countries waiting for you to say which one you want to marry."

As much as Larka didn't want to admit it, Auri was right. There would be no more dancing or midnight visits from Sol. That was over. Now it was time for her to be a queen, and part of being queen was declaring her consort.

Larka truly hadn't decided which suitor she was going to choose. Sol's visit had driven the question into the back of her mind, buried under the cold glide of his fingers on her skin, the way his loose hair spilled over one shoulder, and the whisper of her name in the darkness. Now, she pulled the thought to the front of her mind once again and examined it.

At some point in the night, her unsure feelings and crushing worries had solidified into something certain and unshakable, something she thought she'd known all along but hadn't been brave enough to admit to herself until the time was upon her.

"Larka?" prompted Auri. "Have you decided about

your suitors?"

"Yes," said Larka, squaring her shoulders. "I think I have."

Chapter Twenty-Six

Even though the Council Room was large, it was a tight squeeze to fit both the council and Larka's suitors. A cluster of pages was ordered to cart in more chairs, but even so, several of the suitors ended up lining the walls instead of seated at the table.

Larka sat silently while people swirled in and out of the council chamber. She forced herself to keep still, not to tap her feet or pace or chew her fingernails. She could see the eyes of all her suitors and councilors on her, speculating about the decision she would soon make, and she knew that she couldn't show her nervousness. They would take it for weakness.

This is my choice, she reminded herself. *No one can stop me from deciding who will be my consort. This and this alone is entirely mine.* There was no script, no words to memorize. Her words would be her own, and she knew what she had to say.

At last, after what seemed like a ridiculous amount of fuss, all the councilors and suitors were seated—or, in the case of Aubrey Allard, leaning against the wall in a way she thought was supposed to look seductive but really looked as if he had a back problem. Stefan and Dario, standing together by the door, gave Larka encouraging nods. All of them looked at Larka expectantly.

"My queen," prompted Councilor Davin, "we're ready for your decision."

Larka curled her fingers around the carved armrests of her chair and sat up as straight as she could. "Of course, Councilor." To her suitors, she said, "I thank you for being here today and for being generous enough to offer your hands in marriage to me. It pleases me greatly to know that there are so many people and countries willing to build alliances with Belmarros."

Her suitors bowed their heads and murmured stock phrases about her kindness.

"However," Larka continued, nerves roiling unpleasantly in her stomach, "I must inform you that, at this time, I've decided not to take a consort."

The room erupted in noise. The suitors were all talking at once, their voices filled with confusion and annoyance. The council's desperate attempts to quiet the suitors only added to the chaos. For a solid minute, the council chamber was full of yelling about weddings and alliances and tradition, until Larka grew fed up with them all, stood, and shouted, "Quiet! All of you!" Her voice cut through the dozens of arguing and querying voices, and finally silence reigned again.

Larka sat back down with a thump and steadily met the astonished gaze of the crowd before her. She refused to be ashamed of her decision. She refused to take it back.

"Your Majesty," ventured Councilor Eugenio at last, "what do you mean, you aren't taking a consort?"

"Exactly what it sounds like. I've considered all of the suitors before me, and although I believe they are fine and worthy men, I don't want to marry."

"How can you say that?" protested Varian, the gold-bedecked Astraian merchant. "How can you say that you don't want to marry any of us and yet still call us fine men? What do you have against us that you won't pick a suitor to wed?"

"I came all the way across the sea to become your consort, and you reject me out of hand!" complained Fergus MacKay.

"What an insult!" agreed Aubrey Allard. "I have half a mind to write back to the King of Veanara about this."

"I don't have anything against any of you, and I don't intend this as an insult against any of you," said Larka, exasperated. She'd feared this might happen, that her suitors would make her decision all about themselves instead of her.

"Please let Her Majesty explain herself before any of you jump to conclusions," interjected Stefan. Larka cast him a grateful glance. She should have known that Stefan would support her no matter what decision she made.

Larka took a breath to calm herself. "As I just said, this decision isn't meant as an insult to any of you, the quality of your character, or the countries you all came from. I'm happy to continue forging alliances between our many lands. I just don't want to marry, at least at this time."

"But, Your Majesty, it's tradition," sputtered Councilor Eugenio. "Any ruler not married by the time she ascends the throne picks a consort to reign beside her. It's an excellent way to solidify power and produce heirs."

"You don't need to explain the rules of my own ancestors to me, Councilor. I know as well as you do. But tell me, how many of those rulers have ascended the throne at such a young age as I have?"

Eugenio opened and closed his mouth a few times before reluctantly answering, "Very few. Belmarros has been lucky in that regard."

"So," continued Larka, "very few of my ancestors found it necessary to wed at such a young age. They were able to hold off until they felt prepared to select the best consort for their rule. I see no reason why I can't do the same."

"What about your heirs? A young, untried queen with no heirs is a liability." This from Fergus MacKay, sounding triumphant, as if he had picked a hole in Larka's logic and it would now all come unraveling like a poorly made scarf.

She cast him an icy look. "I have eleven younger sisters, Prince Fergal, who are currently in fine health, and many cousins besides. I think heirs can wait a few years. This is my choice, and I stand by it."

"You've wasted all of our time," complained another suitor.

"I know, and I regret that." Larka really did. She wished she hadn't let things get this far along before being confident enough in herself to cast away a tradition that made her unhappy. "Some of you came to Vaelkarra from very far away, and I'm sorry to break your hopes like this."

"This is hardly fair," spat one suitor, a gray-haired duke easily thirty years older than Larka. "To come such a long way only to be denied by a child."

Larka pushed down her anger as far as it would go. This was no time to lose control. In the most even voice she could manage, she said, "If you think I'm a child, then perhaps you shouldn't have come seeking to marry me in the first place. Besides, all of you knew there was a chance that you wouldn't be chosen anyway. I'm simply not choosing anyone."

"How do we know you aren't misleading us?" spoke Miron Brandt, the first thing he'd said since her announcement. He'd managed to snag a coveted place at the council table and now leaned forward toward Larka.

She blinked at him in confusion. "I'm sorry?"

"How do you we know you aren't lying to us?" repeated Miron. "Have you found another man you prefer, and this is just a way of shuffling off all of your suitors so you don't have to deal with us? Because I, for one, would appre ciate the truth."

"That's no way to talk to a queen," snapped Councilor Trajan. Miron looked suitably cowed.

"Duke Brandt does bring up a good point," Larka conceded. "I promise all of you that I speak the truth when I say there is no one else." It was the truth; even if she could see Sol again, this decision wasn't about him. It was about her, about pushing back against the layers and layers of Belmarrian tradition that threatened to smother her. As queen, she was going to have enough to deal with that she didn't want to add a new husband on top of it. Not when her marriage wasn't necessary yet.

Miron sat back, seemingly satisfied. He hadn't fought as hard as some of the others against her decision, and Larka wondered if a part of him distrusted or feared her, even if he couldn't remember why. Perhaps this was why he'd backed off on courting her in the last few weeks.

"This won't be forever," added Larka. "I understand the necessity of alliances and a royal marriage. In three years or five or ten, or whenever I feel that I'm ready to entertain suitors again, I will welcome back any of you who still wish to become my consort. But right now, this is my choice, and I choose not to marry."

After Larka was finished speaking, the stunned silence in the room slowly thawed into acceptance. Half of the councilors looked as if they wanted to continue arguing, and the suitors had expressions ranging from bafflement to anger, but none of them challenged Larka. They all knew the choosing of the royal consort was a decision made by the ruler of Belmarros and no one else.

"Well," said Councilor Mariana at last. "I can safely say that all of us are surprised by the outcome of this meeting. But although I expected—as I'm sure we all expected—the Little Queen to walk out of here with her future consort on her arm, I respect her decision. As we all must."

A wave of relief crashed over Larka. Win the support of Mariana, and the support of the rest of the council was almost guaranteed. They could not force Larka to marry, not when such an influential voice backed her.

Larka stood, then paused before she began to leave. "Before we leave this room, I want to emphasize, again, that the decision I made is not about any of my suitors. Please don't take offense. I choose not to marry not because I wish you or your countries ill but because I don't think this is the right time for me to do so. After the coronation, I will happily discuss and create alliances with all of you." She inclined her head—just a little bit, for a queen should be dignified. "Thank you for listening. This meeting is adjourned."

Larka walked out of the Council Room alone, but it didn't feel like loneliness. It felt like freedom.

Chapter Twenty-Seven

Larka spent the last few hours before her coronation meditating inside the temple. It was yet another Belmarrian tradition, although this time it was one that she enjoyed. There was something deeply calming about sitting cross-legged in a small, closed-off room of gray stone, concentrating only on breathing peacefully and slowing her thoughts. If the gods had still lived, it would have been a time to pray to them. Instead, Larka was left alone to think back on her past and forward to her coronation.

Now that she had announced her decision not to marry, a huge weight had been lifted off her shoulders that she'd barely even realized she was carrying. The tension that had been wound through her for months was gone. It was as if a part of Larka had been crying out inside her to make the right choice even before she admitted it to herself.

Larka wasn't sure how long she sat and meditated. With no windows in the room, she could only guess by the slow trickle of wax down the candles lining the walls. She thought about many things while she sat there: about her father and his cruel selfishness; about Stefan, who'd had even less preparation than she had before he took charge of a kingdom; about all the ancestors who had sat in this very place and likely also wondered if they would make the right choices for Belmarros.

Finally, there was a knock on the door. Larka stood, rubbing feeling back into her legs and smoothing the heavy folds of her skirts back into their proper shape. She opened the door to find Stefan and Dario on the other side, both of them carefully groomed and dressed in blue and green as well.

"Your Majesty," said Dario, bowing deeply. The gold beads in his hair clinked together.

"I think that's the first time I've ever seen someone use your title without you wincing," noted Stefan.

Larka stepped out of the small room and into the antechamber of the palace. "I suppose that's because I'm starting to feel more like a queen," she said. She rearranged her loose hair until it fell over her shoulders and tried to imagine the weight of the crown that would soon sit there. It wasn't the terrifying prospect she'd always thought it would be.

"That's good, because it's time for you to become one," said Stefan. He came forward and took Larka's hand and bowed over it. "Are you ready?"

"I think I am."

Stefan and Dario escorted her across the antechamber to the massive doors leading to the temple. They depicted the Moon Sisters weeping tears of pure silver over the world. Distantly, beyond the heavy wood doors, Larka heard muffled voices, the sound of a thousand people all waiting for a glimpse of their new queen.

"We leave you here," Stefan said. "And know that I'm proud of you, more than I can say. Dario and I both are. Your parents would be, too, if they were here today."

Larka smiled crookedly. "Because my father's good opinion matters so much, does it?"

Sadness flashed in Stefan's eyes. "You'll be a better ruler than Eldric ever could have dreamed of being. And although I didn't know Marion well, I think she would have been happy to see the kind of queen you grew up to be."

"Good luck," said Dario earnestly. "Stef and I will be in the audience, watching. We believe in you." Then they were both gone, taking a back corridor to their seats in the temple.

Larka took a moment to steady herself. She ran her fingers down the straight scars on her palms from her coming-of-age. That day was so far away from this one that it was difficult to believe it was the same lifetime. She'd had no idea what was to come.

When Larka had steadied her nerves enough, she reached out and pushed open the vast double doors that led to the Temple of the Fallen Gods. Every seat in the red-walled temple was full. Nobles and merchants and servants alike, they had all come to see their new queen. It felt as if the entire city of Vaelkarra was crammed in the temple. The entire country, even. The crowd utterly dwarfed the one that had come for her coming-of-age. There wasn't even room to stand along the walls. And as soon as Larka entered the temple, every person shifted in his seat to catch a glimpse of her. Larka walked up to the altar at a sedate pace so they might look as much as they wanted. It was in that moment, the train of her heavy dress dragging behind her, her head raised high, the eyes of an entire country upon her, that Larka truly felt like a queen.

The priestess of the temple waited at the altar for her. As always, she was clad in robes of a bloody shade of scarlet with a shaved head. Beside her on the altar were the bone-white knife that had scarred Larka's palms at her coming-of-age and the crown of Belmarros.

Though the knife was the same one Ysobel the Founder had carried at her waist when she united the warring tribes into one country, the crown was not the one Ysobel had worn. That one had been lost at sea when Larka's father died. The one before the priestess was a replica, perfectly measured and fitted to resemble the original. It was made of whorls of brightly polished gold that looked like fire—or perhaps waves. Nestled between the spirals of gold were sapphires and emeralds that winked like a dozen eyes.

"My queen," said the priestess with utter calmness, as if this was something she did every day. "Are you ready?"

"Yes," said Larka, and she didn't think she was lying.

"Then first, the blade." The priestess picked up the godbone knife and held it out to Larka hilt-first, perfectly balanced on her open palms. "Your ancestors carried this knife as a reminder that they must defend our country and even go to war on its behalf. Can you say the same, my queen? Will you protect Belmarros with every breath you draw?"

"I will," said Larka, thinking of Aelia, whom she had not saved, and all the people who lived in Belmarros whom she still could. "I swear to carry this blade as a reminder of my promise."

"Then take it."

Larka plucked the knife from the palms of the priestess and held it up to the watching crowd before sliding it home into the scabbard at her waist.

"And now, the crown," said the priestess. "Have you proven your devotion to Belmarros?"

"I have." Larka held up her palms so that the priestess might see the twin white lines that scored her palms. "I have chosen Belmarros with word and with action and with blood. I swear to be its queen as long as I may live."

"Then let the crown be yours." The priestess held out the crown in her pale hands. Larka had known how the ceremony would go, of course, but she still found herself taken aback by how quickly it was going. After a moment's hesitation, she reached out and took the crown. It was nothing like the coronets she used to wear, solid instead of light and comfortable, and she could already imagine the pressure of it on her head.

Let the crown be heavy, Ysobel was said to have commanded the blacksmith forging it, *so that no ruler after me may forget that the weight of their country rests upon them, and all the responsibilities that come with it.*

Some rulers had ignored that weight. Larka had tried to, at first. Now, standing before her gathered people, she vowed that she would never abandon them again. Larka pivoted to face the silent audience before her and raised the crown high into the air so that even those standing far in the back might see that she held it.

"I, Larka," she said, surprised at how clear and focused her own voice sounded, "daughter of Eldric, he who was king before me, and his chosen consort Marion, do come before you to claim my birthright. I have spent my months as Little Queen to learn the workings of this country. I have shown my devotion through blood spilled at this very altar. Is there anyone who would deny my claim?"

The room was utterly quiet.

"Then I shall be queen," she said. It was tradition—dating all the way back to Ysobel and the rival tribes before her—that a new ruler would crown herself. In Dalbrast, the new kaiser was crowned by a priest. In Astraia, the former ruler or a close relative. In Belmarros, though, the kings and queens were beholden to no one but themselves. They would not be influenced by religion nor family. So, Larka lowered the crown upon her own head and made herself queen.

For a split second, the silence in the temple remained. Larka could distantly hear rain from an autumn storm falling on the roof high above. Then the room exploded into noise: cheers and shouts and whistles, cries of celebration for the people's new queen. The crowd rose up as one, clapping and shouting in joy, and Larka found herself swept away in a wave of congratulations. Kath and Karo and Krista, even though they were really too old for such things, bounded up the steps to the altar and flung themselves at her with all the grace and enthusiasm of puppies. Larka caught them, laughing, although she had to be sure not to tip back her head and send the crown crashing to the floor. Already, the weight of it was changing things.

The tide of people carried Larka out of the temple and down the palace halls until they came to the great ballroom on the other side of the castle. It was All Hallows' Eve, and servants waited outside the doors to pass out masks so that the revelers could pretend to be someone else for an evening—another coronation tradition. Larka was handed a peacock mask painted blue and green and gold. Real feathers stuck up from the top of it; they did nothing to disguise the crown on her head, but she slid the mask on anyway as she stepped through the doors to the ballroom.

The ballroom had gone unused for four years, and Larka found herself taken aback by the arching height of the ceiling and the vast stained-glass windows lining the walls. The place was brightly lit and decorated in blue and green. The storm outside seemed a world away.

At the far end of the ballroom was a dais with an empty throne where Larka would soon be expected to sit and hold court. She would receive wishes for a happy reign—whether or not the person behind the wish felt the sentiment—and gifts from her court and perhaps discussion of alliances from ambassadors. But that would come later. For now, it was time for the ball.

Normally, Larka would have danced her first dance as queen with her chosen consort. With no new consort at hand, however, there was a brief, confused pause as the crowd milled around her, clearly wondering who would dance with their new queen instead. Stefan, wearing a fox mask, came forward almost immediately and clasped Larka's hands. Larka smiled at him. In her anxiety over her announcement, she hadn't considered who would dance with her when she chose to marry no one at all.

Larka's first dance as queen was a solemn affair, slow and formal, each step in time to the sound of the swelling orchestra, which played loudly enough to drown out the rain. She and Stefan had the floor to themselves. The rest of her court clustered around the edges of the ballroom and simply watched.

Larka had danced dozens, perhaps hundreds, of dances in the underworld over the last few months, but this one felt different. Stefan's hands in hers were warm and comforting, not the cold, lifeless flesh of the dead. There was a different kind of weight to this dance than any in the underworld. Then she had danced for a god in a lonely, cold world forgotten by everyone. Now her people saw her dance before them as their new queen, tall and strong and unafraid.

Finally, Larka's first dance as queen ended, and Stefan stepped away to leave her alone at the center of the room. She held up her hands and called, "Come, celebrate! Let us dance for all the years Belmarros has stood and all the years it will continue to stand."

People flooded the floor as soon as she spoke. The dance transitioned from something stiff and formal to a merry country dance filled with twirling and swapping of partners and two circles rotating around each other. Larka found herself in the inner circle, and she let herself be lost in the crowd, head tipped back (but not too far back) and skirts swirling around her. The crush of people around her was so big that she saw no one she recognized even as she was passed, laughing, from partner to partner. It made her feel almost anonymous.

The dance then switched again, everyone clapping once before turning to new partners. Larka thought she might have grown bored with dancing after so many nights doing it in Sol's realm, but this dance was a thousand worlds away from the cold solemnness of her underworld nights. This dance was life and heartbeat, laughter and smiles.

Larka reached out blindly behind her to grasp the hand of a new partner, and she froze. The hand that held hers was cold. Inhumanly so, in this hot room with everyone so close together. And it might have been her imagination, but she thought she felt a spark pass between the clasped hands.

Time slowed to a crawl, long enough that the mere seconds she had as her partner spun her around stretched out long enough for her to wonder, *Is it him? It feels like him.*

No, it can't be him. He couldn't leave. He wouldn't come tonight. Would he? Maybe—

Larka finished turning and saw the face of her partner. Despite the long-beaked black and gold mask her partner wore, Larka knew immediately. She didn't need to see Sol's face to know it was him. She had already recognized by his touch, by his breathing, by the way her heart pounded in response to him.

If Larka had felt a spark between their joined hands, now it flared into fire. She thought of Sol in the darkness and the strained way that he had said her name—and Larka jerked back from recalling that *particular* memory. She could feel her cheeks flush even brighter than they already were and hoped that no one could read her thoughts on her face.

Sol smiled at her, a secret sort of smile that she'd never seen on his face before. He was the same as always, white hair and stark tattoos and black robe, but no one dancing around them seemed to notice anything unusual about their queen's new partner.

She had never danced with him before. Not in all of the countless nights she'd spent whirling across the floor of the underworld to the strain of ghostly violins. He'd always sat and watched while she danced in the arms of some long-forgotten shade, and although she'd felt her eyes on him, he had never once stepped down from his throne to take her hand. Yet here he was now.

Sol drew her a little closer, matching her step for step in the dance. "Hello," he said, and despite the music and the noise of the crowd around them, she heard him perfectly.

"Hello," Larka breathed. She didn't know what else to say.

Sol. *Here*, when she'd thought that last night was the last time she'd ever see him. She would have thought she was dreaming if his hand in hers had not felt so real.

As Larka guided him through the dance, she asked, "How are you here?"

She saw him smile again underneath the bird mask.

This time there was a touch of glee in the expression. "It is All Hallows' Eve, a night for the dead. Tonight I may go where I please."

"And you choose to go to a coronation dance?"

"I choose to spend it with you," he corrected gently. The dance around them was impossibly far away. It seemed to Larka that the others were only blurry impressions of movement and color. She and Sol were the only real things in the world.

Sol pulled her a little closer, put his free hand on her waist, and whispered, "Come with me one more time. There is something you must see in the underworld."

Larka knew that she should be thinking about her coronation ball, about all the people who very much wanted to see their queen dance. She should be thinking about her duties and how they meant she couldn't go gallivanting off to the underworld any time she felt like it. But at the moment, she didn't care about any of that. She only cared that she'd thought she would never see Sol again, and now he was here before her.

"Alright," said Larka. "I'll go with you."

Hands still clasped, Sol guided Larka skillfully out of the crowd. No one noticed their queen hand-in-hand with the god of death; he must have been doing something to turn away their attention.

Sol paused in a dim corner of the ballroom behind one of the groaning tables piled high with fruit and sweets. He slid off his mask and let it fall to the floor. Larka did the same. There was no need for disguises between them.

Sol raised a hand and reached out to the shadows, gently, as if they were a skittish cat that he didn't want to frighten away. At his touch, the shadows darkened into a deep black stain that promised something hidden in their depths. They spread across the wall like ivy until the darkness formed an arched doorway flat against the wall.

Larka had rarely seen Sol perform such a blatant act of magic. It made her uneasy—she was more comfortable with him when he *didn't* emphasize that he was a millen nia-old god who could perform feats of magic beyond human understanding.

Before she could think better of her decision to go with him, Sol stepped into the shadows and pulled Larka along with him. Instead of crashing into hard, unforgiving rock, Larka found herself immersed in the same numb darkness through which she'd traveled the previous night. She took one last look back at the bright, laughing celebration, and then she was smothered in shadows.

Shadow-travel was just as unpleasant as Larka remembered it. The only thing that made the endless void between worlds bearable was the knowledge that eventually it would be over. After what seemed like far too long, the shadows loosened their grip on Larka and released her into the underworld.

Larka let go of Sol and fell to her knees, gulping in cold air. Her body was desperate for every breath she couldn't have when in limbo. For a minute, all she could do was crouch on the ground—earth, not stone, so they must not be in Sol's palace—and heave in breath after breath.

When she no longer felt light-headed, Larka rose unsteadily to her feet to find herself in the forest of silver trees. Though she'd walked through it many times since that first night, Larka always found herself a little amazed by the trees and how they looked like the work of the finest silversmith but grew and put out buds and fell to the forest floor when they were tarnished and dead.

Larka brushed dirt off her skirts and tried to regain her dignity. At least her crown hadn't fallen off. "So, why do you want me to come here?"

"Come. I will show you." Sol started off into the silver forest, and Larka followed him though she was filled with trepidation. He led her off the main path that she had traveled so many times and onto a smaller trail that led into the unknown forest. After only a few steps, it felt as if the whole world was made of silver leaves and black dirt.

Not far into the forest, Sol stopped before one of the

trees. He reached up on tiptoe and pulled down one of the branches with the clink of silver leaves brushing together. Larka blinked in surprise. Hidden by the leaves, she had never before noticed that tiny silver fruit lay along the branch as well. Apples, if underworld fruit was the same as normal fruit.

Sol plucked one of the tiny apples—barely more than a mouthful, really—off the branch and held it out to Larka, who looked at it dubiously.

"Am I supposed to eat it?"

"Of course," said Sol, as if it was obvious.

"But it's made of silver!"

"No, it's not." He pushed it closer to her, and she took it, surprised to find that even though it might have looked like silver, the flesh gave under her fingertips as easily as a real apple.

Still hesitant, Larka lifted the apple to her mouth and took a cautious bite. Sweet flavor exploded over her tongue. More than flavor, even. Memories.

She saw a city with white walls higher than treetops, an orchard of apple trees tiny against the vast grandeur.

She saw an island in the midst of a great crashing sea, a single stunted apple tree the only living thing growing upon it.

She saw children with the black tattoos of arcanists throwing apples at each other and laughing, heedless of the magic in their veins.

She saw a king take a single bite of an apple pie and fall down at the foot of his throne, writhing and dying from poison.

She saw an orchard burning thanks to a roving band of soldiers and a woman crouched in the midst of the flames, weeping.

She saw a young soldier clad in bloodstained armor skillfully peel a rich red apple with a few strokes of a knife and devour it in a few bites.

She saw a thousand things across a thousand years,

memories all filled with the sweet fruit of apples.

Larka jerked back to the present day to find herself still standing beneath the silver tree holding an apple in her hand and Sol looking at her with anticipation in his eyes.

"Well?" he said impatiently. "What did you see?"

Larka shook herself. It took a moment to come back to her own skin and not the memories of some long-dead person.

"I saw… memories," she said, haltingly. "Of people eating apples?"

Sol smiled, triumph in the curl of his lips. "Yes. These are the memory-trees. All the dead who pass through this grove leave something of themselves, whether it be one memory or a hundred."

"I don't understand. Why is this important?"

"You'll see." Sol took her by the hand and led her away from the apple tree.

They visited the other two forests of gold and diamond, and in each one, Sol bade her to eat. She ate a golden cherry and had yet more visions, everything from merchants selling fruit to lovers feeding each other by the ocean. In the diamond forest, she bit into a shining peach and saw Queen Ysobel herself eat the fruit as she watched the palace of Belmarros be built. Each time, Larka asked Sol what the point of it all was. And each time, he only smiled and told her that she would see.

After Larka had eaten from the fruit of the diamond forest, she thought this strange test—for she could not quite shake the feeling that this was a test—would be over. But no. Sol only led her further into the forests of the underworld until they reached a clearing in the midst of the glittering diamond forest.

In the center of the clearing grew a short, squat tree with deep green oval leaves and rough bark nearly the same color as the black soil. Hanging from one low branch of the tree was a fruit: a pomegranate, so rich and red and ripe with life that it looked utterly out of place in the land of the dead.

Sol reached up and brushed a finger across the smooth skin of the fruit before plucking it. His expression as he cradled it in his long fingers was reverent. With one sharp gesture, he twisted the fruit in half to reveal the shining white interior and seeds that clung there like tiny drops of blood. When he held out one half to Larka, it was with more ceremony than the previous times, as if this fruit had some special importance that the others did not.

Larka reached out to take it and then hesitated. "What is this?" she asked. "What do you want, Sol? Why this visit to your realm to eat fruit, of all things? The memories are interesting, but I don't see why it's important."

Sol continued to hold out the pomegranate. "It is not just fruit, Larka. I thought you would understand that by now."

"Then what is it? Tell me, or I won't eat. Why did you want me to eat the memory fruit, and why do you want me to eat this?"

A weary expression crossed Sol's face, and he lowered the two halves of the pomegranate. "I told you that I would explain, and I will. The memory fruit was a test."

Even though she'd guessed that on her own, a chill danced down Larka's back. "What kind of test?"

"To see if you could endure the memories."

If Larka had felt chilly before, now she was icy with apprehension. "Endure?"

"It can be overwhelming," Sol explained awkwardly, "to have so many thousands of years of memories dropped upon you at once. The human mind is not meant for bearing the weight of so many years. I wished to see if you were strong enough."

"Strong enough for what?"

"To be a queen," he said simply.

"I'm already a queen," Larka said.

"No. I mean you will be my queen. Queen of the underworld. I will build another throne to match mine, and we will dance without anyone watching, and I will show you the wonders and horrors of this world, wonders and horrors which many mortals may not survive seeing. You will be queen and I will be king, and we will need no one but ourselves." Ferocious loneliness and hope flared to life in Sol's eyes. "I will not be alone anymore."

Larka drew back from his reaching hands. "I don't understand. I—I'm mortal Sol. I'll age and die, and you won't. In a hundred years, I'll be nothing but a memory. How can you want me to be your queen?"

"Eat the fruit," said Sol desperately. "Eat it, and it will make you queen of the underworld."

"How could a pomegranate make me queen of the underworld?" Larka stared with confusion at the fruit he held.

"It is from a tree that was grown in the soil of the underworld and given water from the lake of the dead, and so it has the magic of death inside it. A single seed will strip away any mortality in your blood."

Larka stared at the fruit with a kind of fascinated revulsion, as if it were a bloodied sword or something equally terrible and beautiful. This fruit, so ordinary looking, had power that people would kill for.

"Why me? Why now? Out of everyone in the world who's ever lived, why do you want me to be your queen?"

"Why not you?" said Sol simply. "You are beautiful, Larka, and kind. You do not fear the darkness here as others do. If you were to be my queen, I would never be alone again, and you would be free of having to be queen of Belmarros. We could do as we please, and you would not have to spend the rest of your days as queen of a country that does not care about you."

"I…" said Larka and trailed off. She couldn't take her eyes off the fruit. She imagined the tart juice of the pomegranate bursting against her tongue and almost felt the crunch of the seed against her teeth. It would be so easy to reach out and pluck a single seed….

Larka bit the inside of her cheek hard enough to

draw blood. She felt as if she were standing on the edge of a great precipice. If she stepped off the edge, she might fly or she might fall, and there was no telling which.

"We will be together," said Sol, his words like silk. "We will never be lonely again. We will have everything that we need, if only you eat."

He held out the pomegranate again. Larka took one half from him, pried a single seed from where it nestled against the others, and lifted it to her mouth.

Chapter Twenty-Nine

The moment she placed the seed on her tongue, Larka snapped out of the trance she had fallen into. Rational thought rushed back in like a tidal wave. No matter how lonely Sol seemed, could she really sacrifice her life in the daylight world to keep him company? She might have enjoyed the night she spent with him—more than enjoyed it, if she was honest. That still wasn't enough to resign herself to an immortal lifetime of reigning over the cold and dark, not when there were people in the living world relying on her. Not when they would mourn her disappearance.

Larka closed her eyes, feeling the smooth pomegranate seed on her tongue. She could almost feel it pulsing like a hot coal, reminding her of the magic that waited inside it to be released. The potential of godhood was between her teeth, and she must not bite down.

Larka opened her eyes to find Sol looking at her with something approaching giddiness. He moved toward her and took both of her hands, leaning down until he could rest his forehead against hers. She saw with astonishment that he was weeping, and her stomach lurched unpleasantly when she realized why: He thought she had eaten the pomegranate.

"Oh, Larka. Now I will not be alone anymore." Sol's voice was full of such raw happiness that her heart broke a little, knowing she would have to tell him she couldn't stay in the underworld.

Then, before she could speak the truth, he kissed her. Despite herself, Larka found herself caught up in the careful way he tipped her chin and smoothed a hand over her hair. She kissed him back and couldn't tell herself that she wouldn't miss this.

Larka broke the kiss after a second, guiltily fearing that Sol would notice she still balanced the pomegranate seed under her tongue. Sol didn't seem to realize it, though. He kissed her shoulder, her cheek, the top of her head, the curve of her neck, which made her shiver. He was smiling as she had never seen him smile before.

Larka reached up one hand and wiped away the tears that still spilled down his face. "It's going to be alright," she whispered and hoped she was telling the truth. This time the kiss tasted of salt, and she realized she was crying a little, too, in pity for this god who was full of such aching emptiness and sadness, and that she would likely never see him again now that she would not be his queen.

While she was still trying to think of a way to refuse him, Sol picked her up in his arms and whirled her around. Larka squeaked and clutched at his hair to keep from falling. He laughed and kissed her nose and said joyfully, "My queen."

"Sol," said Larka. It was cruel to drag out his hope like this. She had to tell him the truth. "Put me down, please." He set her back on her feet, and the happiness faded from his face to be replaced by a solemn look.

"What is it?"

Larka licked her lips nervously. "Sol, I'm not—"

Sol held up a hand and tilted back his head, listening. "Wait. I hear something."

"What?" Horribly, she was relieved at the interruption. She wouldn't have to deny him yet.

"Not what. *Who*. Someone is here who should not be. I feel life in this world where there should only be death, and it is not you. Do you hear them coming?"

Larka strained to hear whatever sound Sol spoke of. At first she heard nothing at all, just the unnatural stillness of the underworld. And then she did hear something, the cracking of branches underfoot and the whisper of moving cloth.

Only a second after she first heard the approaching footsteps, the intruders burst into the clearing. Larka saw who had come to the underworld: her sisters, all eleven of them still bedecked in gems and silk for the coronation ball. They crashed out of the forest and stopped abruptly in front of Larka and Sol.

Larka blinked hard to make sure she wasn't hallucinating. But no, when she opened her eyes again, her sisters were still there. All of them, from Rhiannon to tiny Etain held in Gwynna's arms, stood before her.

"What are you doing here?" asked Sol. "Our bargain is done. How did you get here?" Every ounce of joy in his voice had drained away to be replaced by bitterly cold authority. He took a step forward in the slow, powerful way that only someone with all of eternity at his fingertips could.

Rhiannon raised her chin defiantly and met Sol's icy gray eyes with her own soft brown ones, though at the moment they were hard with anger. "We saw you leave with Larka, even if no one else did. We opened the portal and followed you."

"How?" asked Sol in exasperation.

"Larka is our sister," said Rhiannon simply. "We will always be able to find her. Besides, she has the same death magic inside of us as we do. We're bound to the underworld in ways I'm not even sure you entirely understand. Both of those together were enough to make the portal open."

"Very well," said Sol. "I should have realized that. But what are you doing here? I do not need you anymore."

"What, because you have our sister instead?" Gwynna scowled. "You're not keeping her! I don't know what you want with Larka, but we're taking her back."

Sol laughed at that. He tipped his head back and laughed, and Larka thought that he had never sounded more inhuman than in that moment. When he was finished, he said, "Your sister ate the fruit of the underworld. Whatever you came to do, it is too late, for Larka already made her choice. She is queen of the underworld now."

"Actually," said Larka apologetically, "I'm not."

Sol turned toward her. The slow betrayal that traced its way across his face was terrible to behold. "What? But I saw you—"

Larka cupped her hands and spat the pomegranate seed into them. It gleamed blood-red against the skin of her palms, as if taunting her to take it back.

Sol paled, if such a thing was possible. "Why did you not eat?"

"I can't stay here," said Larka, as gently as she could. She dropped the seed onto the ground next to the fruit it had come from and saw Sol's face drop along with it. "We said that we would dance for you to pay our debt, and we have. I don't belong down here in the dark. None of us do, not when we aren't dead yet. Besides, I have responsibilities in Belmarros."

"That is why I wanted you to stay!" Sol protested. "You spoke to me of how unhappy you are, about having to marry and become queen. I thought if you stayed in the underworld, you would be free of that. You could choose to be a queen instead of being forced."

"I was unhappy," Larka admitted. "Horribly, at first. But that was when I felt new at ruling, unsure of myself and tired of being pushed around by everyone at court with an agenda. I didn't believe I could be a good queen. I do now—

or at least that I can become one with time. So, as much as I used to hate my duties, and as much as I feel sorry for you, I'm not staying here." She tried to make her words as soft as possible, but Sol's face still crumpled with despair.

He stared down at the abandoned pomegranate on the ground. "I only wanted you to be happy. I only wanted not to be alone."

"Larka isn't a *thing* you can use to make yourself feel better," protested Auri, coming forward and putting a hand on Larka's shoulder. "She's a person, with her own mind and her own will, and you can't make her stay if she doesn't want to."

"Please," Sol whispered. He got down on his knees, heedless of the dirt soiling his robe, and stretched out his hands toward Larka. "Please, Larka, I beg of you. Stay and keep the dark away."

Larka shook her head, though guilt roiled in her stomach. It wasn't easy to deny someone begging on their knees. "I care about you, I really do. I'm sorry that you're stuck here, but that's not enough to make me stay."

"Was it even about making Larka happy?" Rhiannon, too, came forward to stand next to her sister, and Larka felt strong with the presence of her sisters beside her forming a row. "Are you just lonely and desperate and trying to come up with a reason why someone would want to stay with you?"

Rhiannon's words crystallized the fear that had begun to lurk inside Larka, the fear that maybe Sol was just another person who wanted to use her for his own purposes.

"Did you only see me as a means to an end?" Larka whispered. Had all of it—the dancing, the walk to see the dead, the whispered confessions of secrets, the midnight visit—just been a way to make her eat the pomegranate when the time came?

"No," said Sol, so violently that Larka had to believe him. "I would never. I swear on my dead brothers and sisters that I was never manipulating you. I love you, Larka."

His confession drove all the breath out of Larka, and

she was left clutching at responses that seemed insufficient. *Love.* The word had not come up between them before, and now it was spoken boldly in the open air. Why did he have to use such a word when it was clear that she couldn't stay with him?

Auri gave Sol a dark look. "If you hate it down here so much, then why did you want Larka to stay? That doesn't sound like love. That sounds like selfishness."

Sol closed his eyes. "I'm all alone here, and no one ever comes except the dead. I can feel the darkness pressing on me. The longer I am down here, the more I forget what sunlight looks like or the sound of laughter. If you stayed, you could keep the darkness away. I know you could."

Larka took a step closer to Sol. Before her wasn't someone terrifying and inhuman, just someone frightened, someone forsaken and forgotten by the world. She knelt and laid a hand on Sol's cold arm. He didn't look up at her, only kept staring dejectedly at the ground.

"I'm sorry, Sol," Larka said. "I can barely guess how awful it's been for you now that the other gods are dead. Still, that doesn't mean I'll be your queen. Just as you have responsibilities here that you can't abandon, I can't leave my kingdom in the daylight world forever wondering what happened to their queen. I wouldn't want to leave them. Do you understand?"

He was silent.

"Sol?" she prompted.

"I understand. I told you once that you would become queen and forget all about me. When you said you would never forget me, I hoped that perhaps…" Sol trailed off.

Larka rose and brushed diamond-flecked dirt off the skirt of her coronation dress. It was hard not to pity the god before her, but short of resigning herself to becoming queen of the underworld, she couldn't think of any way to help him.

"You won't be completely alone," she said eventu

ally. "Galen will still help you with the dead, won't he? And there might be others who don't want to move on. They can keep you company."

"But there will be no one else who is alive." Sol put his head in his hands. His next words were muffled and despondent. "What kind of god am I, afraid to be alone and hating my own duties?"

Gwynna had been silent up until that point, preoccupied with holding Etain, who was really getting too large to be passed from sister to sister. Now, Larka saw Gwynna hand Etain to Kath and step forward.

"Sol," Gwynna said hesitantly.

"What is it?" Even with his head still in his hands, the note of irritation in Sol's voice was clear.

"Have you ever considered..." Gwynna paused, then began again. "Have you ever considered that maybe you haven't always been a god?"

Sol jerked his hands away from his face and stood so he could look down on Gwynna from his considerable height. He truly didn't look human in that moment, all graveyard-pale skin and spidery fingers and eerie tattoos, and Larka honestly couldn't understand why her sister would think he was anything other than Death. "What do you mean, little princess? How can I be anything but a god?"

Gwynna dug around in one of the pockets of her violet dress—no matter the occasion, she always insisted on her clothing having pockets—and brought out a few sheets of crumpled parchment. Larka glimpsed Gwynna's familiar handwriting, nearly illegible in her constant rush to put her thoughts to paper.

"There's an old story," said Gwynna, unfolding the parchment. "I never put much faith in it. I always thought it was just another children's tale, like the others I read to Alannah and Etain. But the more I researched the gods, the more it turned up." She waved the paper. "All of these books had variations of this story in it, so many that it couldn't be a coincidence. And I started to think that maybe… maybe it wasn't just a story."

Sol stood in the center of the clearing, hugging himself as if he was cold. "And this story? What did it say?"

"It spoke of a god who lay dying during the war, and the man who came upon him." Gwynna smoothed the wrinkled paper with one nervous hand. "It said that the god gave the man the mantle of godhood as he passed from the world, so that even though the god was gone, his power would remain. The once-man became a god himself, and he watches over this world even after the rest of the pantheon has died."

"And you think I am this god?" asked Sol is disbelief. "Princess, that does not sound like a true story. It sounds like something people tell each other in the depths of night when they sit around a fire and become overwhelmed with the idea that the creators of the world are gone. It sounds like a child's dream."

Gwynna didn't back down. "That's what I thought, too. Until I met you."

"What do you mean, Gwyn?" asked Rhiannon. "There's nothing about Sol that makes me think he was once a man."

Gwynna raised a finger. "That's because you're not looking hard enough. I did look, and there are things that don't line up. Think about it. Sol, why do you feel cold? Why do you fear the darkness and the emptiness?"

"Who would not fear this place?" protested Sol. "You have seen it for yourselves."

"Yes, but you were supposedly born here. These lands—the shining forests, the black lake—are under your control. Shouldn't you be more at home here if this is where you belong? Unless maybe it's the human part of you that doesn't belong here?"

"That is not proof."

"It's really not," added Larka, frowning. "Besides, why didn't you mention this before?"

"I wasn't sure," admitted Gwynna. "But I'm more convinced now than I was before. Sol, why do you hate the underworld enough that you're afraid to be alone here? Maybe it's because there's a part of you that knows you shouldn't be here."

Sol backed away from Gwynna, shaking his head violently. "You're wrong. I... I am not a human. I never have been human. I have only ever been Death."

"Have you?" Gwynna's voice took on a determined note. "If you're only a god, Sol, then why do you have a name? The word for 'death' in the Divine Tongue is—" Gwynna whispered a cold, sharp-edged word that was unfamiliar to Larka. "But you call yourself Sol, and you wear the tattoos of an arcanist—of human magic—even though you claim you've never been human."

"You lie," said Sol, but there was less conviction in his voice than there had been.

"I don't," said Gwynna stubbornly.

"All you have to convince me is a tale for children!"

The two of them might have gone on arguing back and forth fruitlessly all night, but Gwynna's words had dislodged a memory in Larka, of things Sol had once said to her as they walked by the lake, of secrets they had exchanged.

Larka stepped between Sol and Gwynna and held her hands up to keep them from arguing. "Stop it, both of you."

"What?" snapped Gwynna. "I'm just trying to understand—"

"So am I. Let me talk." Larka turned to Sol and lowered her voice. "I don't know if what my sister says is true. I've never heard the story of a man becoming a god before. But I remember you told me once, when we walked by the lake, that you thought there was a part of you that you couldn't remember. You told me the same thing last night, that you felt diminished, like there were parts of you missing."

"I did say that," admitted Sol reluctantly. He tugged on his long braid in an anguished movement. "That does not make it *true*. I think I would remember if I had once been human."

"But you might have been." Larka didn't find the idea as ridiculous as she had when Gwynna first introduced it. Hadn't she thought more than once that there seemed to be two parts to Sol: the one who kissed her hands and had eyes full of grief and the one older and more powerful than she could fathom?

"You still have no proof," said Sol, though doubt was creeping into his voice.

There was silence at that. Sol was right; they had reached an impasse. Larka knew she and her sisters should probably leave. The longer they stayed in the underworld, the more they risked someone in Belmarros noticing that the princesses were missing. Yet she felt that they couldn't leave, not when she knew she would always think of Sol pacing alone in the darkness. He would haunt her as well as any shade.

A flicker of an idea occurred to Larka—a way that they might be able to prove, once and for all, if Sol really had once been human. "Wait," she said. "I think I know how we can figure out the truth."

"Oh?" Sol regarded her with a dubious look.

"Yes. Call for Galen."

Larka knew from the bafflement on Sol's face that he didn't understand her idea. Nevertheless, he tilted his head back and called, "Galen! Galen Dietrich of the Dead, I call you. I am your king, and I command you to come to me."

The response was almost instantaneous. The shadows beneath the boughs of the diamond trees shivered and stirred, and the undead arcanist walked out of the forest. He wore the same plain clothing as always, his brown hair forever short and the silver scars on his cheeks almost gleaming in the unearthly light of the diamonds.

Larka had never asked why Galen and Sol carried the same tattoos on their skin, though one was mortal and the other a god. Had Sol always had them, or were they another mark that he was more than Death?

"You called, Sol?" said Galen. He raised an eyebrow. "What's going on here? I thought your bargain with the princesses was done."

"It's complicated," said Larka, not really in the mood to get into the whole mess of how Sol had tried and failed to convince her to become queen of the underworld. "I wanted your help with something, if you can. You removed Miron Brandt's memories, right?"

Galen nodded. "I still have them, if you want them." He reached into a pocket of his dark brown coat and pulled out the glass ball, memories swirling within its depths.

"Er, no," said Larka. "Actually, I wanted to know if you can do the opposite. Could you find memories that someone has forgotten?"

Galen blinked. "Why? Forgotten something important?"

"No, but I think Sol might have." Larka explained Gwynna's theory to Galen, concluding with, "Sol showed me some of his memories when we first met, but only the ones of being Death. I thought that maybe you could use your magic to see if he's forgotten that he used to be human. At the very least, we could try to find out what exactly happened to him during the War of the Gods. Help us find the truth. Look into his memories and see what's there."

Galen frowned. "I think I could, perhaps.... I know more about removing memories than uncovering them, but there's no harm in trying." He held out a hand to Sol, who took it gingerly, as if he thought Galen's touch would burn him.

"Let Larka be part of this spell, too," said Sol. "I would have her see the truth of me, whatever it is."

"And me," said Gwynna. "I need to know if I'm right."

The four of them stood together in the clearing, forming a square under the low branches of the pomegranate tree. Galen shook his sleeve back to bare the rune he had used to remove Miron's memories. He began to whisper in the Divine Tongue—Larka thought it might be a backward version of the same chant she'd heard him use previously, a version to find memories instead of taking them away.

Sol and Galen squeezed Larka's fingers tightly. Galen sang the chant, and sang and sang, and the power built up between the four like the air crackling before a thunderstorm of terrible proportions. Just when the feeling of power racing through Larka became overwhelming enough that she couldn't stand it any longer, there was a *pull*, and—

She was in his memories again. She saw a hall full of light and gods holding court there. She saw fire falling from the sky and women in the moon weeping tears of quicksilver to put it out. She saw the world fracturing and reforming, continents pulled up from the seabed by one god only to be thrown at another. Then she was alone in the dark, and she was ushering rows of silent dead into the afterlife...

"No," she heard Galen say faintly. "Not this. Go back again."

There was a straining between them, a reaching for something hidden. Galen's magic bore down harder as it searched for the truth. His chant hummed in Larka's ears. Finally, something cracked, a hidden barrier that had lain, unknown, in Sol's mind for hundreds of years, and new memories poured in like a flood.

She saw him, then, a single figure illuminated in the darkness and chaos of swirling memories. Sol. But not the Sol she knew today. He had the tattoos, yes, and the long hair, but there was color in him. His hair was dark blond, his eyes a rich gray like steel. He was golden instead of winter-pale, and freckles dotted his cheeks. Warm blood pulsed under his skin, and his hands were long and slim but not inhumanly so, with only ten fingers. His beauty was a human kind of beauty, not a god-like one. He carried himself differently, too, without the weight of grief and years, without the burden of being King of the Dead. This was Sol young and carefree and human.

"Show me more." Galen's voice pulsed in Larka's

ears, and then he went back to his steady chant.

The memory opened outward, becoming more real. She saw that Sol stood on a long, rocky beach with the sea crashing on one side and a sheer cliff on the other. A dark citadel loomed above the crags.

Before Sol lay a god, brilliant and terrifying as a fallen star.

He was bleeding pure, golden blood onto the coarse sand of the beach. He was so bright that Larka could barely stand to look upon him for more than a few seconds at a time, but from what she could see, he wore shattered armor the color of night and his face was constantly shifting. She recognized a few of the faces: a creature made of ice, an Astraian warrior with blood-red eyes, a man with greasy black hair and gray skin, a monster with the head of a vulture and a skeletal body...

Sol had shown her memories of these aspects the night she had first come to the underworld as proof of who he was. She accepted that he was Death, but she had never wondered why, if another one of his names was The One of Many Faces, Sol had never worn any of the faces she had seen in his memories.

She watched as the human Sol knelt beside the dying god in the same careful way one might approach a wounded predator. "The master arcanists at the citadel say you are dying."

"Yes," said the god in a voice like the rumbling of the earth. "I know I am. My sister Lady Sun betrayed me and stabbed me straight through with a sword of light. I do not need humans to tell me that. Why are you here, little arcanist?"

"The master arcanists say that when you're dead, they will harvest your power, divide it among themselves, and twist it to their own uses. They... they're glad that you fell here so that you'll die within their reach."

The god closed his eyes—they were red as rubies against black skin—and sighed. "You humans never cease to amaze me with your cruelty. Of course they plan to desecrate me. Why tell me this?"

Sol hesitated, twining his hands together in a worried way. "I wanted to know if there was a way I could help you. It doesn't seem a very noble way to die, picked apart by scavengers."

The god breathed in, a terrible wheeze that said there was something punctured and bleeding inside him, something irreversibly damaged. "There is one thing that could be done to keep me from the master arcanists."

"Tell me," said Sol. His face glowed with hopeful curiosity.

The god said, "This body is dying, but I may still pass on the mantle of godhood and all the powers that come with it. I would be born again, in a way. Humanity would not be entirely without the gods."

"Could you really do that?" asked Sol. "I've never heard of a god who could pass on power in such a way."

"I am the only one," said the god. His words were fainter now and labored. "I am Death. It is my curse and my blessing that I alone shall never truly die."

"Then, I'll take your mantle. Pass your godhood on to me so the other arcanists can't steal your power. I don't want all the gods to be dead."

Death laughed hoarsely at this. "Do not lie to me, little human. I know you want this power for yourself and that is why you ask. But, yes, you may take it. You will be made into something other than human, something more. Will you do this for me?"

"Yes," said Sol, sounding both eager and afraid. "Yes, of course!"

"I warn you, human, that you will not remain yourself. You will have not only my powers but my memories as well. You will be Death. Do you still want this?"

"I do," said Sol.

Larka wanted to cry out, to warn him that this decision was greater than he could ever dream, but she had no voice. She was only a spectator to this scene that had played out so long ago.

"Then take my power," said Death. He raised one hand and held it out to Sol, who hesitated. "Drink of my ichor and become the next Death."

The god flapped his hand weakly as if to say, Go on, do it. Golden ichor dripped from his fingertips. Sol bent over the god's hand, putting his lips to one of the wounds at the wrist.

Larka recoiled in revulsion at the sight of the gold blood staining Sol's lips. He drank the divine blood, and she could see the light inside the god draining away to flow into Sol. The light poured through him, so brilliant that she could see the outline of his bones: the curve of his skull, the hollow of his nose, the stubs of his finger bones.

Sol drank and drank and drank. Gleaming blood dripped to the ground from his mouth and stained his clothing. Still, the power flowed into him, and the god before him began to fade. He ceased to shift faces and simply lay on the beach breathing in labored gasps, which themselves slowly died away.

Finally, the rush of power trickled and died. Sol let the god's hand drop. The former Death had become merely a ribbon of dry flesh stretched across flimsy bone. All that had been divine was gone from him.

Sol lifted his head. Larka saw that his mouth was smeared with gold, and his eyes were so dilated that they seemed pure black. There was something inhuman inside him, an immeasurably old and powerful creature that had not been there before drinking divine blood.

Sol's tongue darted out to lick the last few drops of blood away. He lifted his stained fingers to his mouth to clean them. The desiccated body at his feet seemed forgotten entirely.

This was how a new god was made, then: through blood and sacrifice. Through the death of another.

Sol began to get to his feet, but the power seemed to

weigh upon him so heavily that he could barely move. He sat back down beside the dead god, breathing hard as if he had just run a dozen miles. The light inside him was still glowing, barely contained by his mortal form.

As Larka watched, a spasm wracked Sol, sending him sprawling across the rocks of the beach. He thrashed and cried out. His back arched unnaturally as if he was having a seizure. He was still glowing, but now it was less a quiet kind of power than a bonfire that threatened to consume him. He reached up one hand to the sky as if begging now-dead gods to save him, and Larka saw his fingers cracking and elongating to make room for new joints, a sixth finger sprouting alongside the ones already there.

Sol began to scream, and the memory cut out.

Chapter Thirty-One

Larka was yanked back to the present feeling as if someone had taken her brain out, tossed it around a bit, and crammed it unceremoniously back into her skull. It took her several seconds to realize the memory had ended, because Sol had yanked his hands away from the circle and stumbled back. Shock was etched across his face, and there was a distinctly gray undertone to his skin.

"It is not true," he said hoarsely. "I do not believe it. I do not know what arcanist trick this is, but—"

"It is true," interrupted Galen, turning a pitying look on Sol. "You know it is. Memory magic is more reliable than our own minds. It shows only what's really there, even if we've forgotten it."

"I knew it," said Gwynna, more to herself than Larka. "I knew it." She didn't sound triumphant; she sounded sad. Larka could sympathize. It was one thing to hear the stories of dying gods. It was another thing entirely to see one of them die before you, stabbed to death by his own sister. It was a horrible thing, to see an immortal creature dying.

Sol was trembling. "But how could I forget such a thing? How could I forget that I was once a human? How could I forget my very self?"

"So, it's true?" asked Rhiannon. She was standing next to the group that had searched Sol's memories, twisting her hands nervously.

Larka let her hand drop from Galen's grip. "It seems so. We saw that Sol used to be an arcanist. The other arcanists were going to take Death's power and divide it among themselves after he died, and Sol became Death to stop them."

"So, they knew?" cried Karo indignantly. "All these centuries, and the arcanists knew there was still one god alive and never told anyone?"

"Maybe not," pointed out Gwynna. "It didn't seem like anyone knew what Sol was going to do. They just wanted Death's power for their own, and he wanted to stop them. Maybe they guessed what happened, but, well, it's not like Sol was around to tell them."

"Besides, telling anyone else would mean admitting they covered up the death of a god so they could try to steal his power." Auri sounded disgusted, and Larka couldn't blame her. Everyone knew the arcanists treasured power and wealth above all things, but she'd never dreamed they would try to steal it from a dying god.

"The story leaked out somehow, I suppose," said Gwynna softly. "But it became just that: a story."

Sol had been observing the conversation in silence. He seemed to be struggling to comprehend the enormity of the truth had just been revealed to him. Now he said, "I understand how the world could forget about me. What I do not understand is how I could forget who I am."

"I don't understand, either," said Galen patiently. "If you let me continue the spell, we might be able to find out more." He held out his hands again.

Sol clasped hands with them again, and they were plunged into darkness once more. This time it was more an impression of images than anything else.

Sol awakened in the underworld, slowly, over years and decades. Even as he guided the other gods there, he was only half-aware of anything. He was Sol the arcanist and Death the god, yet not quite either of them. He seemed a confused and broken shadow of himself, remembering that he had forgotten something and that he was a lesser god than he had once been but not what he had forgotten or who he had once been.

Sol the arcanist was less present than the god he had taken into himself. They were twined together, two souls in one, but there was more of the god than Sol. Death had simply overwhelmed him. If the god had been an ocean, Sol was an inkwell tipped into it.

And yet, some parts of the human man remained. He shivered in the cold of the underworld that had never bothered the god before him. He wept bitter tears over the fallen pantheon, while the god merely would have accepted that everything must die in time. He slept, and had nightmares, while the god had no need for sleep.

The god had never minded the endless darkness and silence. But for the man who was now part of him, it was unbearable. He felt as if the unchanging blackness around him pressed close to him, wrapping around his body like the vines of a terrible plant that wished to force its way down his throat. The silence of the underworld thundered in his ears, and his own voice was not strong enough to break it for more than a moment or two.

The years passed, then the decades, then the centuries. The sky remained impenetrable and black, the rows of dead crossing the lake endlessly long. The only thing that changed was Sol himself. The color slowly leached from his skin from living in a world without a sun. Despair and loneliness grew in his heart until they consumed him. The scant days every year where he could walk the world were not enough to revive him.

And then came the dancing girls, bringing light and laughter and movement into the dusty corners of his lifeless realm. He clung to the warmth they left for him, like a drowning man. He needed them. He needed the eldest girl the most, with her quick feet and soft voice and the kindness she extended to him as easily as a welcoming hand.

Larka saw herself reflected in Sol's memories and felt an odd lurching sensation at seeing herself through another's eyes. She saw herself moving through the steps of a dance and how Sol wanted to join her but didn't dare. She saw herself lost in the dance, rosy-cheeked and smiling, and holding Sol's hand as he walked with her along the beach of the dead. She saw herself in his bedchamber, practically glowing against the darkness.

More than anything, Larka felt his need, underlying everything as he looked at her. What he needed from her, most of all, was her vitality. She was a reminder that there were still living things in the world, and every time she touched him, it was a reminder that he was still alive, too.

He was not a shade. He was still living even if he was broken and missing something important, and she reminded him of that. When she was close, he could forget that he wasn't whole.

He needed her.

He needed this to last.

He needed her to stay.

One last memory broke into Larka's mind. She saw him rising out of his bed; she saw herself stir and turn toward him, still mostly half-asleep; and she saw Sol bend down to run a hand over her hair and kiss her forehead softly. Then he picked her up, one hand bracing her shoulders and another under her knees, and carried her through the shadows back to her apartments. They arrived just as the first gray light of dawn was peeking over the horizon. He set her gently on the bed and walked back into the darkness.

She saw him walking through the underworld, shoul-

ders slumped and head bowed. The look on his face was the acute misery of someone who has held someone in his arms he desires more than anyone but who knows that it will never happen again.

She saw his aimless pacing lead him through the forests until he reached the clearing with the pomegranate tree. She saw Sol reach up a six-fingered hand to graze the smooth, red fruit, and something like hope sharpened in his eye.

This time Larka was the one who broke the connection. She staggered away from Sol and Galen and would have fallen over completely if Auri and Kath hadn't rushed over and caught her by the elbows.

"Are you alright?" asked Auri.

"You look like you're going to pass out," added Kath helpfully. "Or throw up. Maybe both?"

"I saw everything," said Larka. Her voice rasped as if she had been screaming. "Everything."

She wished she hadn't. The image of Sol thrashing in agony as he went from human to god was stuck in her mind, and the lonely centuries after that were little better.

Sol looked at her solemnly. "Now you see. Now you understand why I cannot stay down here, watching everyone leave except for myself. I cannot keep being Death."

Chapter Thirty-Two

It took Larka a moment to muster the words she had to say. "But we need you, Sol. You're the only god left."

"Without you," Galen added, "people can't get to the afterlife the way they should. I'm not powerful enough to do it on my own. We still need Death."

"I know." Sol's voice broke, and he tugged hard at his hair. "Humanity needs me. And yet I feel that I am going mad down here, only seeing sunlight a few times a year. I cannot keep being Death."

Gwynna folded her arms and looked unmoved. "How? You said so yourself that humanity needs Death. You can't just *stop* guiding people in the afterlife and, I don't know, sit on your throne and cry."

"No," said Sol slowly. "Perhaps I could pass the mantle on to someone else. I had forgotten that it was possible to do so, but now I think it could be an escape..."

Gwynna backed away, seizing Larka's sleeve and

tugging her along. Larka let her sister pull her away until they stood clustered with the rest of the princesses. "No! Absolutely not! You're not keeping my sister down here so she can become Lady Death or something. We already made it clear Larka's coming with us!"

Sol looked taken aback by the suggestion. "I was not referring to your sister, little princess. I meant someone else, someone who is just as familiar with death and darkness and magic as I am." And it was true, he didn't turn and look at Larka.

"Me?" asked Galen, sounding stunned. "You want me to become Death?"

Sol and Galen faced each other: god and shade, separated by centuries yet still bearing the same runes upon their skin.

"If you would take the burden," said Sol, ducking his head.

Galen hesitated. "I've watched you through all the years I've spent down here. I've seen how tired you've become of guiding the dead. After so long, I understand why you would want to give up your duty as King of the Dead and Lord of a Thousand Faces. But… I don't understand why you would want me to become Death after you."

"Why not?" said Sol simply.

"Because I was monstrous when I was alive." Galen ran a hand over the runes on his arm. There was the same soul-deep guilt in his voice that had been present when Larka had danced with him and Galen had first told her of why he didn't pass on with the rest of the dead. She had hoped that her reassurances had helped, but it didn't seem so. "The magic in my veins," he continued, "I used it for cruel, wicked purposes. You've probably guided shades to the afterlife who were killed by me."

"I have," agreed Sol.

"So how could you possibly trust me to take over your duties?"

"I did not know you when you lived, Galen Dietrich." Sol stepped forward and laid a comforting, almost fatherly, hand on Galen's shoulder. "I can only judge the man I see before me, and I see someone who feels such a duty to others that he has kept himself from peace for two hundred years. I see someone to whom, if he is willing, I would very much like to pass on the mantle of godhood."

"I've never thought you were a bad person either," added Larka. "When my sisters and I first came to the underworld, we were frightened. You comforted us and said we had nothing to fear. That's not the mark of a cruel man."

"And you're an excellent dancer," piped Auri.

Galen gave her a weary smile. "Thank you, Auri."

"We do not believe you to be a cruel, wicked man," said Sol. "And if you are willing to do this thing, to become Death in my place, then I would gladly let you do it. So, will you?"

"Are you sure?" insisted Galen.

Sol nodded. "I trust you, Galen Dietrich. And besides that, no matter what kind of man you are, it is impossible to refuse your duties once you have the power. You will be Death because the divine power in your bones will not let you be anything else. I ask you, will you become Death in my stead?"

"Yes," said Galen at last. "I'll become Death."

Sol had the look of a man who had been traveling through a desert for a long time and had only just realized the oasis on the horizon was not a mirage. "Truly?"

Galen nodded. "All I've wanted since I came here was to help the dead find peace. And anyway, I've already spent centuries down here; what are a few more?" He gave Sol a steady, bracing look. "Shall we get on with it? I don't see a reason to delay. The princesses need to go home soon."

"Certainly. There is no point in putting it off." Sol bent to pick up the pomegranate, which still lay on the ground, and then turned to Larka. "May I see the knife you carry at your waist?"

Larka handed over the godbone knife mechanically, not even really thinking about why he might want it. Her mind was still so overwhelmed with memories of raging gods and hollow-eyed dead that she had little room for her own thoughts.

A kind of spark of gold fire leaped between Sol and the blade when his fingers closed around it. He closed his eyes, and the breath that escaped him in one long sigh was somewhere between sad and nostalgic. He touched his finger to the shining tip of the knife, drawing a bead of gold blood, and said, "As I thought. This knife was taken from the thigh bone of my sister War. It will do for the purpose."

"The purpose?" said Larka. His words jolted her, and she very much hoped that he wasn't talking about what she feared he was.

Sol looked at her, gray eyes gleaming. "Of course. Only a god can kill another god. Even though War is dead, her power should remain in this knife. Along with the pomegranate, it should be enough to make a new Death."

"So, you're going to *die*? You're going to let Galen kill you?"

Sol gazed down at the godbone knife he held in his spindly fingers. "Think of it not as dying, Larka, but as setting down a burden that I have carried for too long."

"That doesn't make it any better!" Her throat was raw with the sudden build-up of tears she refused to shed. She didn't want to start weeping.

Sol took a step toward her, shifting the knife to the hand that held the pomegranate so he could cup her face. Even with all the weariness he carried inside him, he still looked at Larka with such tenderness that she swallowed back her weeping even harder. He stroked a finger down her cheek in the place the tears would fall if she had let them.

"Larka," Sol said, so very softly. "I have lived for two thousand years, longer than any mortal could ever dream of, and I would rather die today than live another two thousand years in the dark. Maybe I already died when I became Death, and all the centuries in between were only a long, dragged-out pause before the end. I do know that if this is the only way that I can be free, then so be it."

Larka's throat had closed up. She wasn't sure she could say anything even if she had known what words would help. Every part of her rebelled against the idea of having to see Sol fall and die. She had lost so many people to death, and had fought so hard against slipping into it herself, that she couldn't comprehend someone walking into it willingly. Still, Sol had been right when he said this was the only way to free himself. She couldn't imagine leaving him alone down there.

Sol turned back to Galen. "Are you having second thoughts?"

"No," said Galen. "I understand what needs to be done, and your blood will not be the first I've shed."

"Good." Sol held the knife out to him. "This should do the deed. One god to kill another, as they have always said. Or in this case, the bone of a god."

Galen took the knife without hesitation, hefting the weight of it in his hands easily. He was clearly no stranger to blades. Larka herself shuddered at the gleam of white bone. "Now?"

Sol shrugged. "Now is as good as any other time. Or would you rather have us stand here all night?"

Galen swallowed and angled the knife up, as if practicing for the final strike.

"Come," said Sol. "We both know it is time."

Larka saw Rhiannon and Gwynna cover Alannah and Etain's faces so they wouldn't see what was coming, while Mel buried her face in Auri's skirts. Larka hated that this was about to happen.

"Are you ready?" asked Sol.

Galen swallowed. "As ready as I'll ever be," he said. "Where… where should I strike?"

"The heart," said Sol, indicating with one hand. "Go between the ribs. Ichor from the heart of a god is where the true power resides, so it should be quick."

Galen's hand was steadier than Larka's would have been in the situation. He did not shake in the slightest, not when he walked up to Sol, not when he practiced the motion once, twice, three times.

Sol's eyes met Larka's over Galen's head, full of weariness and apology and a readiness to rest. Then Galen stabbed him.

Sol gasped, a faint, involuntary sound of surprise, even though he had known it was coming, and pressed a hand to his heart as if to see if the knife was really there. Larka went to him. She couldn't help it; she had crossed the ground before she was done thinking the motion through. She caught Sol just before he fell to the ground. The weight of him was so heavy she could barely keep him upright, but she refused to let him collapse.

Sol breathed in. It was a wet, wheezing sound, horribly similar to the noise the first Death had made as he was dying. When Sol coughed, gold edged his lips, and Larka felt the movement shudder through his entire body. Ichor leaked from his wound. It looked so much like liquid light, beautiful and brilliant, that it was hard to believe it was Sol's blood.

"Don't forget… the pomegranate," Sol said. Every word seemed to cost him. Larka could no longer keep him upright, and they fell to the ground together in a heap.

Golden ichor leaked from the wound on Sol's chest, and Galen smeared it on the pomegranate, red and gold mixing in horrible beauty. He ate the fruit in a few bites, heedless of the thick skin, and as he ate, Larka saw the same hunger that had been in Sol's eyes when he transformed, a hunger for divinity so intense that it couldn't be stopped.

But even as Galen ate, even as he became Death, Sol did not die, even though Larka's heart stuttered fearfully with every pause between his breaths. Whatever divinity remained in him was enough to keep him alive for a few more minutes. He kept himself mostly upright with one hand braced on the ground, breathing in long gasps.

At last, Galen was done eating the pomegranate. Larka was glad; the sight of him eating the ichor-covered fruit made her sick. He looked down at Sol, his eyes curiously blank, and said, "Is that all?"

Sol shook his head feebly. "Heart's... blood," he managed. "Take out... the knife."

And Galen pulled the knife from Sol's chest, with a horrible sound of blade on bone that made Larka want to cover her ears. There was curiously little blood, as if it had already drained out of Sol along with his power. Galen ran a finger along the length of the blade and licked the fire-bright blood off. He let the godbone knife fall to the ground, forgotten, as he swallowed. He looked more like a living person than Larka had ever seen him look before. The golden light swimming under the surface of his skin lent color to his cheek and a gleam to his eyes. Instead of dead, he was gloriously alive.

Sol swayed, and she caught his shoulders to keep him sitting upright. "Sorry," he gasped out. His eyes were on Larka, but she wondered if perhaps he was apologizing to everyone, to the world for not being the god they needed.

"It's alright," she soothed, although it really wasn't. It was the only thing she could think to say.

"Help... me," said Sol as he fumbled with the sleeve of his robe. Larka helped Sol push it up to reveal the underside of his tattooed arm. His breath was coming slow and harsh—whatever borrowed minutes the power in his blood had given him were clearly running out.

With shaking, ichor-stained fingers, Sol circled one of the runes on his arm and began to whisper unfamiliar words in the Divine Tongue, stumbling and halting but refusing to stop.

"What are you doing?" hissed Larka. What spell could possibly help him now if he wasn't Death anymore?

"Wait," Sol managed and continued his chant.

A moment later, she saw the results; the leak of ichor

from Sol's wound stemmed, his breathing came more steadily, and he could sit on his own without having to lean his full weight on Larka. Impossible as it seemed, he was healing himself.

"How?" she breathed.

The corner of Sol's mouth turned up in a smile. "I may not be a god anymore, but I am still an arcanist, and I still have the power of one. And—" He held out his arm before him. Larka blinked. She was so used to Sol's six fingers that it took her a moment to see that he had five fingers now instead, five fingers of the normal length and with the normal number of joints.

"I am human again," said Sol softly. "All of Death's power flowed out of me and has left only… me. The person I was before I became a god."

Larka couldn't help herself; she threw her arms around Sol and held him tight, heedless of the ichor still covering his robes. He even felt different. His ice-cold skin was warming to something closer to human skin.

After a moment, she drew back. "Can you stand?"

"If you help me."

She did, and he managed to get to his feet unsteadily.

"Is it over?" asked Auri, hugging herself. The rest of Larka's sisters stood wide-eyed by the edge of the forest.

"I think so," said Larka. She reached up to tuck her hair behind her ears and found to her surprise that she was trembling, the remnants of shock making their way through her body. "Is everyone else alright?"

"Yes," said Yara. "We're fine. Larka, you're glowing."

Yara was right, Larka realized. The ichor on her skirts had a faint golden glow that made her coronation dress look even more beautiful, in a terrible kind of way. It would be difficult to explain that to the court.

"What about Galen? He's just sort of… standing there." Auri pointed, and Larka saw that Galen stood beneath the pomegranate tree, studying the branches with his hands clasped behind his back.

"Galen?" Larka asked cautiously.

"Yes?" He sounded normal, at least. There was no pain in his voice, and he wasn't screaming from the sudden influx of divine power.

"Are you alright?"

"Have you become Death?" added Sol.

Galen turned around. He looked entirely like his normal, plainly-dressed self, but when he unclasped his hands, Larka saw that he now had twelve fingers.

"It worked," she breathed.

"I think so," said Galen. He sounded calm and distant—inhumanly calm, the same way Sol used to speak sometimes, as if he had seen so many impossible things that one more was nothing.

"Does it hurt?" asked Sol. "When I became Death, it was agonizing. I thought I would be ripped apart from the pain alone."

Galen shrugged. "No, actually. Maybe because I was already dead, there was less of me that needed to be transformed to become Death."

"So, you *are* Death now?" said Gwynna, creeping up to stand beside Larka.

"Oh, yes. I have all the memories of Death. It's like…" Galen paused and tilted his head back, looking at what little starless sky could be seen between the branches of the forest. "It's like a tidal wave in my mind. All these memories of people and places that I've never seen before but are somehow *mine*." There was a depth to his eyes that hadn't been there before, thousands of years that now weighed on his mind. Yet there was still a trace of humanity inside him, perhaps the same trace that Larka had seen inside Sol and recognized, however unconsciously.

Galen stepped out from underneath the pomegranate tree. Even his walk was different, more confident, with all of eternity to stride across the lands that were now his.

"We need to go soon," said Larka.

Galen nodded. "Yes, it will be dawn in your world sooner than you think. I can open a portal to the living world for you."

"And..." Larka hesitated, unsure. "May we speak of you? The world should know that one god still lives."

Galen nodded. "There is no use for your silence anymore, so speak freely. I saw how heavily carrying this secret weighed on you. And I believe Death has been forgotten long enough. It does no good for me to hide down here for the rest of eternity."

"And me?" asked Sol. He was twining his braid around one wrist in a nervous gesture.

"Go with them, too," said Galen softly. "You're free, and the underworld is in good hands. Go. Walk the earth. Learn to be human again. Don't worry about me."

Sol bowed his head. "Thank you. I truly thank you upon the names of all the gods."

"There's no need. I made my choice willingly." Galen stuck one hand in his pocket and emerged with the glass globe containing Miron Brandt's memories cupped delicately between his newly elongated fingers. "Princesses, I think this is yours."

Gwynna stepped forward and took the globe from Galen. "What should we do with it?"

"Anything you wish. I have no need for it now. To release the memories back to their owner, only smash the globe."

Gwynna gazed down at the globe. "I think we should give Miron back his memories."

"You do?" said Larka, startled. "You were the one who told Galen to remove them in the first place."

"Yes, but that was when we still had a bargain with Sol. I don't want to hide anymore. I don't want to lie. I think the world deserves to know the truth, that one god still lives and we've met him. There's no need to keep it a secret now." Gwynna's voice was fierce as she slipped the globe into her own pocket.

"And I can tell Janna the truth," said Rhiannon, longing etched on her face.

Larka's sisters clustered around Galen to say their farewells, but she hung back next to Sol. She still couldn't believe that he lived, even though she'd seen the wound in his chest seal over with her own eyes.

Sol turned to Larka, a look of bafflement on his face. "I… I did not expect to survive the transfer of power. I am not quite sure what to do with myself now that I still live, or where to go. I am not sure about… us."

Larka hesitated. "Do you want there to be an us?" She herself wasn't sure what she wanted. Last night, they had been a trapped god and a lonely princess, and they had fallen together as if it was the most natural thing in the world. Now, they were a mortal with the living world at his fingertips and a queen with a country to run. Would that change things too much? Sol had said he loved her, but that was when he had been a god.

She chewed the inside of her cheek. "I… I understand if you'd rather be on your own—"

Sol shook his head fiercely enough that his braid swung back and forth. "I meant what I said. I loved you when I lived in darkness. I think I could love you in the light as well. But… I do not remember who I am anymore. Not entirely. I want to try and remember who I was, and perhaps go back to the arcanists to try and find answers. I want to see the world—properly, not for a few days each year."

"There's no hurry," said Larka. "Live the life you would have had if you hadn't become Death. Remember how to be human. There will always be a place for you in Belmarros if you want it. I promise."

Sol ducked his head and looked at her almost shyly. "And could there be a place at your side as well?"

"I informed my suitors that I don't intend to take a consort any time soon," admitted Larka. "I meant it. I want to learn how to be a good queen before getting married and having children." She placed a gentle hand on Sol's arm. "And I told you once that I didn't want to forget you, and I meant it. So, yes, there could be a place for you at my side."

Sol smiled at her, and there was something sweet and human about it that had been absent when he was Death. "Then I will make a promise of my own, that no matter where I go, I will come back to Belmarros. I will come back to you, if we both still wish it."

There was an ache in Larka's heart again but not the unpleasant sort. All she could think of to say was, "Don't be gone too long."

Larka's sisters had finished their goodbyes to Galen, who now looked at Larka and Sol.

"I don't regret this," Galen said finally. "I made my choice, and I'm glad it will set you free. And please don't be offended if I wish not to see any of you again for a long, long time."

"We understand, and we hope the same," said Gwynna, a touch grimly.

Larka hoped it, too. She had found a kind of beauty in this realm over the months of dancing there. Still, the beauty of silver forests and black lakes was not a human kind of beauty. It was nothing compared to sunlight and laughter and the smell of autumn on the wind.

Her crown waited above, and her kingdom and the rest of her family. There was nothing left for her in the underworld, not with the bargain over and the god they had made it with turned human again. Galen was Death now, standing solemnly under the branches of the pomegranate tree, and he did not need her.

So, Larka set her shoulders straight, turned to her sisters and Sol, and began the long walk up to the daylight world and the life that she had there. And if the shadows clung close to her, as if begging her to stay, she fixed her eyes ahead on the light that she knew would be there.

Glossary of Names

PLACES

BELMARROS: kingdom where the princesses live and where Larka is soon to be queen; capital is Vaelkarra.

GALLOW'S DANCE: poor neighborhood of Vaelkarra, where Larka's mother was from.

ASTRAIA: tropical archipelago allied to Belmarros, homeland of Queen-Consort Asha.

DALBRAST: kingdom across the sea ruled by a kaiser known to be rigid and harsh.

VEANARA: island kingdom known for its decadent ways.

DREKKARIA: island stronghold of the arcanists, beholden to no other kingdom; school is known as the Citadel of Ink.

LIMMAR AND MARETH: also known as the Crescent Islands, homeland of Queen-Consort Eithne.

CHARACTERS

THE PRINCESSES

LARKA: the eldest, 18, daughter of Eldric and Marion.

RHIANNON: 17, daughter of Eldric and Asha, also called Rhee.

GWYNNA: 16, daughter of Eldric and Asha, also called Gwyn.

AURIANA: 15, daughter of Eldric and Auriana, also called Auri.

KATHARINE: 14, daughter of Eldric and Asha, triplet to Kristina and Karolina, also called Kath.

KRISTINA: 14, triplet, also called Krista.

KAROLINA: 14, triplet, also called Karo.

YARA: 12, daughter of Eldric and Iris.

TALIA: 10, daughter of Eldric and Iris.

MELINA: 8, daughter of Eldric and Iris, also called Mel.

ALANNAH: 5, daughter of Eldric and Eithne.

ETAIN: 3, daughter of Eldric and Eithne, born after her father's death.

OTHER FAMILY MEMBERS

KING ELDRIC: father of the princesses, died at sea four years previously.

STEFAN: 28, Eldric's younger half-brother and uncle to the princesses, regent for Larka until she comes of age.

DARIO: 29, Stefan's husband, nobility from the southern provinces.

MARION: Larka's mother and former lower-class actress, died after miscarrying her second child.

ASHA: mother of Rhiannon, Gwynna, Katharine, Kristina, and Karolina; former Astraian princess; died of a lingering illness after birth of the triplets.

AURIANA: Eldric's third wife, married to him after she became pregnant with Auriana; died after hitting her head in a fall.

IRIS: mother of Talia, Yara, and Melina; died of a tumor in her breast.

EITHNE: Eldric's last wife, died in childbirth, mother Allanah and Etain

AT COURT

LORD AENGUS BRADDOCK: leading member of a political faction that would see Larka denied the throne.

DUKE MIRON BRANDT: Dalbrasti suitor of Larka.

JANNA BRANDT: Miron's younger sister.

MARIANA: member of the Royal Council of Belmarros.

TRAJAN: member of the Royal Council, ex-general.

DAVIN: youngest member of the Royal Council.

EUGENIO: member of the Royal Council.

EDANA: member of the Royal Council.

CORBIN: member of the Royal Council.

AUBREY ALLARD: suitor of Larka's from Veanara.

FERGAL MACKAY: suitor from the Crescent Islands.

VARIAN VALONOS: suitor from Astraia.

LADY ETTA: a gossipy female courtier.

IN THE UNDERWORLD

SOL: the forgotten and lonely god of death, who saves the lives of the princesses through mysterious magic.

GALEN: one of the restless dead, a shade who feels he can't move into the afterlife.

AELIA: a young Belmarrian woman who died an untimely death along with her children.

ACKNOWLEDGMENTS

I've been dreaming of writing a book for pretty much my entire life, and now I have. It's a bit surreal that I've finally done it. However, I didn't do it on my own, and I never would have gotten this far without everyone who supported me and my writing. Some thank-yous are definitely in order, and I'd like to give them to the following:

The Telling Room, which has been a place for me to explore and grow as a writer over the years. I wouldn't be the writer or person I am today without the countless summer camps and writing opportunities they've given me.

Kathryn Williams, for making me feel like I knew where I was headed and how to get there, and for being a great leader during my time in the Young Emerging Authors program. And also for the snacks.

My mentor, Jenny Siler, for not only listening to a lot of semi-incomprehensible rambling about what I wanted my book to be, but for understanding what I meant, figuring out how everything should fit together, and helping me make this book way better than I ever could have on my own.

My fellow members of YEA, Catherine and Christopher and Lulu, for loving writing so much and reminding me that I wasn't alone in this process. This program wouldn't have been half as fun without you guys. Also, I would know far less facts about quantum physics.

Amy Raina, second reader and book designer; Molly McGrath, publisher; Molly Haley, photographer; and everyone else who helped put the finishing touches on my book.

My creative writing teachers throughout the years, Ms. Agell and Ms. O'Neill and Ms. Tommaso. From middle school through high school, your classes and clubs were a place where I learned so much more about writing than I ever could have dreamed. Ms. Agell in particular supported my writing when I was just starting out in middle school, even when I never finished things and had a new story every week.

My parents, who have always told me they're proud that both their daughters are writers. Mom, thank you for putting up with me talking (complaining) about writing a lot and always asking me what I was working on. Mitch, thank you for your enthusiasm for everything I've written and for encouraging me to share it with the world.

Finally, fairy tales and the Brothers Grimm, for giving me the original backbone off of which I built the rest of this book.

ABOUT THE AUTHOR

Eleanor M. Rasor, nicknamed Pie for long and complicated reasons, is a graduate of Yarmouth High School and plans to attend Mount Holyoke College, where she hopes to keep writing. She currently lives in Yarmouth, Maine, with her parents, twin sister, and two disobedient but fuzzy cats. She's been writing stories filled with things such as magic, dragons, and girls with swords for almost as long as she can remember. When not writing, she can be found reading, swimming in the ocean, riding her bike, or over-analyzing action movies.

THE TELLING ROOM

At The Telling Room, we empower youth through writing and share their voices with the world.

We seek to build confidence and strengthen literacy and leadership skills in the youth we serve and provide real audiences for their writing. We believe the power of creative expression can change communities and propel youth toward future success as published authors, community leaders, and agents of positive change.

Our writing and publishing programs focus primarily on youth, ages 6 to 18. We welcome collaborations with other organizations as they make for exciting programs and events that would be impossible to produce alone.

The Telling Room
225 Commercial Street, Suite 201
Portland, ME 04101
www.tellingroom.org
207-774-6064

YOUNG EMERGING AUTHORS FELLOWSHIP

This book was produced as part of the Young Emerging Authors Fellowship, a Telling Room writing and publishing program that offers successful applicants the chance to plan, write, edit, design, and publish their own books in a single year. In weekly sessions at The Telling Room, fellows work collaboratively, writing and sharing their work, and independently with professionals in the writing and publishing industries, including authors, editors, agents, designers, and publishers.

TELLINGROOM.ORG/PROGRAMS/YEA

THANK YOU

The Young Emerging Authors Fellowship program could not have taken place without the generous support of our individual donors, corporate partners, and grants from: the Conway Charitable Trust; the Frog Crossing Foundation; the Hoehl Family Foundation; component funds of the Maine Community Foundation; the Rona Jaffe Foundation; the Sam L. Cohen Foundation; and the TD Charitable Foundation. Special thanks go as well to Eimskip and their selection committee partners for honoring The Telling Room as the 2018 Scandinavian Northern Lights Christmas Charity Event beneficiary. We thank you all.

STAFF

Executive Director: Celine Kuhn
Communications Manager: Blaire Knight-Graves
Development Director: Sarah Schneider
Program Director: Nick Whiston
Publications Director: Molly McGrath
Lead Teacher: Marjolaine Whittlesey
Lead Teacher: Kathryn Williams
Lead Teacher and Book Designer: Amy Raina
Young Writers & Leaders Program Lead: Sonya Tomlinson Young
Program/Volunteer Coordinator: Peyton Black
Publications & Community Engagement Coordinator: Clare LaVergne
Development Assistant / Office Manager: Rachele Ryan
Publications Intern: Evgeniya Dame

AMBASSADORS

Telling Room Ambassadors extend our impact in the community. In addition to speaking at events of all types, the ambassadors meet quarterly to advise on Telling Room strategy. Our ambassadors are high school students and alumni who have been published in at least one Telling Room publication and have participated in at least one of our core writing and publishing programs.

Edna Thecla
Akimana Aruna Kenyi
Gracia Bareti
Liam Swift
Judica'elle Irakoze
Rhode Niangasa Phambu
Hussein Maow
Nafviso Ali
Cameron Jury
Siri Pierce
Richard Akera
Zainab Almatwari
Maryam Abdullah
Salim Salim

VOLUNTEERS

Volunteers are essential to our organization. They sit side-by- side with youth, write with them, ask questions, and help them develop and publish their stories or poems. They help us run field trips in the city, lead residencies in classrooms around Maine, edit pieces for publication, and can be found at events selling and distributing books by our authors. We could not do anything we do without our volunteers.

WRITING PROGRAMS

Our suite of innovative writing programs is at the heart of our organization. All of the programs we provide during the school year are 100% free to youth and their families, ensuring that those who need our services most, and who may be least likely to have a voice in our local community, can participate.

We conduct multi-week IN-SCHOOL RESIDENCIES, in which Telling Room teaching artists and community volunteers work in classrooms throughout Maine to write, edit, and publish stories and poems in original chapbooks.

We offer a variety of SUMMER CAMPS (and scholarships for them) for writers of all ages and interests on topics ranging from food writing to sports writing and everything in between and beyond.

And at our studio spaces in downtown Portland, we offer a full complement of core writing and publishing programs each year, including:

LITERARY FIELD TRIPS, where students come to our writing center for the morning with their classmates and teachers to engage as working writers;

YOUNG WRITERS & LEADERS, a free, afterschool literary arts program for international multilingual high school students;

WRITERS BLOCK, a fun and supportive program in which youth develop writing among a group of peers;

THE YOUNG EMERGING AUTHORS FELLOWSHIP, our writing and publishing program that offers successful applicants the chance to plan, write, edit, design, and publish their own books in a single year;

And PUBLISHING WORKSHOP, where participants receive a working tutorial on the book publishing industry.

PUBLICATIONS

The Telling Room is a leader in youth publishing, an emerging niche of the publishing industry and a unique and inspiring model in the field of literary arts education and creative youth development. Our publications and events support The Telling Room's suite of writing programs and send youth voices out to audiences across Maine, the U.S., and around the world.

We produce carefully edited, beautifully designed, and locally printed books of our students' stories, poems, and personal narratives. In addition to this publication, The Telling Room has launched over 150 other titles and has published over 4,000 authors in our books.

Each year, all of our programs are linked by a new theme, and the best student writing from the year is published in a "best of" anthology, released every spring at a community event attended by hundreds of supporters. We also publish ten chapbooks per year, four single-authored titles from the YEA program, and special projects.

The publications team works hard to distribute books to schools, bookstores, and libraries, at special events, and out in the community through READ WHILE YOU WAIT, an initiative that places books in offices and shops where people might read them while they wait, and then leave the books behind for others to enjoy.

Aside from publishing books like these of student writing through our writing and publishing programs, we encourage the publication of student work in a number of other ways:

Writers ages 6-18 from anywhere in the world can submit their work to our online publication, STORIES.

We keep a current list of PLACES TO PUBLISH for young writers who wish to be published beyond The Telling Room.

We hold a WRITING CONTEST, on an annual theme, for Maine youth.

We submit student work each year to local and national awards programs such as the SCHOLASTIC ART & WRITING AWARDS.

GET PUBLISHED!

Stories is an online publishing spacefor children and teen writers ages 6-18 from around the world. Submit your writing to:

TELLINGROOM.ORG/STORIES

BUY A BOOK!

We do all of the great work we do when people like you support us and our young writers and authors. If you liked this book, please let us know, or share it with someone else. You can also buy other Telling Room books: www.tellingroom.org/store. Your purchase supports kids, books, literacy, leadership development, creative thinking, youth empowerment, teachers, the arts, and much more, and you or your recipient gets a great book, or a library of them—what's better than that?

JOIN OUR AMAZING SUPPORTERS

You can help us amplify the voices of Maine's youth, whether by making a financial contribution to help keep our programs free for youth; sharing a book with a friend, teacher, or young person you know; volunteering your time in one of our programs; or showing up to hear students present their work at one of our community events.

VOLUNTEER

To learn how you can become a volunteer visit:

WWW.TELLINGROOM.ORG/VOLUNTEER

BE IN OUR AUDIENCE

Attend an event! Find out what's happening at:
WWW.TELLINGROOM.ORG/EVENTS

MAKE A CONTRIBUTION

A financial gift of any size makes a big difference. You can make a secure donation at tellingroom.org./give, or mail your check to: The Telling Room, 225 Commercial Street, Suite 201, Portland, ME 04101. We are a registered 501(c)(3) organization, so all donations are tax deductible.

BUNDLE OF BOOKS SUBSCRIPTION

Become a Bundle of Books subscriber, and get a bundle of The Telling Room's newest books delivered right to your door.

Pay $100 per year (tax deductible), and receive five brand new Telling Room books and a special surprise gift. Bundle of Books subscriptions include the latest release from our prize-winning annual anthology series, the newest Young Emerging Author titles, and more....

Subscribe by sending an email to MOLLY@TELLINGROOM.ORG and include "Bundle of Books Subscription" in the heading.

ALSO AVAILABLE FROM THE TELLING ROOM

Atomic Tangerine
Because, Why Not Write?
Between Two Rivers
Beyond the Picket Fence
Can I Call You Cheesecake?
Exit 13
The First Rule of Dancing
Forced
Fufu and Fresh Strawberries
Hemingway's Ghost
How to Climb Trees
How to Eat Green Crab
I Carry It Everywhere
I Remember Warm Rain
Illumination
Little Bird's Flock
Once
An Open Letter to Ophelia
The Presumpscot Baptism of a Jewish Girl
Quantum Mechanics for Kids
Quick
The Road to Terrencefield
A Season for Building Houses
The Secrets They Left Behind
The Sky at 5 AM
Sleeping Through Thunder
Simona
Songs in the Parking Lot
Sparks
Speak Up
The Stars are the Same Everywhere
The Story I Want to Tell
Tearing Down the Playground
Tell Me the Future
Untranslatable Honeyed Bruises
When the Ocean Meets the Sky
When the Sea Spoke
Yellow Apocalypse

Find these books at tellingroom.org/store or your favorite local bookseller. All proceeds from the sale of Telling Room books support our free writing programs for Maine youth.

THANK YOU!

Thank you for investing in our youth and believing in their work.